ABOUT THE AUTHOR

Jay Strongman is a renowned international DJ and a long-time writer on popular and underground culture. Like many of his generation growing up in 1960s and '70s Britain, Jay was heavily influenced by the American TV shows, movies and music that permeated British culture at the time. That love of mid-20th Century Americana led him to starting London's first neo-Rockabilly clothing store, "Rock-A-Cha", in 1979 and fronting a rockabilly band called the El-Trains the same year. A few years later he started DJ'ing and his pioneering mix of music led to him becoming one of the first DJs-as-popstars, working on radio and in nightclubs around the world. Besides his thirty-plus year career as a DJ, Jay has also been a regular writer on music and fashion for such publications as the *Face Magazine*, the *Sunday Times*, *i-D Magazine* and *Vogue*. He has written two art books on popular culture - *Tiki Mugs – Cult Artifacts of Polynesian Pop* (Korero Books) and the highly acclaimed *Steampunk – The Art Of Victorian Futurism* (Korero Books). *Ritual Of The Savage* is his first novel and was inspired by rainy Sunday afternoons as a child watching Bogart and Bacall films on TV and reading Raymond Chandler, Ray Bradbury and Jonathan Latimer novels late into the night. Jay currently spends his time between his newly adopted homeland of Southern California and his first love, London Town.

To Sannah, with thanks.

COMING SOON BY JAY STRONGMAN

To Kill a Cure

Martian Eye

jaystrongman.wordpress.com

www.hungryeyebooks.com

RITUAL OF THE SAVAGE

Jay Strongman

First published in 2015

Hungry Eye Books
157 Mornington Road, Leytonstone, London E11 3DT
www.hungryeyebooks.com

Cover design by
Rian Hughes, www.devicefonts.co.uk

A CIP record for this book is avaiable from the British Library

ISBN: 978-0-9931866-0-8 (hardback)

ISBN: 978-0-9931866-1-5 (paperback)

ISBN: 978-0-9931866-2-2 (ebook)

RITUAL OF THE SAVAGE

Jay Strongman

Contents

Zombies at the Luau

Light, too much damned light! The afternoon sun shone in harsh, unforgiving bars through the blinds and across my eyes. Suddenly, I was awake and I didn't want to be. Squinting against the daylight, I lifted my aching head and glanced down at my body. It wasn't a pretty sight. From the edge of my boxer shorts to my ankles ran a line of angry purple and brown bruises. There was dried blood on my stomach and what looked like bite marks on my left hand. I shut my eyes again, trying to block out the glare, trying to pull my ragged thoughts together. Gradually, my memory shifted into gear and I began to feel even worse.

It had been an unremarkable day and I was way over on Sunset, on business. It was hot and by early evening, I really needed a drink. The Blue Cat Lounge was my kind of place. They ran me a tab, served a good Martini and kept out the kids. It suited me fine. Sure, it looked nothing special from the street, but inside it was sleek, comfortable and discreetly lit. I was enjoying the air-conditioning and shooting the breeze with Gene, the head barman, when I got distracted.

She was a bottle blonde in a pink summer dress, wearing a shade too much make-up, but young enough, and cute enough, to get away with it. She sauntered over to the far end of the bar, made a big deal out of sitting down just so, and gave me a smile. Like a moth to the flame, I was attracted. I know nice girls don't go to bars alone, but I was too loaded to want a nice girl. I pulled up a stool next to her and introduced myself. She talked; I listened. I joked; she laughed. Sometime after my third drink, I vaguely recall her telling me that her boyfriend was the jealous type, but by then I was nibbling her neck and whispering into her ear. I'd also found out she was twenty-two, lived with her mother in Studio City, and worked as a receptionist for an insurance company; but none of that interested me. I got her phone number and then convinced her she had to see my apartment. She acted coy at first so I told her about my hi-fi set up. It was either the thought of hearing my Sensaround Stereo or my hand massaging the soft skin of her upper thigh above her stocking top that changed her mind. Whatever it was, her resistance was suddenly low.

Much as I enjoyed the change of pace, I don't usually go for public smooching. It might give people the wrong idea about me. So, peeling her off me, I told her I'd get the car from the lot and pick her up out front. I was dimly aware that two or three guys were walking in off the street as I whispered in her ear, but I didn't pay them much attention. I figured the death ray one of them was beaming at me was because he didn't like my suit. I'm a sharp guy, clothes-wise, and most other men seem to find that annoying. Anyway, as I headed out the back door I wasn't really thinking about anything except the blonde. Her hot Juicy Fruit breath in my ear, and the way she'd shivered when I stroked her leg, had my mind kind of distracted.

That's the trouble with sex, when you're close to getting it very little else matters. Actually, when you're *real* close to getting it, *nothing* else matters. Whether it was that, or the alcohol, I don't know, but I didn't hear the three guys following me out to the parking lot. I should have been alert but I wasn't. Stupid. *Stupid*. If you act like there's no tomorrow, one day soon there will be no tomorrow. Doc Stevens told me that in Hawaii back in '45 and, with hindsight, I guess the old boy was right.

I was just opening the car door when the first guy hit me from behind. After that, it was just a blur of fists, shoe leather and booze-softened pain. I'm pretty sure one of them said something about leaving his woman alone. And I'm pretty damned sure I heard Tony, one of the bar's bus boys, calling out that the cops were coming. A few more hurried kicks and then I was left alone, slumped behind the steering wheel—bruised, bloody and battered. I guess it could have been worse, but the way my Chevy was parked next to a fire red Buick thankfully gave the goons little space to get at me. That much I remembered, and Tony giving me a wet cloth for my cuts, but the drive home from Los Feliz to North Formosa Drive was a blank. How the hell I did that without getting pulled over was anybody's guess. Maybe it was some basic Marine survival instinct. Perhaps, it was just luck. Perhaps, the whole damned thing was a dream.

I opened my eyes again. The sunlight was brighter than ever, and the pain wasn't letting up. My mouth tasted like hell, and I was sweating up the sheets. No, it wasn't a dream. I grabbed the alarm clock and held it about six inches from my face while my eyes slowly began to focus. It was five in the afternoon. I had to get myself into the shower and let the water kick-start my brain. I had a big meeting with my ex-wife at six and I couldn't be late for that. I swung my feet to the floor and slowly stood up. It wasn't easy. My legs felt like they were made of rubber, and my head was filled with lead. What a combination. Meet 20th Century Man—rubber, lead and a gallon of Vermouth.

Standing there, half-awake and gently swaying, I noticed my suit lying crumpled on the carpet. Jesus! Seventy-five bucks for a suit and I'd dumped the damned thing on the floor like garbage. I shuffled over to it and, with a groan, bent down and scooped up the jacket. It was fine, not a scuff or blood spot anywhere on the powder blue fabric. Even the pants were okay, the creases were still sharp and my wallet was still in the back pocket. Maybe there was a patron saint of tailors. My shirt was a mess though. It hadn't been cheap but now three buttons were missing and several splashes of blood had ruined the white-on-white sheen of the fabric. Walking to the bathroom, I balled it up and dumped it in the trash. What a waste!

So there I was, thirty-three years old, beat-up, hung-over and alone, with blood on my shirt and bruises the colors of a Technicolor epic all over me. Meanwhile, most of my old Marine buddies had houses in the suburbs, wives, kids, and late model, four-door, family sedans. They had weekends at the beach, bridge nights on Wednesdays, bowling leagues on Fridays, and balling their secretaries every lunch break. Okay, I made the last bit up, but you can't blame me for being bitter. For some damned reason I'd always taken the road less travelled, and this time that road had left me clinging to the sink for support at five in the afternoon while I checked my face for cuts and bruises. A couple of years back, a little cutie I picked up on a weekend down in San Juan Capistrano told me I looked like Jimmy Dean. Well, young James had been gone a while and, according to my bathroom mirror, I wasn't swinging movie star looks anymore by any stretch of the imagination. One eye was a little puffed up, there were two bloodied scrapes on my cheeks, a big, dark, bruise on my forehead and a cut on my chin. But at least my nose was still straight and my teeth were all there. I stared deeply into my eyes, but my reflection was giving nothing away.

Ten minutes later, I was out of the shower and ready for coffee. I gently pulled on a pair of black gabardine slacks, a black casual shirt with a monogrammed pocket and my brand new flecked sport coat. It was cream with black and pearl grey flecks. I'd seen it in *Esquire* magazine and ordered one the next day. It made me feel good about myself and for that reason, alone, it was worth every buck I'd paid for it. My fridge was empty, so I headed down the block to the Village West Coffee Shop. The sunlight hit me hard at first but a gentle breeze helped offset the afternoon heat. I noticed I'd parked the Chevy really badly, but it didn't have a scratch on it, maybe there was a patron saint for Detroit metal too. About a year ago the Village West had been a real beat joint—the whole scene, "daddy-o"—with poetry readings, bongo players and little rich kids dressing up poor in sandals and black sweaters. It was always good for laughs and easy pick-ups though, and Angelo, the owner, got a kick out of charging would-be stars and starlets 30 cents a cup of coffee. Anyhow, the whole Bohemian thing eventually moved to Sunset Strip and Angelo's clientele had gotten older and less interesting, which meant I fit in pretty well. When I walked in, Angelo whistled as he saw my face. Old world Italian with a grey goatee that made him look like some medieval count, Angelo was a good guy, one of life's gentlemen, but he could also be painfully honest.

"You crazy, crazy! What the hell you do this time? If you can't hold your booze you shouldna drink! You need some ice for those bruises?"

I cracked what I hoped passed for a smile.

"No ice, Angelo, but this crazy guy really needs a coffee."

He waved at me to sit down so I slid in to one of the booths overlooking the street. Angelo brought over the coffee, but before he could give me the third degree, a couple of fruits in matching grey slack suits swished through the door. I'd never seen them before but Angelo treated them like regulars and so, thankfully, he left me alone.

The java was good and strong. My mind started functioning again and wicked thoughts stalked my imagination. Part of me wanted to find Blondie's boyfriend and his pals and give them a little payback for the job they'd done on me. It wouldn't be hard to track them down. I was supposed to be a private detective for God's sake. I was also a vengeful guy, biblical even. I believed in an eye for an eye, a tooth for a tooth. We hadn't turned the other cheek after Pearl Harbor and now the Japs were playing baseball, dancing to jazz, and buying our cars. Revenge worked, revenge was good, and revenge was part of the American Way.

But I had something very important to attend to and Vicki, my ex-wife, hated me to be late. I left some change on the table, nodded to Angelo and walked stiffly back up the street. The sun was getting low in the sky, I wanted a drink and from the way my gut was rumbling, I knew I needed food. Luckily I was going somewhere that had both, in spades. An actor I worked for back in '55 had introduced me to the Luau and it had been one of my favorite watering holes ever since. It was, basically, a glorified up-market Polynesian shack, but the drinks were good and the company was cordial. According to legend, Steve Crane, the owner, had made out with almost every starlet in Hollywood, but in the Luau there was usually plenty of action left over for us mere mortals. But action, of any kind, was the last thing on my mind as I eased into the Chevy and very carefully joined the rush hour traffic heading west. The sun was in my eyes the whole trip, and by the time I reached Rodeo Drive I was in a bad way. I valet parked, nodded to the doorman and brushed past the ferns into the Luau's air-conditioned interior. It was early and the place was virtually empty, so I chose a table over by the tropical pool at the back of the room. It was secluded, but I could still see everyone who came in and, if they were looking, they could see me. The gentle sound of the mini waterfall behind me helped soothe my nerves, but something told me they wouldn't stay that way long.

I ordered food and a Zombie cocktail. In my state the Zombie seemed appropriate. The waitress who served me seemed worried by my appearance, so, after she left I shifted my chair back so my face was more in shadow. Maybe people would think I was one of the wooden Tikis that were dotted around the place. The Zombie tasted good and I was half way through it when the food arrived. The world was slowly starting to seem like a better place and then, half an hour late, Vicki arrived. She looked great in a well-tailored, figure-hugging cream pencil skirt and matching jacket. Her naturally blonde hair was cut shoulder-length, waved and full. Two years, and God knows how many more women later, and I still got shook up when she was near.

She glanced around the room, picked me out and hurried over. We'd first met in 1950. I was bumming around from one dead end job to another, still using the war as an excuse for screwing up. She was a rich man's daughter who had the good sense to know she'd been spoiled rotten. We were both in Canter's Deli at three in the morning one aimless Friday night. She was dressed in rolled-up jeans and bobby sox with a bunch of giggling girlfriends. I was on my lonesome, hunched over a cold coffee and a slice of apple pie covered in the gloop that was once a scoop of ice cream. She reached over to my booth and asked to borrow the sugar. I said something smart and she said something smarter. She joined me at my table. Her eyes were blue-green, her sun-kissed blonde hair was in a ponytail. An hour later, I was in love.

"Why do we always have to meet here?" she said as she reached the table, "It's always full of Hollywood phonies and hookers who think they're Ava Gardner."

She was always angry with me and even angrier with herself for being in the same room as me. I stood up to kiss her hello and she saw my face. Noticing the bruises, her voice softened slightly.

"What the hell happened to you?"

"It's nothing, just an accident. I walked into a door. No big deal."

Before she could say anything, the waitress appeared at the table.

I ordered another Zombie and a Martini for Vicki. As soon as the waitress left, her mood darkened.

"God, J.D., just look at your face. When are you going to grow up? You're like a big child, getting into fights at your age. Every time I start to think you're going to make it as a decent human being, you act like some juvenile delinquent. I suppose you were making out with some little honey from Hollywood High. Were you and she on the back seat of your car with Elvis playing on the radio? How romantic! Did her father give you a beating?"

Her voice was trembling but I didn't say a word. I read somewhere that you should never interrupt when someone's praising you. I've also learned to do the same when someone's insulting you. You never know what you're going to find out about yourself. This was like a rerun of all our past meetings since the big split. But, there was something more in her tone this time, not just the usual exasperation and contempt.

"For God's sake, why can't you be more reliable? I really need your help right now, and I despise myself for even telling you this."

The words ended in tears and part of me melted. She was a tough cookie and tears didn't come easily to her. Even during our worst times, the tears were rare. I moved closer and put an arm around her shoulders. A surge of pity swept over me. I kissed her head and whispered the kind of stupid nothings you whisper when you try to get a girl to stop weeping. As I held her, the scent of Chanel filled my senses. A fat guy in a loud checked jacket was staring at us from a couple of tables over. I glared back and he quickly looked away. I wished I had chosen somewhere more private for this meeting. I wished the Chanel didn't remind me of so many things.

"Honey," I said softly, "do you want to go? Let's drive somewhere else." She sat back and dabbed at the tears with the handkerchief I gave her.

"Don't call me honey, you bastard. You know what that does to me." She didn't say it nastily. It was almost sweet. She took a sip from her Martini. "It's Eddie. He's in very bad trouble. Someone tried to kill him and now he's in hiding somewhere and we don't know what the hell is happening."

She struggled to keep her composure. Eddie was her kid brother. I'd liked him. Back in the good old days, during the summers of '53 and '54, we took him and his fake ID card down the coast to the Lighthouse in Hermosa Beach almost every Sunday. Chet Baker, Art Pepper, Shelly Mane, Eddie loved them all. Me, I could take them or leave them—at least it wasn't that be-bop crap—but Eddie flipped on West Coast jazz. He read *Downbeat*, memorized chord structures, bought albums and dressed Ivy League like Brubeck. The only thing he liked more than music was science. Eddie was made for the Atomic Age. As a kid, he goofed around with home chemistry sets and could tell you the compounds for every metal known. He was head of his school's science club from 9th grade onwards. So, it was no big surprise when he went to Stanford University as a science major, and then landed a good job with some big chemical company. He was the last guy I'd ever imagine to be in serious trouble.

"Who the hell would want to kill Eddie? What was it over? Money? A girl?"

She looked irritated.

"You know Eddie would never need money. And it's not a girl. He told me that much. But he sounded so scared when he last called me. He didn't want the family involved. He said he was going to lay low for a few weeks. Oh, God, if anything happens to him…" The tears started again.

"Okay. Okay. Take it easy now. Why hasn't he called the cops?"

She pulled herself together. I could tell it wasn't easy but she managed it. Why had I let her go?

"He doesn't trust them. He doesn't trust anyone except you. He said you were the only person who could help."

She paused and I knew what was coming before she said it.

"Johnny, I'm begging you, please help us."

I had no choice. I'd do anything for her. I think she knew it, too. I was also kind of flattered that Eddie trusted me that much; and my battered ego needed all the help it could get, because the private eye thing was going nowhere, fast. The last few months I'd been living off inheritance money and a top dollar payment for a job of which I wasn't particularly proud. Sherlock Holmes would never have taken the case, but Sherlock never had to pay the monthly installments on a '58 Chevy. A swish Hollywood producer wanted proof that his live-in boyfriend was making time with some hot-shot director from another studio. It was a basic tailing and surveillance number. It had meant posing as a fag to get into certain clubs, sitting through God knows how many Frances Faye sets at the Crescendo, and long hours parked outside trashy motels in bad neighborhoods. Anyway, I got the evidence I needed and old producer X was so grateful that I'd handled the case discreetly; he added an extra zero to my fee. It didn't hurt that his latest movie had just won an Oscar and the studio was throwing more money at him than he could handle.

But, since then, I hadn't been trying. Vicki was right—I hadn't grown up. I'd played at everything I'd done since 1945. Fighting the Japs had turned me from a kid into a man, but since the war ended, I'd regressed.

The post-war me wanted easy women, smart clothes, a swank apartment and white wall wheels. Hey, I was the ad man's ideal, they dreamed about guys like me on Madison Ave. Electric razors? I'll take the latest model. High Fidelity systems? I'll take the latest model. New girl in town? I'll take the latest model. I'd been kidding along all this time and now Vicki was giving me when-push-comes-to-shove reality. I took a deep breath and jumped in with both feet. The Tiki statues behind her stared at me impassively but, as we got up to leave, I could have sworn that one of them smiled. It knew I was in trouble.

Palm Springs

Two hours later, I was east of Pasadena, driving towards the desert. I had a suitcase in the trunk and Julie London on the radio. Her sultry voice normally made me think of sex, but that evening there was a whirlwind where my brain should have been. Before we left the Luau, Vicki had filled me in on Eddie's movements over the previous few weeks. He hadn't been his usual laid-back self, and had seemed increasingly anxious about something. All he would tell her was that a new project he was working on at Star Crest Chemicals wasn't going well. The last time they spoke, Eddie had called from a payphone and was on the verge of hysteria. He claimed he'd been followed for days, and that a truck had tried to run him down on an empty street. Despite Vicki's pleading, he'd refused to come back to LA. That was when he told her to contact me and that he'd call from a safe place. We figured that place was Palm Springs. Vicki's Uncle Bradley was a director at the Lockheed Corporation. In '51, he'd bought a parcel of land out in the desert and built his dream home on it. "If it's good enough for Bing Crosby and Bob Hope, it's good enough for me'," he never got tired of telling everyone. The desert summers were too hot for Vicki's aunt though, and they kept their Bel Air mansion and only used Uncle's dream home five or six times a year. That had made it a handy getaway for Vicki and me while we were dating. Uncle Bradley didn't mind us using the place, as he actually approved of me. He was a West Pointer and my being a veteran made me some kind of war hero in his eyes. He naively trusted me to take his niece to Palm Springs and behave like a gentleman. Anyway, I figured Eddie would be there at the house. We'd talk, fix his problems over a drink or two and everything would be just hunky dory. I'd return to LA—and Vicki—the conquering hero. She would forgive my past indiscretions, and my life would be back on track. That was the theory anyway.

The late evening traffic was light and by eleven, I was in open desert. After two hours behind the wheel, I needed to stretch out. My legs were sore from the beating I'd taken the night before and I wanted to get the blood circulating to help the bruising heal faster. There was a big, full moon in the sky and I could see a turn-off ahead of me. I took it and ended up on a dirt track that snaked diagonally away from the highway. I bumped along for a couple of minutes and eased the Chevy forward until it was on a bluff overlooking the valley below. I switched off the engine and let the silence sink in as I drank a cup of java from the thermos. I got out of the car and let the cold of the night and the hot coffee help clear the cobwebs from my brain. I leaned back against the warmth of the hood and slowly inhaled the clean desert air. It was good to get out of LA, away from the smog, the noise, and the madness.

I'd always liked the desert. Something about the sheer scale and majesty of the place made it easy to feel truly alone. Being in the wilderness always made me think of that Nat King Cole song, "Nature Boy." The moon was bright, bright enough for me to walk around the car without needing a flashlight. I tried to rub some of the pain out of my legs as I moved, but it didn't help much. I sat back on the hood and let my mind wander. The star-studded sky that stretched above and over me seemed so close I felt I could just reach up and grab a handful of stardust. I could be on another world, on Mars perhaps. Mountains, endless deserts and strange alien shapes loomed out in the vast, moonlit wilderness. This was Ray Bradbury territory. A backdrop to the "Martian Chronicles" that I'd read about a dozen times since they were first published. For a few minutes, I stared out at the Martian landscape and then my mind betrayed me and I remembered my last time in desert country.

It had been a clear summer night, about a year before, and I was heading back from Vegas with a chorus girl I'd met that weekend. She was a dancer at the Dunes' Aladdin Room and one of the wildest women I'd ever dated. It didn't take either of us long to realize what we had was just animal attraction, but we had a fun and exhausting few weeks working that out. Anyway, there we were, doing 70 mph on an empty stretch of road outside of Barstow, when suddenly the darkness was blasted away by a brilliant flash of light. For a few seconds of eternity, everything was bright as day and stark white with harsh black shadows. And then there was a clap of distant thunder.

Carol had been almost asleep when the midnight sun struck. She grabbed my arm and screamed and then it was night again. I thought it was the end of the world. The Russians had finally done it. No four-minute warning, just BOOM! But the world hadn't ended. It was one of our own A-Bombs, detonated somewhere out in the desert. They said later, on the radio, that it was the biggest ever tested, about twenty times bigger than the Fat Boy they dropped on Hiroshima. It was only after I'd swung the automobile off the tarmac and onto the desert sand that I realized what the flash really was. They'd been doing tests every year since the war, but I must have missed the warning about this baby. I tried calming Carol down but she was almost hysterical.

"Oh, my God! It was so bright, so quick. What chance would we have had if it was the real thing?"

"Don't worry, it'll never happen," I kept saying, but my heart was pounding and part of me knew I was lying. It *could* happen. Anytime. It made me feel helpless and insignificant. I'd felt that way before but in different circumstances. Once, on Iwo Jima, the Navy opened up with its big guns on a ridge full of Japs just two hundred yards from where we were curled up in our fox holes. The ground shook as the shells thudded home, and I felt like an ant caught in the path of a bulldozer. But, though my insides were quaking, I knew, without even thinking about it, that back home everything was like it had always been. Away from the war, back in the States, people were driving, shopping, and walking down their little neighborhood streets, just living. The Bomb, though, that was different. When the time came, it would be *sayonara* everything. Goodbye cruel world.

There were no bomb tests as I stood in the high desert above Palm Springs, worrying about young Eddie, but the images of mushroom clouds in my head meant the Martian landscape suddenly lost its exotic appeal. My surroundings had abruptly become eerie and desolate. I shivered. If World War III had started right then I would have been out there on my own, alone in a dead world. It suddenly seemed really important that I be back amongst people, to be part of the human race again. From where I stood, I could make out the tiny, twinkling lights of houses in the Coachella Valley. I wanted to be down there among those lights.

The solitude of the desert night had crept up on me and done strange things to my mind. I climbed back into the car, and as soon as the engine growled to life I felt more relaxed. Five minutes later, I was back on the highway. As I picked up speed, a Coca Cola truck came rolling alongside me and I felt strangely comforted having its lit-up silver and red bulk blocking out the desert to my right hand side. The end of the world became just a figment of a strange distant nightmare. The familiar Coca Cola logo, the truck's shiny panels and the smell of gasoline were life-affirming reality. I followed the Coke truck right into town. The guy drove like an idiot, but I was still disappointed when he turned off before I did. Although it was past midnight as I cruised down Palm Canyon Drive, there were plenty of other automobiles on the move. Outside one restaurant, a bunch of smooth looking guys in white tuxedos and dolled-up women in cocktail dresses were piling into a line of Cadillacs, with much shouting and laughter. A couple of photographers were popping flashes and everybody seemed to love the attention. Perhaps Sinatra was in town. A block south of the restaurant party, two Kim Novak look-a-likes in gold Capri pants swayed from a red convertible to the entrance of the Silver Slipper Lounge Bar. For a couple of seconds I took my foot off the gas and my eyes off the road. I didn't stop though and, putting temptation back in its cage, I left the bars and cars of the main drag behind me and turned off into a quiet residential district. The lawns were impeccable; tall, stately palms lined the sidewalks and the streets reeked of money.

Uncle Bradley's place was at the end of a cul-de-sac, with the mountains as an impressive backdrop. The house was a low-roofed, sleek modern number, with boulders and cacti arranged artfully around it. It all looked very natural, but I knew for a fact some dinky Hollywood landscape gardener had charged a couple of thousand bucks to create that just-part-of-the-desert look. The Flintstones would have lived here, if Fred had been a millionaire and not a dumb-ass quarry man. In fact, the whole damned neighborhood looked like a space age Bedrock with brand new Imperials and Lincoln Continentals in every driveway. I parked on the street and walked slowly to the front door. The curtains were drawn on the big windows, and there was no sign of any light behind them. I rang the doorbell three times and waited. Nothing happened so I fished out the front-door keys Vicki had given me, jiggled the lock and stepped inside.

As I came into the entrance hall, I stumbled over something big and bulky lying on the floor. Catching my balance, I groped for the light-switch. Stretched in front of me was a body. It was a shock, but a shock tempered by realizing that at least the corpse wasn't Eddie. I carefully stepped over the lifeless form, bent down and stared into the face of death. In this case, death was an overweight, slightly balding guy in his late 40s. He was wearing a crumpled shirt and tie, grey business suit, scuffed black shoes and an expression of pure horror on his face. It was the facial grimace that hit me hardest. I'd seen dead men before, in the Pacific, but even among those who had died slowly, blood-soaked in agony, I hadn't seen a look of such fear.

The house was in silence. I could see no obvious signs of injury on the man in the grey flannel suit. There was no blood anywhere and I couldn't detect any bruising to the head or neck. I knelt by the body. From the smell of alcohol wafting up at me it seemed like the deceased had been drinking pretty heavily. I carefully removed a wallet from his jacket's inside breast pocket. I flipped it open and checked his ID. The fat man was one Clifford B. Rhodes, head of the Star Crest Chemical Corporation's security division. That wasn't good. For Vicki's and Eddie's sake, I wanted to be on that bluff overlooking the valley again, daydreaming under the starlight. But I wasn't. I was in Uncle Bradley's dream home, confused, and alone with a corpse. I figured the first thing to do was get the late Mister Rhodes as far away from the house as possible. I quickly checked his other pockets and found a few coins and a pack of Chester-fields. The wallet had about two hundred bucks in tens and twenties, a photo of what I presumed were Rhodes' wife and kids on Santa Monica pier, a membership card to the Elk's Club, a California driving license and a couple of folded letters written on Star Crest Chemical note paper. One was a list of names and places that meant nothing to me; the other was a signed letter from Eddie to a "Dearest Justine".

I kept the letters and put everything else back where I'd found them. I was trying to be as methodical as possible, but I was tired. I checked the rest of the house. There were no broken windows, no signs of a struggle and no Eddie. A pile of LPs, an empty vodka bottle, and two highball glasses on the blonde wood coffee table in the living room were the only indication that he might have been there in the last twenty-four hours. I grabbed a blanket from a cupboard in one of the guest rooms and wrapped Rhodes in it. I wanted to hide the look on that face as quickly as possible. I stepped outside and looked across the street. There was no sign of life in either of the two other houses in the cul-de-sac. I was pretty sure that the boulders and cacti shielded me from any prying eyes, so I switched my suitcase to the back seat of the Chevy and dragged the body out to the sidewalk. I'd forgotten how heavy a corpse could be, and I almost killed myself lifting it into the trunk. I was shaking and sweating when I got back into the car. I kept the headlights off until I reached South Palm Canyon Drive and then I headed east towards the open desert.

I wasn't happy. I'd been in Palm Springs less than an hour and I was attempting to dispose of what was possibly a murder victim. I wasn't thinking straight. I needed sleep, but first I had to lose Rhodes somewhere and get back to the house. I was getting so damned tired I wasn't even aware of the mechanics of driving. I just kept looking at the motels on either side of the road and desperately wondering if any of them would be a safe place to dump the body. I didn't want to leave it out in the desert where no one would find it. The man had a family, for God's sake, and they deserved to know what had happened. But what the hell *had* happened and how was Eddie involved?

While I was puzzling that out, I rolled my window down and leaned my face into the rush of air for a few seconds. The chill wind helped me focus and I stepped on the gas as I headed towards the city limits. The buildings and bright neon signs petered out and soon there was only desert and the occasional building site on either side of the road. Then, five minutes later I saw what I needed. About a hundred yards ahead of me was a huge, cantilever sign advertising the Desert Knight Diner. The diner itself was set back from the road and looked closed, so, I pulled up in front of the chrome steps that led up to the entrance and killed the engine.

For five minutes I sat there in the silence of the night and then, cursing my aching legs, I got out of the car and checked the back of the building. There was no one around, just piles of empty cardboard boxes and the smell of kitchen grease and disinfectant. I walked back to the car, praying there would be no passing traffic, and set to work. I half-carried, half-dragged the body onto the steps of the diner, bundled the blanket back into the trunk and hit the road. Luck was on my side and no other vehicles were in sight as I sped away. I glanced round once and could vaguely make out the dark shape slumped against the chrome steps. I hoped the diner opened early and they'd find Rhodes before something crept out of the wilderness looking for an easy meal.

I headed back into town, was briefly lost, and spent forty minutes cutting across quiet residential streets to reach Palm Canyon Drive again. The cul-de-sac was still deserted as I took my revolver from its compartment under the dashboard, got my suitcase from the rear seat and went back into the house. Except for a few drag marks on the carpet in the hall, you'd never know that somebody had died there. I brushed the carpet's fibers back into place with my foot and went into the den. I felt dirty and sad—sad for Rhodes, sad for Eddie, and sad for myself. I opened up the drinks cabinet and poured myself a brandy. I felt I deserved it. I downed the amber liquid in one swallow and let the heat work its way down to my gut. Gun still in hand; I went through the dining area to the big floor-to-ceiling windows at the back of the house. With the light of the moon flooding in on the carpet, I checked the locks on the back door. They were fine, so I took a deep breath and stood staring out at the pool. The moon reflected off the water and created eerie shadows on the trunks of the palm trees that stood like sentinels at the edge of the concrete decking. Uncle Bradley had brought them in from Pasadena to give the garden that authentic, naturally tropical look. Beyond the palms were more boulders and then the shrub and sand of the desert. And beyond all that was the mountain. It sat brooding, a giant black shadow that blotted out most of the star-lit sky to the West. I looked at the mountain for a long time though it didn't tell me anything I didn't already know. There was still a lot to take care of, but I was beat. I went around the house turning out lights and then hit the sack. I slept in the master bedroom with the revolver on the bedside table and the drapes pulled to hide the mountain.

Justine

I slept well, and probably would have gone on sleeping if Vicki hadn't called. I fumbled for the phone, remembering, too late, that maybe I shouldn't have answered it.

"Johnny, is that you?"

I grunted in reply.

"Are you okay? What's going on?

I didn't know which question to answer first so I made up my own.

"Hi, what time is it?"

"It's eight. I was getting worried. You said you'd call first thing in the morning. How's Eddie? Did you two talk, yet?"

I stretched out in the bed. It was the most comfortable bed I'd ever slept in. Maybe money couldn't buy you everything but it sure gave you a good night's sleep.

"Slow down. Slow down. I'm still waking up. I haven't spoken to Eddie because he's not here. I think he…"

Before I could finish she cut in on me. "He's not there? Then where is he? Why aren't you out looking for him? Oh, God, please tell me you haven't got some little tramp there with you. Johnny, if you have, so help me I'll kill you!"

"Jesus! Just hold it a minute!" I probably shouted too loudly but it shut her up. "I got here late. Eddie wasn't here, but it looks like he was earlier. Has he called you?"

"No, of course not. You know I would have told you that." She was angry and I guess I couldn't really blame her but I had my hands tied. I couldn't tell her about Rhodes yet but I had to give her something.

"I've got a feeling Eddie got lonely out here and spent the night at a hotel somewhere. I'll start calling them and ask if he's checked in at any of them. But for all I know, he could show up here any second."

I guess the tone of my voice calmed her down. She told me to call the minute I heard from Eddie and to take care of myself. She even sounded like she meant it. I hung up and padded into the en-suite bathroom.

There was one of those little, flat weighing machines on the floor, and out of vanity, I climbed on. I clocked in at 190 lbs., which wasn't bad, I guess. Most of it was still muscle but I needed toning up. The bruises on my legs were changing color and the scar on my side from the Jap shrapnel that took me out of the war looked redder than it had been for some time. I didn't know what that meant, but I knew I needed some sun.

After a shower and a shave, I dressed in my white Keds, a pair of chinos and a white sports shirt. It was going to be one hell of a hot day and I wanted to be prepared. The sky was that electric blue that you only get in the desert and, even with the automatic air-conditioning on, I could sense the heat pounding the walls and roof. The house's maid service must have been in recently because the Frigidaire in the kitchen was pretty well stocked. I whipped up some scrambled eggs, downed a mug of coffee and tried to think. I didn't know yet what kind of mess Eddie was in, but I knew he was in deep. The head of Star Crest security had died in the house. God only knew who else was aware he'd been there or if he'd driven out from Fontana by himself. In his wallet, he had a letter from Eddie to some girl, so he'd obviously been doing his research. From the two highball glasses on the coffee table I guessed that Eddie had been in the house too. I didn't have Eddie down for a killer, so, who or what had snuffed Rhodes? And if it was a heart attack, what had put that look of terror on his face?

I gazed out at the pool. It looked cool and inviting, but questions kept fizzing like Alka-Seltzer in my brain. I laid out the letter and the page of notes that had been in Rhodes' wallet and poured myself some orange juice. The notes were lists of names and places, some crossed out, some underlined. Top of the list was the name Justine Moore and in brackets after that were the words "Research and Development". The next item was the phrase *Ritual of the Savage* with three big question marks after it. One or two of the other names on the list were familiar, like the Royal Hawaiian Restaurant in Laguna Beach, and disturbingly, 1705 San Jacinto Drive, which was exactly where I was sitting. The other underlined names—Pacific Art Supplies on Pico Boulevard, the Jive Hive on Sunset Strip, and The Opening Door of Perception—meant nothing to me. Eddie's letter to Justine was a lot more interesting. It was dated a few days previously:

My Dearest Justine. I don't know where to start. Everything has become so crazy lately. You're the only good thing to have happened to me since Menlo Park. You've opened my mind to so many things, but the more I find out, the more I'm confused. You told me you loved me and I've listened to you every step of the way but now everything seems out of whack. I feel threatened by everyone and everything—that's why I've decided to get away for a while. I've got to get my mind straightened out and deal with things without Star Crest breathing down my neck. I would give anything right now to have you next to me, your sweet face smiling at me. Please call me, or better still, meet me in Palm Springs. I've started something that I've lost all control of, and I need you by my side. So long as I know I have you, everything else will be worthwhile. Rhodes is sniffing around and I wonder all the time if I've done the right thing. When you're with me, it all makes sense. But alone, I don't know what's right or wrong. Please, sweet Justine, call me on the number I gave you. Let me know you'll see me soon. I can't wait to hold you again or kiss your beautiful lips. I need you. I love you.

Yours always,
Eddie.

Jesus. The kid had it bad and whatever trouble he was in, this Justine seemed a big part of it. I also wondered what was going on at Star Crest that had made Eddie take off so suddenly. They were no two-bit operation but one of the biggest pharmaceutical companies in the country. While I was pondering that question, I couldn't help thinking that, at that very moment, Rhodes' body was probably being examined by a police forensics expert. Once Star Crest had been informed, they'd undoubtedly connect Eddie with the death and then he would need all the help he could get, but where the hell was he?

I drifted into the den, the empty vodka bottle and glasses sat there taunting me. It was then that I noticed something about the pile of LPs haphazardly stacked on the table. Uncle Bradley's music collection was still neatly stored in the shelves beneath his expensive phonograph. The twenty or so albums dumped on the table had to be music that Eddie had brought with him. The top two albums on the pile confirmed this; Eddie's name, and the date of their purchase, was scrawled on the back of each record sleeve. Sifting through the albums it became even more obvious they weren't Uncle Bradley's records. The old guy's taste was strictly classical. These LPs had titles like *Jungle Jazz*, *Lure Of The Tropics* and *Voodoo Suite*. Why had Eddie dragged his record collection to Palm Springs with him? I also couldn't figure out why he'd suddenly gotten into this exotic mood music. What had happened to all the serious jazz he used to go crazy for?

I worked my way down the pile until I found an album I'd seen before in record stores. The cover was a painting of a brunette in a low-cut gown, half-embracing, half-resisting some horny looking guy, while all around them these creepy tribal masks stared out into space. It was a weird cover, the expression on the brunette's face made her look more frightened than ecstatic and the masks hinted at some primitive evil. But it wasn't so much the cover art that attracted my attention. The title, *Ritual of the Savage* was the same phrase that appeared on Rhodes' list. I picked it up and flipped it over. The back of the album had the usual dramatic liner notes. All that *Do the mysteries of native rituals intrigue you? Does the haunting beat of savage drums fascinate you?* bullshit. Sad but true, that kind of stuff vaguely interested me because I'd found that some women actually love that exotic musical journey stuff. Especially when they'd had a couple of cocktails, the lights were low and the bedroom was only a few inebriated steps away from the hi-fi. *Playboy* magazine had just written about it, calling it "Seduction music—the bringing out of the pagan beast lurking behind the lipstick, powder, and paint of the hot-blooded American female." I wasn't going to argue with Hugh Hefner, but it didn't seem like this kind of seduction was Eddie's style.

More interesting were the countless scribbles and jottings that Eddie had scrawled on the back cover in his tiny, intense handwriting. Half of it made no sense at all; mathematical formulas and the names of chemical compounds I'd never heard of. But amongst all the mad scientist jargon there were things that intrigued me. The words *Doors of Perception* were there as they had been on Rhodes' list. So, too, were other phrases that had me wondering about Eddie's sanity, *The exporting of evil and the saving of a dream from Menlo Park* and *A time bomb of the mind that opens a phone line to God?* were two of the more colorful ones. *Phone line to God.* What the hell was he thinking?

Maybe they were clues to help me find him, or maybe they were just the drunken ramblings of a lovesick scientist. Some of the track listings had been circled in red ink, but this was no more help than the rest of the babble. "Sophisticated Savage", "Busy Port", and "The Ritual" meant nothing to me. Was there a message in the music itself? I went to slide out the disc and a brown envelope came out with it. The envelope had been sealed at some point, but it wasn't any more. Stamped on both sides was a printed warning *Property of Star Crest Chemicals Research & Development Department. Not to be removed from R & D laboratories under ANY circumstances.*

Beneath the warning, on the front of the envelope, was a white square of paper headed *Menlo Park Veterans Hospital Test Results—January through May 1958*. Under that were Eddie's real name, "Edward Hastings", and his title, "Project Director—The Huxley Experiment". What really grabbed my interest though, was the typed line in very large font at the bottom of the white paper. *Department of Defense—Classified Military Intelligence. To be opened only in the presence of an assigned officer.*

Great, the kid was in possession of classified US Government documents! I shook out the contents of the envelope and a dozen or so sheets of typewritten paper, all stamped "Top Secret", fluttered to the floor. I skimmed through the endless lines of text looking for meaning, but for all I understood of it, it may as well have been in Martian. There were references to "tolerance levels" and pages of formulae and dosages. Here and there, Eddie's handwritten notes popped up, again in a scrawl so tiny I couldn't make out some of the words. Whatever else it was, it seemed too important to be left lying around, so I replaced the contents of the envelope and put it back inside the sleeve of the album. Then I checked out the rest of Eddie's LPs for scribbled notes or hidden envelopes. I found nothing. I then thought of one place where Eddie's special little package would be safe for at least a short while.

As I stepped outside onto the poolside patio, the heat hit me like a wave breaking on a beach. It must have been at least 110 degrees. I shaded my eyes from the noonday sun and walked round the water's edge to a cluster of small rocks that lay at the base of the nearest palm tree. The junction box for the night-lights in the pool was hidden beneath them. The rocks were hot to my touch as I moved them to one side and flipped open the lid of the metal container. Carefully, I squeezed the *Ritual of the Savage* down the side of the electrical casings and replaced the box lid and the rocks. I was walking back into the welcoming shade of the house when I heard an automobile pull up outside. My mind was racing as I dashed into the bedroom, grabbed my revolver and headed for the front door. Was this Eddie at last? The cops? I reached the entrance hall as a key clicked in the lock and the door opened.

The intensity of the daylight blinded me to the identity of the intruder but it couldn't disguise the fact that it was a woman. She had a shape Kim Novak would have been proud of and she was tall. She was so busy looking down at the floor as she carefully pushed the door open that she didn't notice me at first. I just had time to stuff the revolver into the back waistband of my pants and under my shirt before she saw me. When she did, she literally jumped with fright. She put her hands over her heart, took in a deep breath and slowly let it out. Then she spoke.

"Who the hell are you? You almost scared me to death."

"I'm Johnny. I'm a friend of the family," I smiled as I said it. "And who the hell are *you*?"

She relaxed half a notch. Even nervous, she was one of the most gorgeous women I'd ever laid eyes on. She had glossy red hair pulled back into a bun on top of her head but it wasn't the kind of red you see on white-skinned Irish girls. This was a tawny color that accented the pale honey tan of her skin. Her face was angular with full lips and almond shaped eyes. She wore high heels, skin-tight Capri pants on long legs, and a white blouse tied up at her slender waist. The skin of her belly was firm and tanned. She looked like the French actress Agnes Laurent. She looked like a sleek, golden animal. I wanted her. I hoped my eyes didn't show it but I wasn't counting on it.

31

"Oh *you're* Johnny! Eddie talks about you all the time." Her eyes widened a little, "from the way he spoke about you I thought you were a lot older."

"I usually am," I replied, "the desert air does wonders for my complexion."

Despite the anxiety that flickered across her face, she giggled. She had the whitest teeth. She was a smooth operator too. She had gone from shock to easy familiarity in a few seconds. I had to be careful.

"I'm guessing you're Justine. Am I right?"

She extended a slim wristed arm. We shook hands.

"Yes. You're one hundred per cent right. Justine Moore. I'm Eddie's girlfriend, but I guess you'd gathered that."

I nodded. She was standing inches from me now and I could smell her perfume.

"Well, aren't you going to invite me in? I could really do with a cold Coke."

She flashed those teeth again.

"I'm sorry. Please come in. I guess you know where the kitchen is?"

She pushed the front door shut with her foot and eased past me. I followed her into the den. She swayed with an easy grace and I found my eyes fixed to the curves of her hips. From the way her ass moved, I knew she'd be good in bed. It occurred to me that was a line I'd once read in a cheap paperback and I felt guilty that it had leaped into my head at that moment. This was Eddie's girl after all. I had to try and remember that. It was difficult though, the Capri pants were skin-tight and I couldn't see a panty line.

"So where is Eddie?" I asked, "His sister said he'd be here."

She reached the chrome door of the Frigidaire, tugged it open, and bending slightly at the waist, she reached inside for a Coke. She turned and offered me the bottle. I shook my head. That stuff had way too many damned bubbles for me. She shrugged, flipped the lid off using the bottle opener on the wall and perched cutely on one of the kitchen counter stools. She raised the bottle and sipped at the Coke. I guess she tilted the bottle back a little too far and too fast because as the liquid fizzed into her mouth a couple of amber drops fell from her lips onto

32

her white Capri pants, landing where the material stretched tight over her calf muscles. She bent forward to wipe at the tiny stains and as she angled forward her breasts swelled against the fabric of her blouse. Sweat started prickling on my upper lip.

It was crazy. She'd obviously expected to find Rhodes' body when she stepped in to the house. She also must have guessed that I knew where the body had gone. But here we were like two teenagers flitting around each other on a first date. I pulled up a stool across the counter from her and waited for her to stop fussing with the Coke stain. She straightened up and smiled at me. Her expression was so innocent that I almost felt guilty for my thoughts.

"I'm sorry. What were you saying?"

"Eddie. Where is he?" I asked it nicely, but slow enough to show I meant business. She sipped at her drink, more carefully this time, with no spills. I couldn't help but be disappointed.

"Oh, he'll be here any minute. We went out to get some breakfast this morning and afterwards he decided to go to a bookstore and buy some magazines. You know Eddie, he has to have his *Science Today* journal. I got bored waiting for him so I got a cab back here first."

She had tried to bluff me and she'd gotten it badly wrong. She must have assumed I'd only just arrived. I didn't know why she was lying, but I was glad she was. She wasn't perfect after all. I tried her again.

"Seriously, where's Eddie? I really need to know."

She took a longer drink from the Coke bottle and didn't act flustered.

"I just told you. He's in town but he'll be here any minute."

"Uh, huh."

I got up and gently took the bottle from her hot little hand. She looked surprised. I acted hurt.

"Justine, Justine... I thought we could be friends, as we're both friends of the family..."

She started to speak but I put a finger to her mouth.

"Shhh, let me finish. You're not telling me the truth. We can't be friends if you keep lying to me. I'm here to help Eddie. We've been pretty polite, so far, but now I'm going to ask you again and this time I'll let you know something. I've been here all night and the body you expected to find has been disposed of."

She suddenly looked defeated. She raised a hand to her temple and shook her head.

"Oh, God. I knew this would go all wrong. Okay, Johnny, I'm so sorry I lied to you, but Eddie and I are in big trouble."

"No kidding?"

"I wasn't sure what to tell you. There're crazy things going on at Star Crest and we had to get away. Eddie said we should come here. He wanted some time to work out whether we should speak to the newspapers or to the police. But last night the head of Star Crest security turned up and said we'd stolen research papers. We kept trying to tell him we had nothing, but he wouldn't listen. At first he was kind of friendly, Eddie gave him a couple of drinks but then he started slapping Eddie around and I ran into the bedroom to call the police. While I was trying to get through, I heard a crash. I thought it was Eddie, so I ran back to the den. He was okay… but the security man was lying in the hallway, dead."

She looked genuinely upset. If it was all an act, it was a good one.

"We thought he'd had a heart attack but we were too frightened to call an ambulance. It was so awful. Eddie drove us to a motel. He said we should figure out what to do from there. But I think the big ape really hurt Eddie because this morning the poor darling couldn't get out of bed. I came back here to check if he'd really died—the security man, I mean. If he had, Eddie and I agreed that I'd go back to the motel and we'd call the police and just… tell them the truth…"

She sounded plausible enough. As she spoke, I tried to figure out how old she was. Her composure said late twenties but her face said younger. In some things, at least, Eddie was a lucky boy. As she finished she reached over to me and put her hand on my forearm.

"But now you're here you can help us. You can back up our story."

Her soft hand gently squeezed my arm. It felt good.

"Sure, Justine, I'll help you. Rhodes *is* dead and I agree it looks like a heart attack. I dumped the body late last night because I didn't want Eddie's family getting mixed up with the police in such an awkward way. Now I know what happened here, I guess I'll have to call them;

but I have to talk to Eddie first. I need to know what was happening at Star Crest that made you both take off. I don't understand why Eddie was so scared if he'd done nothing wrong. And what about those papers Rhodes thought you had stolen? Was he right? Were you two selling company secrets?"

She made to answer but I talked over her.

"I also don't get why Rhodes came down here himself. Why didn't he just call the local cops to pick you up? A big company like Star Crest is going to carry a lot of weight with the Palm Springs Police Department. Care to explain any of that?"

She frowned. "I don't know why he thought we were thieves—and it sounds like you don't believe us, either."

"I didn't say I didn't believe you, but there's…"

"You're supposed to be Eddie's friend, and while he's lying injured in a crummy motel room, you're giving me the third degree!"

Her beautifully full lower lip started trembling and her eyes filled with tears.

"We're being persecuted because we found out that one of Star Crest's products could be harmful to the public. We tried warning them but all they care about is their profit margins. Eddie tried to talk to them and now he's probably got a fractured rib and they'll blame us for that Mister Rhodes dying and…"

Her shoulders were shaking with emotion. The tears rolling down her cheeks and her big, wet eyes made her look like a lost little kid. She stepped forward into my arms and really started sobbing. I hate it when women cry, it fogs my judgment and makes me do dumb things. I hugged her and tried to feel like a knight in shining armor comforting the damsel in distress. But all I could really feel was her warm, soft body pressed against my chest and the way her breasts pushed at me as she gulped down air between sobs. With great reluctance, I eased her away from me and fished out my handkerchief so she could dry her face.

"Listen, Justine, we'll drive over to Eddie, I'll talk to him, I'll call the medics if he needs them. Then we'll call the cops and get this whole damned thing sorted out. Eddie's family has money, they'll get the best lawyers in California and everything will be fine. Now, come on, stop crying. Let's go see him."

As I said it, I knew she was a liar. I'd seen the Star Crest documents that Eddie had hidden in his exotica album. I also couldn't help thinking that in the space of less than twenty-four hours, two beautiful women had shed tears over poor, misunderstood Eddie. I felt a tinge of envy.

Justine dabbed away the last of the tears and smiled.

"Thanks, Johnny. Eddie was right about you."

As she said it, she leaned forward and kissed me on the cheek. Her lips lingered for a second or two and I fought the impulse to turn my head just two lousy inches and put my mouth to hers. I forced myself to remember that she was Eddie's girlfriend. It was all too complicated.

The Sundowner

Despite my nagging conscience, my fevered imagination was working overtime as I unlocked the door of the Chevy. The Impala's a swell ride and I felt proud of the way she purred into life as I started the ignition. Justine's white outfit and tanned skin contrasted nicely with the pale blue leather of the upholstery and, under other circumstances, it would've been my idea of a perfect date but life is never quite that simple. The noonday heat was baking off the ground in shimmery waves as we cruised past fantastically landscaped modern houses, towering palm trees, and open stretches of scrub desert. The Sundowner Motel was only ten minutes from San Jacinto Drive and we didn't talk much as I drove over there. I was trying to stop the fantasies running through my mind while the unknowing participant in them sat next to me, quiet as you like.

Despite Justine's earlier comment, the motel didn't look too crummy to me. Shielded from the road by a white concrete-block sunscreen of interlocking small circles, it was a two-story affair with the obligatory kidney-shaped swimming pool and feather-like palms. I spotted Eddie's beige, soft-top Thunderbird parked at one end of the building and pulled up next to it. There was only one other car parked in the whole lot. It was July after all, and few tourists could face the desert heat until after Labor Day at the earliest.

"We're on the second floor," Justine said.

She then arched her back, lifting her hips off the car seat. I was wondering what the hell she was doing until she stuck her hand into the slanted front pocket of her tight-fitting Capri pants. I watched enraptured as she used the tips of her fingers to tug out a key with a tiny brass tag attached.

"Room 22. At the top of the stairs," she said and pointed to a flight of steps next to Eddie's T-bird. I took the key, swung my door open, and started getting out of the car. A thought suddenly occurred to me.

"What about you. You're coming up too, aren't you?"

I waited for an answer. She slowly repeated the arching movement of her hips and pulled a lipstick from her other pocket. She smiled sweetly up at me.

"I just want to retouch my lipstick. I'll be there in a second."

I nodded, pretending to understand female logic. I was also wondering if she knew what effect she'd had on me when she did that thing with her hips. As I started climbing the stairs I was startled by the sharp blast of the Chevy's horn cutting into the afternoon's quietness. I swung around. Justine was standing by the driver's side of the car waving sweetly.

"I'm ready now," she called and began strolling over to the bottom of the steps.

I reached the landing and opened the door to Room 22. A mambo song was playing on the radio, and the sunlight streamed in from behind me. The blinds were shut, but I could plainly make out someone lying on one of the room's twin beds. As I walked over, I realized it was Eddie and he didn't look good. His grey slacks and white T-shirt were creased and dirty, like he'd been wearing them for days. His unshaven face was deathly pale, his eyes were sunken and shut and his mouth was twitching. I leaned over the bed and spoke softly.

"Jesus, Eddie! What the hell have you been up to, kid?"

In response, his eyelids struggled open. His normally clear blue eyes were cloudy and bloodshot. He reached out and grabbed my arm. His mouth was trying to form words but there was just a dry whispering sound. I leaned a little closer.

I understood the next words I heard, but they weren't Eddie's. As the voice began, I felt the cold, hard steel of a gun barrel jammed into the back of my neck.

"Okay, big guy. Let's play this nice and easy and we'll get along just fine."

The voice was thick and deep. It was accompanied by the potent smell of stale sweat and cheap cigars. The son-of-a-bitch must have been lurking behind the door. He was damned good, I'd give him that.

Wondering where Justine was, as I hoped her arrival might give me the distraction I needed to turn the tables on Stinky, I stalled for time.

"Hey! I'm just a friend of the kid's. I don't want any trouble."

The gun barrel was jabbed into my neck again, really hard. It was beginning to hurt. The deep voice growled at me.

"Don't try turning round. Just put your hands on your head real slow and easy and then kneel on the floor."

As he said it, a new mambo song started on the radio. It was one I recognized. It was a girl singing "Bei Mer Bist Du Schon". It was a great version that really swung and was faster than the Andrews Sisters' recording. I liked it a lot but I didn't care for the gun in my neck. I had a bad feeling about it, like the guy behind me was going to use it whatever I did. Just then a shadow half blotted out the long rectangle of sunshine that flooded though the open door from the landing. Justine, at last! For a second I felt the pressure of the gun lessen against my neck. Seizing my chance, I jerked my shoulders to one side and turned quickly, punching the gun upward and away from my neck. I moved fast, but not fast enough to prevent the heavy metal of the butt smashing against my cheekbone. The pain galvanized me into action and, with everything I had, I straight-armed my fist into the face in front of me.

I got lucky and caught him between his mouth and nose. I registered black, greasy hair and pain on a chubby, olive face. I didn't notice much else because I was intent on keeping the gun pointing away from me. He was off balance now and, as he tried to bring the gun back around in my direction, I charged into him—head down. He staggered backwards but still managed to slam the gun butt down on my head. In a blind, pain-filled rage, I kept pushing him backwards until he crashed into a low chest of drawers. Everything on the chest—mirror, lamp, radio—fell to the floor. The volume of the music jumped loudly and the gunman's head whiplashed back into the wall while the mambo girl sang; "Bella, bella, even say Wunderbar…" As he struggled to stay on his feet, I jerked my head up as fast as I could. The top of my skull caught him full in the face with a sickening crunch. I felt dizzy with the pain, but the body in front of me went limp and started to slide to one side. Out of the corner of one eye, I saw the black shape of the gun drop to the carpet. I straightened up as my attacker slumped to a prone position against the chest of drawers. He was wearing a short-sleeved, black and red striped shirt, and black sharkskin pants. He looked like Vic Damone's older, uglier brother. Blood oozed from his nose and mouth. He didn't look out cold though, just stunned. I picked up the gun with one hand and rubbed the sore spot of top of my head with the other. The mambo finished and the announcer was babbling about the show's sponsors, Colgate dental cream, when I heard a car engine revving into life out in the parking lot. I ran to the landing and, shielding my eyes from the sun, I saw Justine driving Eddie's Thunderbird as it screeched out of its parking space and headed for the exit.

Back in the room, Eddie was still motionless on the bed and the tough guy was stirring against the chest of drawers. A wave of agony swept from the top of my battered skull to my eyes and, for a couple of moments, the room spun. I needed to sit down so I kicked the door shut and pulled up a chair. I was about seven feet from my friend in the striped shirt, close enough to stop him doing anything rash. I was angry and confused. Angry because I was hot, sweaty and in pain, confused because I didn't know if Justine had set me up or not. Was the blast on the horn a warning? If it wasn't, why had she taken off like she did? I found myself making excuses for her. Like maybe she had been frightened by the sudden violence. I had a mental picture of her hips rolling in front of me and I was sorry she'd gone. Man, I hated myself. I hated myself so much that I got up and kicked buddy boy real hard in the guts. It wasn't a nice thing to do, but I did it anyway.

While he was breathless, I yanked out a flashy gold wallet from the back pocket of his pants. According to his driver's license he was one Joseph Safarini. There was a bunch of other crap in there but what really grabbed me was a plastic security pass.

It was for the Star Crest Chemical Corporation. Joseph was a night watchman at the company's Fontana plant. Well, things were getting crazier by the minute. I grabbed a tumbler of water from the bathroom and splashed it in his face. He shook his head, spat a couple of times, and sat up. His nose was still bleeding so I threw him a handful of Kleenex from the box in the bathroom.

"Here, Joseph. Your nose is bleeding, clean it up."

He sluggishly tried to catch the wad of tissues but missed them and they crumpled onto his lap. Picking one up, he gingerly dabbed at his nose and scowled at me. His lips were starting to puff up and he had trouble speaking. He wasn't happy with me.

"You son-of-a-bitch, whaddaya kick me for? I got a bad ulcer. You had no call to kick me when I was lying here."

I waved the gun in his general direction.

"I guess I don't like guys sticking guns in the back of my head. I'm sorry about your ulcer. Try drinking more milk."

He muttered a string of cuss words back at me and spat blood on my white Keds. That got me angry all over again. I raised the gun to smack him in the mouth but managed to control myself. He saw my movement and started to put his arm up to cover his head. From the way he moved I could tell he was still pretty dazed. I stepped in close and pressed the snub nose of the revolver against the space between his nostrils and his upper lip. He winced. I guess that part of his face was pretty sore. I pressed harder.

"Okay, Joe. Here's the deal. Take it or leave it. You give me some answers to some very simple questions and I don't start knocking out your teeth. So, you either talk, or you're facing six months of dental work. Understand?"

His eyes, though dulled by pain, were still filled with hatred. I didn't like his attitude and I was inclined to hit him first and ask questions after but I knew my heart wouldn't be in it. I was still feeling guilty about kicking him. Before I could make my mind up, a piercing scream filled the room. It took me a couple of seconds to realize it was coming from Eddie. I left Joseph alone and lurched to the far side of the bed. Eddie was curled in a fetal position, his hand over his eyes. The scream subsided to sobs.

"Oh, God. Please make it stop. Make it go away. I can't take any more! Help me! Help me!"

He was shaking and grinding his fists into his eyes. I pulled at his wrists but it took most of my strength to drag his hands down to his sides.

"What's the matter, Eddie? Listen, it's me, Johnny. You remember me. Remember the Lighthouse at Hermosa Beach? You know, Johnny and Vicki? I'm going to help you, but you have to tell me what's wrong."

The moaning stopped. He grabbed me with both arms and stared at me with the intensity of a lunatic. His voice was calmer.

"Johnny, you've got to help me. I've done something stupid. You have to help me put it right. We've got to stop them. What have I done? What have I done?"

The whole thing gave me the creeps. I tried to move back from the bed but he was clinging to me like his life depended on it. I was still trying to break his hold on me when I saw Joseph stagger to the door of the room. I turned to go get him but Eddie pulled my left arm so hard that I stumbled against the bed. By the time I broke free, Joseph had wrenched open the door and was half running, half stumbling along the landing, heading to the staircase at the reception office end of the block.

Before I could follow him, I noticed two guys walking briskly from the far end of the building towards the Chevy. One of them looked like a cop. They didn't notice Joseph lurching by on the landing above them but they spotted me. I slipped back into the room and tried to tidy up as best I could. I'd just kicked Joe's gun under the bed when they walked in. The first guy was in his fifties with sparse sandy hair, a sparse sandy moustache and a not so sparse belly. A silver badge on his chest read *Arthur Kirkland, General Manager*. The other guy, tall and rangy, had on the khaki colored uniform of the Palm Springs Police Department. He spoke first.

"Say, what's going on here? We've had reports of a fight."

Before I could answer him, the manager added his five cents worth.

"You know, officer, this gentleman's not even a guest at the motel. There was a girl here before, but I saw her drive off about ten minutes ago."

His sense of time was off whack but I let it slide.

"No, there wasn't a fight, officer. I'm afraid my young buddy here has got a bad case of sunstroke. The three of us hit the taverns pretty hard last night and the mixture of heat and alcohol hit him really bad. He was determined to go swimming in the pool here, but I figured that wasn't a great idea considering the state he was in. He wouldn't listen to me though, and it took all my strength to hold him down. I'm assuming that was the fight you heard, Mr. Kirkland."

The cop looked at me slow and hard, and then at Eddie. The poor kid had started babbling again but much quieter this time. Outside, I could hear a car pulling away from the building. It seemed that Joseph had recovered from his tangle with me pretty fast, but at least I had his wallet.

"But you're not checked in here!" Kirkland insisted.

"That's correct, I'm not. I'm staying over at a friend's place. Eddie here is my brother-in-law. He and his wife drove down from Los Angeles yesterday. They spent the evening with me before coming over here about midnight. Justine's just gone down to the drug store to pick up some painkillers. She'll be back any minute."

Thankfully, Kirkland at least bought the story. He didn't mention old Joseph so the bastard had obviously kept a very low profile.

"That's right. They turned up at about 12.30 last night. Most inconvenient for me but they did pay three days in advance".

The cop was still giving me the once over. Finally, he pushed back his cap, scratched his forehead and spoke.

"Well, as there's no damage done, I'll get going. But you better tell this guy" he nodded at Eddie, "to lay off the drink and stay out of the sun. You folks should have more sense, coming out here in the middle of July."

He shook his head at our stupidity and walked out. Meantime, Kirkland was examining the bloodstains on the carpet by the chest of drawers. Before he could complain I pressed a fifty-dollar bill into his hands.

"Look, I'm sorry about the noise. I'm going to check Eddie out now and get him over to my place and call out a doctor. You can keep the three days advance money and please accept this to cover the cost of the cleaning."

The money worked because he smiled and tucked the note into his shirt pocket. "Thank you kindly, we're all good here. I'll let you folks get packed up."

I smiled back until he walked out the door.

It took me awhile to clear the room of Eddie, his few belongings and Joe's gun. Eddie had calmed down enough for me to manhandle him into the Chevy and once he looked settled I high-tailed it to the house on San Jacinto Drive. I dragged him into one of the guest bedrooms and the second I swung his legs onto the bed he was out cold. I then phoned Vicki. We spoke briefly and the relief in her voice after I told her that I had Eddie made everything seem worthwhile. All I could do for the next few hours was sit tight. Vicki was calling Uncle Bradley's doctor in Palm Springs to visit us before she headed down from LA.

Five minutes after I spoke to Vicki, a Doctor McFarlane phoned and said he'd be over in half an hour. I wandered through to the den to get a drink. The room was a mess with the pile of albums that had been on the coffee table strewn across the floor. Records and inner sleeves had been pulled from their covers and dumped on the carpet. So, Justine had come back, searching for the record and envelope I'd hidden out by the pool. She hadn't had time to do a proper search, and the fact that the vodka bottle and two highball glasses had been smashed against the wall surrounding the fireplace, suggested she wasn't too happy about it. I made sure the *Ritual* album was where I'd left it and then went back inside and cleared up the broken glass. Then I tidied Eddie's LPs into one pile and switched on the radio that was part of the phonograph set-up. They were playing a Mel Torme number. I could live with that. As the man they called the "Velvet Fog" crooned about unrequited love, I strolled into the kitchen and mixed myself a large vodka and orange juice with plenty of ice. Back in the living room, I stretched out on the cream-and-black, wall-length sofa and tried to relax. It wasn't easy. I swirled the ice in the glass, pressed its coldness to the bruises on my face, and hoped the vodka would give me answers. Two drinks later, and all I had were more questions.

The doctor arrived late but I wasn't holding it against him. His crew-cut white hair and bearing made me think he had a military background and sure enough it turned out we'd both seen duty in the South Pacific. I led him in to see Eddie and mentioned the fit at the motel. The doc seemed to know what he was doing so I left him to it. As I settled down on the sofa the radio was broadcasting the local news. The lead story was the death of a Star Crest "executive" on the steps of the Desert Knight diner. The report concluded that as the dead man had died of natural causes the police weren't treating the case as foul play. Relief and shame danced a slow, cautious waltz through my mind. If the cops really thought Rhodes had died at the diner, then Eddie and I had one less problem to deal with. On the other hand, I knew that he'd actually croaked at the house with Eddie and Justine present. How directly involved they were in the death was something I could only guess at. The news ended and I switched the radio off. It didn't seem appropriate to have music playing while a doctor was on house call. While I waited, I emptied out Joe Safarini's wallet. The guy didn't have a very full life. Besides a tattered membership card for a Fontana bowling league, a photo of a girl signed "To Dad" and an empty matchbook advertising a burlesque joint in Vegas and a couple of Star Crest pay-slips, there was only one item of interest. It was a business card for a company called Pacific Arts Supplies—the same company that Rhodes had included on his research list on Eddie; someone called Rudy had signed it on the back. The legend on the front read *Exotic Materials for Tropical Decor—Polynesian Sculptures, Our Specialty.* I was still wondering how the hell a tropical decor company fit in with what was going on, when the good doctor walked in. He looked troubled so I offered him a drink. He took a whiskey and soda and sat down with a sigh. He sipped the whiskey and cleared his throat.

"This is most unusual, Mister Davis. I have to tell you straight off the bat that I've never seen anything quite like this. Do you know if young Eddie had been on any medication recently? Had he been in the hospital for any reason?"

I shook my head

"Sorry, Doc, I can't help you. As far as I know, he hasn't been in hospital this year, but as for medication, I've no idea. Why? What do you think it is?"

"Well, without getting him over to a specialist for further tests I can't be sure. The nearest thing I've seen to his symptoms before, are the hallucinations some patients undergo when they're allergic to morphine. But I've not seen this slipping in and out of lucidity before. The main thing is that all his vital signs are normal. I don't think we have anything life threatening here. To be on the safe side, though, I'd like to bring him over to the hospital and get blood tests done. I can arrange for an ambulance to pick him up first thing tomorrow morning. Will you be able to look after him until then?"

"Sure, Vicki will be down later this evening. I'm sure she'll want whatever's best for Eddie, so, go ahead and arrange whatever needs to be done."

He stood up to leave. "Yes, I think the hospital is the best bet in the circumstances. I've given him a gentle sedative to stop him getting into mischief tonight. He should sleep right through to morning. Call me if there're any problems, and tell Vicki I'm sorry to have missed her."

I Love Lucy was on the TV when Vicki finally arrived. Lucille Ball was wondering what surprise gift to get Desi Arnaz for his birthday. The studio audience thought the whole thing was a blast, but I couldn't get too excited about it. Vicki looked tired when I let her in. She hated driving long distances, especially at night. She became mesmerized by oncoming headlights and developed sick headaches if she had to do it for too long. But the second she stepped through the door, she gave me the biggest hug I'd had from her for five years. I squeezed her back. We stood like that for a while, holding on to each other and not saying a word. But then, an image of Justine's face as she'd kissed me flickered uninvited across my subconscious and the whole moment was tainted.

We went in to check on Eddie. He was sleeping soundly. Back in the den, we had a bite to eat before I mixed a couple of Martinis and we curled up on the sofa. I told Vicki everything that had happened except the effect Justine had had on me. Between the two of us we tried to make sense of it all but didn't make much headway. Another brace of Martinis took us through to midnight. Through the floor-to-ceiling windows we could see the clear night sky and those perpetually bright Palm Springs stars. Vicki leaned against me as I draped my arm over her shoulder. Her head rested on my chest and it was like the early days of our marriage with just the two of us inside, with the lights low and the desert just beyond the plate glass. It felt good. I started humming "Two Sleepy People" and she turned her face up to me. Her eyes were wet but she was smiling. When we had our first apartment together, we played our 78 rpm copy of that song until the shellac had almost worn through, but, by then, we'd memorized every last line. Sure, I was no

46

Bob Hope and Vicki wasn't Shirley Ross but we only sang for each other, so it didn't matter.

"We'll always have that song, won't we?" she whispered.

"Yeah, gorgeous. We'll always have that."

She nuzzled in closer.

"Don't stop now. Sing me some more."

I don't know who kissed whom first, but suddenly we were all over each other. As our mouths mashed together, our hands pulled at each other's clothing. Vicki was underneath me, lying on the sofa, her hips grinding up at me, her skirt round her waist. The sex was intense and passionate, the kind of fast, frantic coupling you get before marriage makes everything comfortable. The wham-bam sex you have when you're teenagers. When it's sheer, sweet agony trying to keep your hands off each other all week and finally you get to be alone. And even while you're doing it, you know that the opportunity for such intimacy probably won't occur again anytime soon. When we'd finished we lay there entangled, too tired to move. Vicki spoke first.

"Maybe we shouldn't have done that."

I sat up and stroked her messed-up blonde hair.

"Why not? It was what we wanted wasn't it?"

"Yes, but when we're like this, I want us to be together again…" she paused for a moment. "But if we got back together I know we'd end up fighting and then we'd be back to square one." Her voice was resigned.

I could have told her that I'd changed, that if she took me back I'd be a good, faithful husband. But I didn't trust myself enough to believe it, so I kept my mouth shut and gently kissed her forehead. I think she was too tired to pursue her train of thought because she didn't say anything else. Instead she struggled off the sofa and headed for the bathroom to get ready for bed. While she was gone, I lay there wondering why she still cared for me. The first three years we were together were the best of my life. There was nothing else, no one else for those thirty-six months. We were inseparable and, for our friends, we were probably unbearable. But we didn't care. We got married after our first year together. Our honeymoon was in Hawaii and lasted five glorious weeks. Vicki's father paid for every damned thing and I never guessed that life could be so perfect. During the day we'd lie on pure white sand on hidden beaches, the palm trees gently rustling in the trade winds above our heads. And at night, after a couple of Mai Tai's, we'd cuddle in hammocks, whispering to each other until we fell asleep beneath a big old tropical moon. As we lay, gazing up at the universe, I didn't think anything could ever spoil what we had.

The end started on a weekend break in La Jolla. We'd been man and wife two years. We were at a pretty drunken beach barbecue one evening and I found myself flirting with a pouty, young brunette we'd met at our hotel. While everyone else was hunting driftwood for the fire, we ended up making out behind an outcrop of rocks. No one else knew what we'd done and I couldn't get over the surge of excitement the whole scene had given me. Driving home the next day, my mind was in turmoil. I blamed the rum grogs we'd been drinking. I blamed the brunette for coming on so strong—all flashing eyes and whispered encouragements. I blamed the moon and the sea for casting their spell on me. I blamed myself for being weak. I even blamed Vicki for not paying me enough attention that evening. But however much blame I threw around, I couldn't forget how good it had felt and how the guilt had made it more exciting.

Back in LA I tried to think only of Vicki but there was always temptation. Everywhere I looked there were beautiful girls—in shops, restaurants, bars and nightclubs. Everywhere. Waitresses who looked like Rita Hayworth, sales assistants who sashayed like Ava Gardner, and car-hops shaped like Monroe. Beautiful blondes gazed at me from huge roadside billboards. Models pouted at me from the pages of magazines in full glossy color, their photographs fixing them forever in perpetual come-hither poses. Half-dressed vixens smiled at me from record covers and racy newsstand paperbacks. High School girls, knowing beyond their years, would strut past me at the beach or poolside, their tanned breasts and legs always tantalizing. From the screens of movie theatres and drive-ins, gorgeous faces thirty foot by fifty foot, eyes moist with longing, stared down at me.

I tried to resist temptation, but LA isn't a town built on saying "no." I fought my baser instincts for months, but it was a battle I couldn't win. I applied the Madison Avenue concept of "new is good" to sex, and I was lost. I had a passionate fling with the willing blonde who worked in the office across from my mine and I was hooked. Like a hophead needing just one more fix to keep me satisfied I had one affair after another. I did my damnedest to be discreet but eventually, of course, Vicki found out. She was beyond hurt and I felt like the lowest of the low. I promised her it would never happen again and I think I even believed it when I said it. But Vicki couldn't forget what I'd done and our life together was never the same. She was continuously suspicious and on edge and I couldn't blame her. I'd ruined the best thing that had ever happened to me, and the guilt ate at me morning, noon and night. So I drank. But when I drank, I ended up becoming amorous. And when I got amorous there was always someone around to give me a shapely shoulder to cry on. Sex was a temporary relief from the guilt, and I was caught up in a cycle and a sickness of my own making. Vicki gave me enough chances, but in the fall of '56 she finally left me. Was Palm Springs giving me one last chance?

The Doors of Perception

We slept in the master bedroom that night. Curled together like spoons, her cool back was against my chest; and I held on to her as she slept, and tried to make sense of things. I lay awake until my mind calmed down enough for sleep, but it was only a temporary escape. My dreams were vivid and unsettling. I was at a party in a big modern house with a huge cantilevered roof, panoramic glass windows and that sleek, low-slung furniture that is great to look at but murder to sit on. People were dancing the Mambo and I was out on the floor with Justine. I pulled her close and started chewing on her neck while Vicki and Eddie were standing in a doorway oblivious to my actions. Justine was guiding my hand to her breast and Eddie suddenly wasn't Eddie anymore, but Rhodes. He was pointing at me and Vicki was crying. I dragged Justine outside to a big blue swimming pool and undressed her. She lay there waiting for me to take her but before I could undress myself, a huge mushroom cloud lit up the horizon. Everyone from the party came outside to stare at the cloud and Vicki saw us lying by the pool and looked at me with such despair that I felt like dirt. Someone inside the house started shouting at me and I tried to stand up but couldn't. The shouting got louder.

Then I was awake. Dream over. It was still dark, Vicki was still asleep and I realized the shouting was coming from inside the house. For a moment I felt my insides tighten. I calmed myself down with a couple of deep breaths. Then it clicked where the noise was coming from. It was Eddie, shouting from the other bedroom. I pulled on my boxer shorts, and staggered, barely conscious, down the corridor and switched on the lights in the guest room. The poor kid was sitting bolt upright in bed, a look of blind panic on his face. As soon as he saw me, he stopped yelling. I sat on the bed next to him and tried to sound soothing.

"Eddie, calm down. It's okay."

"Where am I? What's going on?"

"Hey, relax. You're at Uncle Bradley's. It's all okay."

He stared at me intensely.

"Johnny, what's happening?"

At least he had recognized me. That was a start.

"You've been pretty sick but the doctor says you're going to be fine. You just need to relax a little."

"No. I can't relax. People are trying to hurt me. I've done some stupid, stupid things. I've seen some horrible things and I don't even know if they were real or not!"

I tried to reassure him but my heart wasn't in it. God only knew what was going on in his head.

"Come on, Eddie. You're safe now. Whatever you've done, we'll get you through this."

"I don't think it's going to be that easy. I've upset a lot of people. Some of them will never forgive me but I have to find a way to make things better."

He spoke slowly and deliberately, whilst nodding his head like he'd just cracked a really complex math equation. He paused for a moment and then turned to me.

"Is Justine here? No, don't tell me. I know she isn't. Oh, God! I've really messed everything up!"

"Whatever you've done, you need to get some rest. You've been ill and the doctor says you need hospital treatment so that you get better. Do you understand?"

He ignored me and put his face in his hands. I could barely make out what he was saying, let alone understand it.

"We did an amazing thing, Johnny. We've opened the door. We've found a way in. Huxley knew. All those Indians in the South West taking peyote knew. Going into trances, communicating with their gods through mescaline and their rituals. But we aren't savages squatting round the medicine man. We don't need the smoke and the mumbo-jumbo. This isn't voodoo—it's pure science. We've opened the door, Johnny, with science, with chemicals. We've opened the door!"

I didn't want to be having this conversation, not at six in the morning, anyway. I tried to pay attention, not knowing if Eddie was even aware of what he was saying, or if it was supposed to make sense. I gently pulled his hands from his face so I could hear him better.

"What door is it, Eddie. What door have you opened?"

"Didn't I explain? It's the door of perception. The human mind is locked in a prison of its own making and we don't realize that we're only using a tenth of our brains. A tenth! We're still these big apes wandering around, not realizing what we've really got up here in our heads. All that potential being wasted."

He shook his head in sorrow before he continued.

"But now, we've created a doorway though to the other nine tenths, Johnny. It's so, so simple really. We can change the way we think and the way we see things and it's all down to Lysergic Acid Diethylamide. It's the chemical that takes us through the doors. A drug that's as simple to take as aspirin. Do you understand?"

It was obviously important to him that I understood, so I nodded.

"Is this what you and Justine were hiding from Star Crest? Is this the secret in your envelope? "

"No, no. They've known about Lysergic Acid for years. They sent me to Menlo Park to administer the drug to people. It didn't hurt them, just shook them a little. They went through the doors for seven or eight hours but they always came back. But then I made some changes to the formula. It was supposed to enhance it. It should have made the journey easier, but it was too intense, way too intense…"

He began shivering slightly. I tried to drape a blanket over his shoulders but he shrugged me off. His manner was more urgent now.

"I made it easier for people to go through that door, Johnny, but some of them didn't come back. Those people are damaged forever. That's what's in the envelope. It's my formula. They want to use it but it's not right, it's too dangerous. No one should have it. We've got to hide it from everyone. Justine wanted others to have it so that it wouldn't be just our secret, but now, I think she's wrong. She's angry with me. Tell her I didn't mean to upset her…"

He was crying, his mind veering off at a tangent. I didn't want to hear about Justine, not after she'd been in my dreams, naked and willing by the pool, and now taunting me via Eddie's hysterics. I needed to know more about his secret. Why he'd run from Star Crest. Why Rhodes had died. Why a night watchman had pulled a gun on me. So I lied.

"Justine's okay, Eddie. She's gone to stay with a friend of mine in LA and she's going to call you soon. But we have to sort out this problem with Star Crest first. You have to tell me why the military are involved."

"The military?"

"Yeah, why them? And who did Justine want to give the formula to?"

His face creased with agitation. I was worried that any second he would start yelling incoherently again. Vicki saved the situation. She padded into the room yawning and dressed in one of my shirts. Her bare legs looked so good I just wanted to forget Eddie and drag her back to bed again. She rushed over to her brother and gave him a hug.

"Oh, Eddie. You had me really scared. I was at my wit's end."

He gave her a gentle, confused smile

"Hey, sis, what are you doing here?"

"I came down to see you, of course. We've been worried sick about you. Don't you remember you called me?"

"Yes, yes. But that was ages ago, wasn't it? I was just telling Johnny what's been happening. Forgive me, sis, I got really messed up."

I was getting impatient. I hadn't slept well, and a shaft of bright sunlight cutting through the drapes told me a hot new day in the desert had already started. There were still too many questions that needed answers.

"Eddie, listen! We both forgive you. But, you have to tell us exactly what you *have* done. What's been going on? Just try to concentrate, and tell us!"

Vicki gave me a harsh look but Eddie began talking. He was suddenly like the old Eddie, lucid and coherent. It was as though his normal personality had walked out of a dense fog into the sunshine.

"My last year at Stanford I met a researcher called Max Rinkel. He was working on a drug that the Swiss had developed back in 1945. He was convinced it would offer a new treatment for schizophrenia. I thought what he was doing was very important and I managed to get involved in the project. You have to understand, it felt like we were explorers charting new territory and that we were doing something that could actually help people."

He stopped and asked for water. Vicki brought him a glass from the kitchen. He took a couple of long gulps and then continued.

"Star Crest liked what I was doing and offered me a position with them once I'd graduated, on condition I carried on researching Max's work. I think they saw it as a potential gold mine. I mean, imagine, if you could develop a drug that could help all the mentally ill people in the world!"

Eddie's face took on the look of the truly zealous, another man convinced he was going to change the world. He continued, earnestly explaining how he had worked with human guinea pigs from Stanford University's student body and young volunteer GIs, giving them different doses of this new wonder drug. He was starting to get agitated again, when I heard noises at the front of the house. I told Vicki to try and remember everything Eddie said and I went into the study. Pulling the Shantung silk drapes back an inch or two, I glanced outside. Sitting at curbside was a white and red ambulance complete with tail fins. Two white-coated medics were busy unloading a gurney from its rear doors.

The ambulance was expected but the two black sedans that were parking just behind it weren't. The front door of the first sedan opened and I was momentarily blinded by the sunlight reflecting off its window. By the time my eyes had recovered from the glare, three guys in grey suits were out of the car and staring at the house. Two more joined them from the second sedan and together they approached the front door. They were too well dressed to be cops. They looked serious and I knew they were trouble. Shouting to Vicki that we had company, I ran to the bedroom and pulled on chinos and a t-shirt. Then, with a sinking feeling in my gut, I walked down the hallway. I was prepared for the worst. The dark figures of the men outside were visible now through the frosted glass. I paused, counted slowly to ten, and unlocked the door. I think I caught them by surprise because they were still discussing something when I swung the door wide open. All five faces looked half-bemused—half-disappointed that I was wide-awake. They were dawn-raid men. They probably figured we'd still be in bed. It's always a good way to catch people out. Most folks are not at their best before breakfast and the first coffee of the day. They're easy to boss around, easy to intimidate. But I'd caught these guys out and, to rub it in, I gave them a big smile and a warm friendly greeting.

"Good morning, gentlemen. Can I be of any assistance?"

There was a long silence. I guess it was their way of telling me they weren't buying my bullshit. The three guys from the first car were all in their mid to late twenties, undoubtedly Feds, and everything about them said Ivy League. They were tanned, clean-cut and gave off aggression like a hobo gives off body odor.

The two guys from the other sedan were older by twenty years or so. They had hard faces and looked bored as hell. The young guy nearest me fished out a wallet from his coat pocket and flipped it open about six inches from my face. I caught a glimpse of a gold badge and an ID card before he whisked it away and returned it to his pocket. He seemed sore about something.

"I'm Agent Rycroft, FBI. These are Agents Dunn and Whiteside. We're here to question Edward Hastings and Justine Moore on a matter of industrial espionage. We have a warrant to search the house."

As he spoke, one of the other guys flashed an official looking document embossed with a seal from the Palm Springs DA's office. It looked real enough. The two older guys said nothing. I kept the smile on my face and gestured into the hallway.

"Well, that all seems to be in order. Won't you please come in?"

Rycroft made no attempt to hide a sneer and stepped passed me. I guess he figured they were coming in whether I invited them in or not. As the others followed him in, the two ambulance men wheeled their gurney up to the house. The leading medic looked anxious. Like me, he was probably wondering what all these other people were doing there so early in the morning.

"Excuse me, Mister. We're here to transfer an Edward Hastings to the Roosevelt Memorial Hospital. Doctor McFarlane left instructions for us last night. He said that the patient wasn't in any condition to move around but, well, it looks like you're doing fine right now."

He stood uneasily with his hand on the gurney as though awaiting instructions. I tried to put his mind at rest.

"No, no, I'm not the patient. Mister Hastings is still in bed and he will definitely need your assistance. Follow me."

The medics trailed me into the den where the others were waiting. The whole scene was starting to look like an old Marx Brothers comedy. All it needed was a couple of delivery boys, a few nurses and someone shouting "Camera! Action!" and we would have been in business. Instead, Agent Rycroft glared at me and tried to sound commanding.

"Okay. Three questions. Who are you, what are you doing here, and where are Hastings and Moore?"

I met his stare and held it long enough for him to develop a sudden interest in a point slightly to my right. I'd be damned if I was going to let a scrubbed-up, college boy in a Brooks Brothers suit try and intimidate me.

"My name's Davis. I'm here because my wife's uncle owns this property and I'm an invited guest. My wife and I are down here because *Eddie* Hastings, my brother-in-law, is seriously ill and his doctor has recommended that he be taken in for observation. That's why these gentlemen are here." I gestured at the medics.

"As for *Miss* Moore, she dropped Eddie off here yesterday and then took off in his car. We haven't seen her since then, and I've no idea where she is."

I figured I had to lie about Justine, as I didn't know where things were headed. Hell, I wasn't under oath or anything. No one spoke so I just carried on.

"My wife is tending to Eddie right now. He's in a really bad way. Anything else that you'd like to know?"

One of the two older guys stepped forward.

"All right, Mister Davis. Thanks for your help. We won't keep you or your wife any longer than necessary. If you'd like to show us where Mister Hastings is we'll try and clear this up."

He spoke with the air of someone who was used to being obeyed. I'd met plenty of officers like him in the Marines, some good, some bad. I didn't really care which he was, I just didn't want him or his friends around for any longer than was necessary. As I led them down the corridor to Eddie, Dunn and Whiteside dropped back and started checking out the other bedrooms. Vicki met us at the door to Eddie's room.

"Johnny, what's going on? Who are these men?"

"This is Agent Rycroft of the FBI. I haven't been introduced to these other two gentleman yet but they all want to see lucky ole Eddie."

Rycroft stepped around me.

"We're sorry to barge in on you like this, ma'am, but I'm afraid your brother has got some serious questions to answer." As he spoke, his eyes just ate Vicki up. I didn't know what burned me up more—his sudden, creepy politeness or his leering stare. I resisted an impulse to slam a fist into the back of his neck and instead brushed past him and guided Vicki back into the bedroom.

Eddie had taken a turn for the worse again and was lying flat out, muttering and trembling. We stood around the bed for a moment, watching him. One of the older guys spoke first.

"How long has he been like this?"

Vicki and I went to speak at the same time. She let me finish.

"As far as we know he's been like this for at least two days. The doctor saw him yesterday and couldn't figure out what it was. He thinks it might be some kind of an allergic reaction. That's why he arranged for the ambulance to pick him up this morning. They want him at the hospital so they can run some tests on him. But, if you still want to question him now—go ahead."

From the cold, baleful stares I got from our suited guests, I knew I shouldn't have added that last comment, but I couldn't help myself. Something about guys in authority rubs me the wrong way. It was bad enough in the Marines, and since the war, it had gotten worse. It was also difficult because, although the two older guys were obviously the ones in charge, I had no idea who they were. Naturally the bastards weren't volunteering any information about themselves either. But the law is the law and you can't buck it, you just have to try and live with it as best you can. As their little hate rays beamed in on me, Vicki broke the momentary silence.

"Please, can't we just let Eddie go to the hospital? He's not in a fit state to talk or do anything rational. He needs help, not questions."

She made sense and everyone knew it. Rycroft reluctantly beckoned the waiting medics to come in. They carefully placed Eddie on their gurney while Rycroft checked on which hospital they were taking him. He then escorted them out to the front door. I went with them. Dunn was told to ride in the ambulance to the hospital and, while Rycroft gave him more instructions, one of the medics went ahead to open the ambulance's rear doors. I looked down at Eddie who was still mumbling to himself. As I reached down to give him a farewell pat on the shoulder, his eyes opened. He peered up at me and gave me a wink and a smile. I smiled back at him. The clever, little son-of-a-bitch, he'd fooled us all.

Once Eddie had gone, we all ended up in the lounge. Rycroft couldn't keep his eyes off Vicki's bare legs and I could hear the jungle drums of anger beginning to beat in my skull. Just then, Whiteside strolled back in. He looked pleased as punch. He was holding my .45.

"I found this in one of the bedrooms. It's fully loaded."

I tried not to smile as I pulled my permit from my wallet. I held it out to the two older guys, ignoring Rycroft completely.

"The gun's mine. This is the permit."

One of them nodded dully.

"I've got a private investigator's license from the City of Los Angeles attorney's office that allows me to carry it."

Rycroft sneered. "Wow. A real life Mike Hammer, or is Sam Spade more your speed, Davis?"

Before I could open my mouth to reply, Vicki cut in.

"While you're in my uncle's house you'll damned well address my husband as *Mister* Davis, if you don't mind. He's not under arrest is he?"

"No, ma'am"

"In that case show him some respect."

Her voice carried enough authority and scorn to make Rycroft blush a little. You don't grow up a blueblood in California without knowing how to throw your weight around when circumstances demanded and Vicki could mix it with the best of them at those times. I was pleased, too, that she didn't bring up the fact that we'd been separated for some two years. As things stood, it was probably better that we came across as man and wife.

One of the older guys apologized on Rycroft's behalf and switched the conversation around to Eddie.

"I'm sorry we didn't introduce ourselves before, but it's something the ambulance men didn't need to know. My name is Charles Adams and this is Oscar Forester. We're with the Central Intelligence Agency. We're here with our friends from the FBI concerning a very serious matter. As you may be aware, industrial espionage is a growing problem in this country. Some of our biggest corporations are losing millions due to rival companies stealing their product designs. It's bad enough when this is done by other American firms, but we have evidence that Mister Hastings and his girlfriend were approaching foreign interests with Star Crest documents."

Once again, Vicki beat me to the punch.

"I hope you've got evidence to back up these claims. I can't believe Eddie would ever knowingly get involved in something like that—and I'm sure you're aware that my father has one of the best legal teams in the State."

Adams nodded.

"I realize your family would defend any charges with the utmost vigor, Mrs. Davis, but we have photographic, and tape, evidence that shows Justine Moore was dealing with stolen information. In fact, we have bank statements that indicate she's been selling off Star Crest papers for the last year or so. We've been doing a lot of checking into her activities recently, and we found documents at her home that only your brother could have accessed. The internal security people at Star Crest were also monitoring calls between Moore and your brother. All this leads us to believe that he was a willing participant in smuggling documents out of Star Crest headquarters."

The other CIA operative, Forester, cleared his throat and piled on the pressure.

"In fact, the head of Star Crest security was recently here in Palm Springs, trying to find your brother and Miss Moore. His body was found yesterday in what we'd call unusual circumstances…"

Vicki frowned as I tried to look as if this was news to me as well.

"Now, we're not accusing your brother of any involvement in his death, of course, but the whole situation is looking pretty messy. Any information either of you can give us about Eddie's movements over the last week or so could be helpful. As things stand, he's looking at criminal charges that could destroy his career—whether he's found guilty or not."

I thought it was time to butt in.

"Look, you've seen the state Eddie's in. He's not well and I'm sure there's an explanation for whatever he's supposedly done. The thing I don't understand is why you didn't pick up this girl up months ago, if you have all this evidence against her."

"The answer's simple. Star Crest wasn't aware of her activities until very recently and that's when they called us in. Of course, once we began looking into her affairs, it quickly became apparent that she'd made thousands from illicit payments—payments that started late last year. Not only that, but we discovered that Eddie and Miss Moore had been conducting a pretty public affair for over five months now."

As he carried on speaking, I looked past him at the pool. I had an overwhelming urge to take a running dive into the cool blue water. I'd come to Palm Springs expecting Eddie to be in some mix-up over a girl. Sure, there was a girl, but now Rhodes, Joe Safarini, the Army, the CIA, and the Feds were all involved as well. I was beginning to feel like the guy who turned into a goddamned fly in that crazy sci-fi story in *Playboy*. I was trapped in a web yelling "Help!" but no one was listening. As much as I wanted out of the whole mess though, I couldn't help wondering why neither Adams nor Forester had mentioned the classified military documents that Eddie had hidden in the *Ritual of the Savage* sleeve? There was more to this than simple industrial espionage. How much more, I could only guess, but I knew for damned sure that most hospital patients don't usually get FBI escorts. So, for those reasons, I decided to keep quiet about finding Rhodes' body at the house. While Forester jawed away, Rycroft and his remaining FBI pal went off to finish searching the house. They drifted outside, walked slowly once round the pool and then came back in. My nerves were starting to fray around the edges. I couldn't imagine that they'd discover the pool lighting box and the envelope but I knew I couldn't relax until they'd gone. For the next twenty minutes the two CIA guys questioned us about Eddie and Justine. Vicki knew a little, but told them nothing. I knew a lot more, but played dumb. Finally, after taking statements from both of us, the agents left. After they'd gone, my first feeling was relief. My second was unease: Justine, the girl I was lusting after, was on the CIA's most-wanted list.

Summertime Blues

By the time the agents left, I'd been awake almost three hours and I hadn't eaten a thing. Vicki knew me well enough to drag me to the kitchen and fix eggs, hash browns and bacon for both of us. While I ate and drained a couple of mugs of coffee, Vicki had so much to say she hardly touched her food.

"You know, while you were letting those FBI men in, Eddie told me the most amazing things. I just don't know how much I can believe."

"Go ahead, shoot. Every goddamned thing I've heard today is unbelievable. Any little extras aren't going to throw me."

"Try this for size, then. He told me that that girl, Justine, killed Rhodes. He was sure she slipped some capsules into his drink just before his heart attack. Eddie also thinks that she did the same thing to him but he has no idea why. He's convinced that at least three of the GI volunteers he worked with died, too, and several had nervous breakdowns but Star Crest hushed it all up!"

"No wonder Eddie doesn't want anyone to have that formula, if that's what it does to people. Did he say anything else?"

"Not much that made any sense. I think the effects of that drug made it hard for him to concentrate. But he did tell me he'd already tried it on himself in small doses."

"Well, well. So he wasn't content to just watch others swing through the doors of perception, he had to do it for himself. That's obviously why he's been so screwed up lately."

"Maybe, maybe not."

She lit up a cigarette. I poured us both more java. I took another gulp and tried not to sound too irritable.

"This little caper is getting crazier and crazier. Honey, what have you gotten me into?"

I raised my hand in apology as she went to speak.

"I know it's not your fault. I'm just feeling out of my depth with this stuff."

"It *is* frightening," she insisted.

"Well, it's certainly strange. Eddie tells us he's developed a new wonder drug that helps people, but is also dangerous. He doesn't want anyone to have it, not even his girlfriend, but he thinks it's some kind of break-through for mankind."

"Do you think it really could be?" she asked, as if it mattered.

"Maybe, but meanwhile, his girlfriend is peddling Star Crest secrets to the highest bidder, and Eddie may or may not be a willing accomplice. The research he's working on is with the military, and he's got an envelope of their classified documents hidden in a record sleeve. They're important enough for Justine to kill Rhodes—if that's what's happened—and for her to return here to try and get them. Yet, neither those CIA spooks nor that Fed creep, Rycroft, even mentioned them."

After I finished, Vicki sat for a moment and then picked up the phone and started dialing. She put her hand over the receiver and whispered.

"I'm calling Daddy. Eddie's going to need a good lawyer."

I couldn't argue with that, Eddie was going to need all the help he could get. I let her get on with breaking the news to Mister Hastings, Senior, while I slipped out to the pool. The temperature must have been in the 80s and it wasn't even nine yet. I pulled off my clothes and dove in. The water was still cold from the desert night and I gasped as I came up for air. I swam a couple of lengths and then rested my elbows on the edge of the pool while the sun warmed my shoulders. It felt good. I closed my eyes and laid my face on my arms. Cool water, hot sun. A few, fleeting moments snatched from the rat race. Life should always be so simple. My mind drifted back fourteen years.

My platoon was catching some R & R. We were on a secluded white sand beach on a small nameless island in a chain of nameless South Seas islands. We drank beer, sprawled on the sand, splashed about in the clear salt water and talked about women. We were six days and five hundred miles from the war. The ocean lay before us, pristine lush jungle lay behind us, and the cloudless canopy of the biggest sky on Earth stretched above everything. The sheer beauty of the place made me think there was a God and if there had been women there, it would have been heaven.

Anyway, we drank more beer, goofed around, and then, as the afternoon heated up, we moved into the shade of the palms and just lazed there, at peace with the world. Our minds were as distant from reality as I guess most of us would ever get. Then, someone noticed the dark shapes gently riding the swell of the tide in towards us. They looked like clumps of seaweed at first or maybe palm leaves that had been swept out to sea after some tropical storm. But then the shapes, bobbing carelessly on the lazy waves, moved closer and started to look wrong. One or two of the guys got up and waded into the water to check them out. Seconds later they splashed back onto the sand cussing and shouting. The dark shapes weren't seaweed at all. They were the bodies of nine badly burned, badly decomposed sailors. We had to drag them onto the beach and check them for dog tags and other identification. They were all young guys, fellow Americans. And while we'd been resting on the sand thinking there was no prettier place on God's Earth, the bodies of those poor, brave kids had been out there rotting in the beautiful Pacific.

Vicki dove in near me, splashing me back to the present. Like me, she was naked. That was one of the reasons I first fell in love with her—she was so spontaneous. A lot of women would never get naked outside in broad daylight, even in such a private spot, but Vicki could care less— she was a born-and-bred Californian, a real life nature girl. We horsed around for a while and then, as we trod water with the sun sparkling off the ripples around us, we discussed what the hell we were going to do about Eddie. It took us a while and my shoulders were getting red by the time we talked ourselves into a plan and got out of the pool. The previous twelve hours were the closest I'd felt to her for a couple of years, and yet some small, obsessed part of me still had Justine, thief, conspirator and possible murderess, floating around my imagination. I needed therapy.

There's a big billboard on the outskirts of Palm Springs. It's where the desert rises to the West and the winds buffet the traffic on the open highway. It says *The wind is just nature's way of telling you not to leave Beautiful Palm Springs. Come Back Soon.* Well, if nature had anything to do with it, I'd have turned the car around and gone straight back to

Vicki. But not much any of us do these days is natural, so I floored the accelerator and carried on speeding towards Los Angeles.

We'd decided earlier that Vicki was going to stay in Palm Springs to be near Eddie. Her father was flying down from Beverly Hills with a couple of expensive lawyers to meet up with her. That was going to take a few hours though. I didn't want her to be alone in Uncle Bradley's house, so she went to stay with some friends of her parents who had a place out near the Thunderbird Country Club. As we left the house in our respective cars, a police cruiser pulled up across the street and sat there—a silent witness—as we drove off. I suppose the Feds wanted the place under surveillance. But I bet the two cops who watched us drive away had no idea that I had an LP sleeve loaded with classified papers hidden under the Chevy's back seat.

I wasn't sure what I was going to do with those documents. I wasn't sure yet of anything. I just knew I had to get back home. If there were any answers, they had to be in LA. For all I knew, the Feds were on the point of picking up both Justine and Joe Safarini. Vicki and her father could look after Eddie; the only useful thing I could do was check into the Pacific Arts Supplies connection. Rhodes had listed it, Safarini had one of their business cards and Eddie had chosen to hide classified papers in an album featuring what looked like masks from the South Pacific. There had to be something there.

I chewed gum, wove in and out of the afternoon traffic and tried to concentrate on the road. It was difficult. At the back of my mind, hidden away in the darkness, something was stirring. It took me until Fontana to work out what it was. For the first time since the war I really felt I was doing something useful again. It felt so good that I almost headed east to Vegas to celebrate. I didn't, though, and my good mood diminished as the traffic got heavier the farther west I drove.

The California sun was baking the suburbs as I hit the usual snarl-up outside Pasadena. A road crew was digging the highway up again and we were bumper to shiny bumper for a good couple of miles. The car directly in front of me was a pale green convertible full of high school kids, three guys and three girls, all having the time of their lives. The radio was blasting out noise, the guys were laughing those big show-off laughs that teenagers always have and the girls were screeching up a storm. They didn't have a care in the world and I hated them. That wasn't a good sign. It meant I was getting old. I'd have to watch that. It took almost half an hour to get through Pasadena and I was stuck behind those kids the whole way along Colorado Boulevard. The radio station they were listening to had one of those intense forty-year-old DJs who spoke like a teenage retard on amphetamines. He had a name like "Hotdog Horace" or something equally dumb and he sounded so excited I kept expecting him to explode on air. Every other word yelled out of his mouth was "cool" or "crazy". Every record was heading for "hitsville" and every station ident was for "the big boss sound of KWXYZ" or whatever the hell it was. Besides a severely restricted vocabulary, old "Hotdog" didn't seem to have much of a record collection either. He played the same rock and roll song at least five times in a row. It took me all five plays to make out the words because the singer was yet another hillbilly kid trying to be Elvis. The words I did understand made sense though.

"Sometimes I wonder what I'm a gonna do
'Cos there ain't no cure for the summertime blues…"

He'd gotten that damned right. As the traffic finally picked up speed on the western outskirts of the city, the high school kids turned off to the north. As they pulled away from me, I could hear the fading noise of "Hotdog" hollering that we'd be hearing this brand new disc on every jukebox across the country very soon. I could hardly wait.

Hollywood was certainly full of the summertime blues by the time I finally pulled up on North Formosa. The heat had sucked the good humor out of the place, and left people tired and cranky. On the corner of La Brea and Sunset, a small truck had rear-ended a brand new Oldsmobile coupe, and two cops were struggling to keep the drivers from tearing each other apart. Heat waves shimmered off the sidewalks and little old ladies tottered along holding umbrellas to keep the sun's glare off their little old heads. The smog stung my eyes and made my lungs feel like they were half-filled with sand. Even the palms on the corner of my street looked exhausted. It was the kind of weather that turned bar room discussions into brawls and normally quiet men into potential killers. I was beginning to feel like the latter.

I parked the Chevy, grabbed my case out of the trunk and strolled over to my apartment building. I decided to leave the Star Crest documents under the back seat until it got dark. I didn't know if I was being watched or not but I figured it wasn't worth taking any chances. Once I was in the apartment I thanked God that I'd decided to pay the extra rental fee for air-conditioning, and mixed myself a very dry Martini. I make an excellent Martini, it's one of my few good points. It tasted so good that I downed it too quickly, and had to make a second to keep me company in the lounge.

I put an Eartha Kitt album on the hi-fi, flipped through the latest *Esquire* and tried not to think. But even the combination of the sultry voice floating from the speakers of my hi-fi and the chilled nectar of my second Martini couldn't relax me. I tried to get enthusiastic about a preview of the latest, lightweight summer suits but that didn't work either. I closed my eyes. Sleep felt like a good option but it wasn't going to happen. All I could think about was my insane forty-eight hours in Palm Springs.

Coffee at Angelo's

I finished my Martini and forced myself to get up. I had to be doing something. I was tired and hungry so I took a shower, changed into a pair of white loafers, pearl grey slacks, a white short-sleeved shirt and headed out. I thought of driving to Musso's for one of their steak dinners but the idea of getting caught up in the evening traffic changed my mind. The Village West Coffee Shop was nearer and anyway, Angelo was always friendlier than the miserable stuffed shirts who waited the tables at Musso's.

It was too hot to walk so I drove the couple of blocks to Angelo's and parked in the rear lot. Just the short stroll from the Chevy to the entrance of the building made me feel sweaty and dirty again. Maybe it was time to bid Los Angeles a fond farewell and find somewhere cleaner to relax a little. Laguna Beach maybe, where I could hang out in the artists' colony and try and grab some culture before I got too old. I was still weighing up the pros and cons of beachside-living as I stepped into the welcoming shade of the coffee shop. Angelo was standing at the counter nearest the door. He looked real excited about something. Maybe he'd missed me. As I walked over to him, he glanced quickly down to the far end of the seating area and gestured at me to move closer.

"Ciao, bello. Come here, quick. There's a very beautiful dame waiting for you. She's a-been waiting for over an hour. She asked when you come in here. She came in this morning, too. Said she's a really special friend of yours. You old son-of-a-gun."

He gave my cheek a friendly squeeze. I glanced over to the booths along the window. There was a table of four old guys half-way along, a couple of middle aged women on the table after them, and then, at the last booth, was a woman in a blue silk head scarf and a pair of oversized sun glasses. Her head was bent low over a magazine. I didn't recognize her. Angelo sensed my hesitation.

"Whassa matter? You don't know her? She ain't the one who you got beat up over the other night, is she? I'm real sorry, Johnny. I told her you come here often. I knew I should've kept my big mouth shut. But she is so beautiful. She spoke so nice."

The poor guy looked so concerned I almost laughed.

"Hey, Angelo, don't sweat it. I just don't recognize her. Maybe she stopped by my office and Gladys told her I hang out here."

As I said it, I felt a twinge of guilt. I hadn't called Gladys—my receptionist, answering-service and secretary—for over three days. One more thing to do, one more thing I'd probably forget by morning.

After calming Angelo down, I ordered a hamburger and a cup of java and went to meet my mystery woman. She didn't look up as I approached the table so I just slid into the seat opposite her and gave a little theatrical cough.

"Hi there, I hear you wanted to see me?"

She quickly raised her head from the magazine and smiled. A slim elegant hand carefully removed the shades from her face—before they'd even gone I knew it was Justine! The first—and last—person I wanted to see. It was one of the few times in my life when I was genuinely lost for words. She smiled a million dollar smile and I tried my damnedest to stay cool. If she'd wanted to surprise me, she'd done an A-1 job. I searched for the right phrase, the right tone and I failed miserably.

"Well, well, we meet again."

"Is that it, Johnny? You're not going to scream at me for what happened back in Palm Springs?"

As she spoke, I noticed there were shadows under her cloudy green-gold eyes. And there was an air of vulnerability about her. Maybe something had changed in the last twenty-four hours.

"Well, what the hell *did* happen in Palm Springs? You took off pretty damned quickly at the Sundowner."

I thought I already knew the answer to the question, but I threw it in anyway, just to get her side of the story. She hesitated before answering me, and pulled out a pack of smokes. She offered me one but I shook my head. It was a habit I'd never picked up. I always carried my service Zippo though because you never knew when a lady would want a light. She carefully tapped a cigarette from the packet and placed it in her mouth. I instinctively reached for the lighter and sparked the flame into life. She leaned forward and I watched as she slowly hollowed her cheeks and inhaled to get the cigarette lit. She took a deep mouthful of smoke and I noticed that her hand was trembling, just oh-so-slightly. She exhaled the smoke and stared me straight in the eye. Through the soft focus halo of smoke, she looked like some silver screen vision.

"Don't hate me. I want to explain what's been going on. None of this was meant to happen—I didn't want Rhodes to die, I didn't want you fighting with Joseph. And I definitely didn't want to hurt Eddie."

"Yeah, sure—but all those things *did* happen, and I'd really like to know why. And then I'll know whether to hate you or not."

I gave her a big smile. Looking into those eyes, and being all too aware of the moistness of her lips and the way she held her cigarette, I knew that hate was the last thing on my mind. I was doing my damnedest to put on a tough exterior but it was hard work.

She took another drag on her smoke, and then abruptly stubbed it out in the already crowded ashtray.

"Look, it's not what it seems. I had to get out of Palm Springs because I was scared. As soon as I got into town I realized how stupid I'd been, and I began tracking you down because I wanted you to know the truth."

"Justine. For God's sake, cut the crap. You left Palm Springs because the FBI were after you. They turned up at the house this morning with some CIA agents."

She frowned but I carried on.

"They made you sound like Public Enemy Number One. Come to think of it, how do I know you're not? Maybe I should get Angelo there to call the cops right now and do my duty as a citizen. What do you think?"

For a split second her catlike almond eyes showed a touch of fear, but that emotion quickly passed, and she went on the offensive.

"Go ahead, then. If that's what you want to do. I just thought that you were the kind of man who would give people a chance. But, since you figure you know everything, call the cops."

Maybe I shouldn't have teased her with that threat to turn her in, but I needed to keep her as off-balance as I was. She was still glaring at me when Angelo came over with my burger. He asked Justine if she wanted anything else and she gave him a cold but polite "no". Reluctantly, he moved away from the table. I got the feeling he was half expecting me to invite him to join us. That was part of his charm; he wanted to be in on everything.

I ate the burger while Justine looked bored. She adjusted her headscarf a couple of times, and then took out another cigarette. I could tell it was bugging her that I wasn't saying anything, but I carried on eating just the same. Finally, her patience snapped.

"Look, I didn't come here to watch you eat. I could just as easily…"

I cut her off before she could finish.

"Then why the hell did you come here? You're after Eddie's copy of *Ritual of the Savage*, right? The one with the special classified inner sleeve? Well, I hate to tell you this but it's somewhere safe and you can't have it. You see, I know about Eddie's wonder drug and about your little habit of selling company secrets. I know why Rhodes had his heart attack and I also know that you took young Eddie for a sucker. Now, can I finish my meal?"

I'd come on strong but I was suddenly sick of playing games. Justine sat across from me, open-mouthed. For a second she looked in shock, like I'd just slapped her. I waited a moment or two for her to respond and then, when she didn't, I took a mouthful of java and rose to leave. It wasn't something I really wanted to do but if she wasn't going to play ball there was no point hanging around. I didn't even get halfway out of the booth before she reached over and grabbed my arm.

"Johnny, I'm sorry. Please sit down."

I didn't need much prompting so I sat.

"Okay. Now tell me something I don't know."

She grabbed my lighter, lit the cigarette and lowered her voice to a whisper. I had to lean closer to hear her. I could feel her breath against my face. I tried not to let the smoke bother me.

"I'm in big trouble aren't I?"

She actually sounded scared.

"I'm not going to lie to you, Justine. You're in pretty deep, but if you let me know how all this got started maybe I could help. How about it?"

"I need those documents, Johnny, the ones in the record sleeve. I need to get away and I can use them to get out of the country. They've got the flask now. I can't get that back so the only way I can get out of this whole mess is to give them the documents, get the money and disappear."

Her composure seemed to be in tatters. She looked like a frightened kid. I actually felt sorry for her but I was confused. What was the flask she'd mentioned? The Feds hadn't talked about any goddamned flask. I decided to pretend I was in the know though. I grabbed the cigarette from her hand and crushed it into the ashtray. I was getting tired of the smoke in my eyes.

"I can get the flask back. You have to trust me on that. But take me through everything from the start. And I mean *everything*. I need to know if the Feds missed anything."

She went to take out another cigarette. I took her hand and held it on the table.

"No more stalling. You can smoke later."

She stared at me for a moment and then she talked.

"It was about a year ago. I was in debt. I thought Star Crest would help me out, give me an advance or a raise or something. But no, they wouldn't help. I was getting so desperate that I would have done almost anything to get some cash. Anyhow, one night I was working late and Joe Safarini came by my office. He was very friendly and, at first, I just assumed he was trying to proposition me. I was about to ask him to leave when he told me he'd heard I needed money. God knows how he knew that but he knew all right. He asked me how I'd like to get paid just for copying information."

That didn't sound one hundred per cent—old Joey seemed like too much of a gorilla to be the brains behind anything but I kept quiet.

"I had nothing to lose so I listened. He told me to get hold of any research documents I came across and make copies of them. I had to leave the copies in my desk and Joe would pick them up on his shift as a night watchman. I did what he said, and a couple of weeks later he gave me an envelope with two hundred dollars in it. It was so easy. So from then on I'd pass on anything I could get my hands on. I didn't think I was hurting anyone."

It was my turn to frown. She carried on.

"Star Crest is making millions, more money than any other pharmaceutical company in the country. How much could it hurt if a competitor got to know some of their silly flu remedies?"

"C'mon, Justine—I thought you were going to level with me. You knew what the hell you were doing was illegal. The CIA wouldn't be involved if this was just about cold cures."

"I know that and I know it became more serious than that. I'm not defending what I've done. I'm just trying to explain to you how it all happened. How it all got out of control."

She was being petulant again. Her bottom lip jutted out and she almost pouted as she spoke. I tried not to get distracted. She continued.

"All those slimy departmental heads at Fontana never stopped making goo goo eyes at me, so it was easy to get any information I thought Joe could use. Everything was going well until Eddie was transferred to the building I worked in. I know you're going to laugh, but I really liked Eddie."

Liked, she had said. What did that mean?

"He was so decent and earnest. He wasn't like all the other creeps who worked for Star Crest. Married men who'd show me pictures of their kids and then—seconds later—ask me to go on weekend "business trips" with them. Eddie was different. He'd talk about his music and work and how much they meant to him. He'd ask me how I was, and what I thought of things. Pretty soon, we were meeting for lunch and coffee every day. It wasn't long after that we became closer."

She paused and looked enquiringly at me, as if to see my reaction. I stared back as if I didn't care less.

"Once we started dating, Eddie told me more and more about this new project he was working on. At first he was very excited by it, but then he became concerned that the company was going to try and keep the drug from the public."

"Why would they do that? I thought their job was to sell the product."

"I don't know why. But he seemed convinced Star Crest would over-price it, that they would put their profits ahead of helping sick people. I told him that I could help get papers to other companies and then there would be a price war that would make this drug cheap for everyone."

I tried not to sneer.

"So, now you're saying that you did all this to help humanity? That the money suddenly wasn't important?"

She shook her head.

"No, of course the money was important. I'm just saying that Eddie helped me because he didn't trust Star Crest. And then, of course, the military got involved and everything just became crazy. Eddie was sick with worry because they were talking about using the drug as some kind of weapon. He told me that they were trying to turn his new formula into a liquid spray that could be spread over a wide area."

She said it as though it was something I should be shocked by. I shrugged my shoulders again.

"Big deal. So they could spray it, so what?"

"It *is* a big deal because a pint of Eddie's formula in vapor form could affect thousands of people. Imagine it sprayed over a whole town. They wouldn't know what had hit them. Eddie must have told you what happened to those poor soldiers who died after being given too strong a dose."

I nodded. They must have been the three GIs that Vicki mentioned back in Palm Springs.

"Well, Eddie heard that the officers in charge of the experiments had the soldiers' bodies put in a truck and set it on fire. Their families were told they'd died in a road crash. He was angry that a formula he'd worked on to help people was being twisted into something that could harm them. I think he realized then that he couldn't work on the drug anymore. There was only one flask of the liquid made up and he smuggled it out of the laboratories up at Menlo Park and gave it to Joseph."

"Why the hell did he do that?" I asked.

"He told me that he wanted it out of harm's way. He thought Joe would put it somewhere safe while Eddie made his mind up what to do with it. But Joe, being Joe, sold it to his contacts. Eddie took it really bad. The trouble was that he had already tried too much of the initial drug the new formula was based on. He became kind of paranoid. He decided he couldn't trust anyone and took all the research documents with him and ran off to Palm Springs. I knew then that we were all going to be in serious trouble."

"Well, you guessed that right. Didn't it occur to you that you were bound to get caught once you started selling military secrets?"

"Look, Johnny, I didn't know it was government business until *after* we'd already passed on all the initial research details. I was making money, which I needed, and Eddie was salving his conscience. I didn't know the military would get involved. I wish now I'd never started the whole lousy business."

"Sure, sure. You said that before. But who the hell are these people that Joseph sold the flask to? And while we're on the subject, how big a cut did you get?"

"I got nothing for the flask. Selling the flask was Joseph's idea and I honestly don't know who those people are. I think they're some kind of gangsters. Joseph always dealt with that end of things. He told me that they said he'd get paid for the flask once they had Eddie's written formula as well."

I laughed.

"Doesn't sound like Joseph is too good a businessman. Giving them a flask like that on the promise of payment later."

Her voice was bitter.

"I know it. Joe really fouled things up. But they'd always paid up before, so he thought they could be trusted."

"Did he figure they'd protect him or you from the FBI?"

Her eyes began to well up with big crystal tears. I knew then, with certainty, that I wanted to solve this thing as much for her sake as for Vicki's—or Eddie's. I realized I was doomed to play out the private eye scene, right up until the bitter end. I thought again of that *Playboy* story about the guy who got transformed into a fly and ended up trapped in a spider's web, screaming for help. I was stuck in that web and I knew I was powerless even to want to try and escape. I looked into Justine's wet eyes and felt what was left of my will-power ebb away. She pulled a tiny handkerchief from her purse and dabbed at her tears.

I switched my gaze momentarily to the heat-baked sidewalk just outside the diner's window. Two little kids in dungarees were trotting alongside a woman who was old enough to be their grandmother. She was hot and bothered but the kids were having the time of their lives. They were carrying hula-hoops and chatting away to each other like there was no tomorrow. They'd either been somewhere very exciting or were on their way to it. Maybe a friend's birthday party. The scene was like a TV commercial, but it made me sad. For that golden moment in time they had no cares in the world. Give it a few years though and maybe the girl would be worrying if she was pregnant or not and the boy might be just another juvenile delinquent with a grudge against the world. Or maybe he'd end up sitting in a diner with a gorgeous girl who was in deep, deep trouble. A girl who might really need his help but all he could think about was how she'd be in bed. I turned my eyes back to Justine. She had another cigarette in her hand but seemed composed again. I weighed in with a half-hearted question.

"Okay, once Eddie wigged out and skipped to Palm Springs, what happened then?"

"Once he left Star Crest I knew I wouldn't be safe. I thought that if we returned the flask, then I wouldn't be in so much trouble. Joe said it was impossible. His contacts were keeping the flask but they would pay us ten thousand dollars for the written formula. I had to agree to help get it. With my share, I could take care of things here and start again in Rio de Janeiro or Buenos Aires. I didn't want to spend time in a women's prison. Anyway, Eddie finally called me and we agreed to meet in Palm Springs. Joe was going to wait in the motel. I was supposed to get Eddie over there and we were going to grab the papers from him."

I couldn't help sneering. She didn't much care for the sneer and let me know it.

"What does that face mean?"

"It means that I'm surprised at how ready you were to sell Eddie out. I guess the course of true love doesn't run straight when it comes to business."

"I didn't ever say I was in love with Eddie. I'm really, really fond of him, but love didn't come into it."

"So, do you make a habit of sleeping with guys you're just fond of?"

It was a cheap crack. I couldn't tell if she was hurt or angry but her voice was ice.

"Actually, no, I don't. Did you love every woman you've bedded? From what Eddie told me there's been quite a few, even while you were married. Were they all love at first sight?"

I had it coming but I still didn't like it. The girl knew how to draw blood. This was getting too much like a lover's tiff.

"Okay. Let's try and keep this cordial."

She gave me a little half-smile that meant nothing. I needed a drink. I needed to be on my own to think. I needed to grab her face and kiss her. But, to my credit, what I actually did was pay attention to what she was saying.

"The trouble was, after I arrived at the house in Palm Springs, Rhodes turned up. He told us we had to give back the flask and the papers. He let me know pretty quickly that he thought I was the one to blame for everything. He said I might do time in a State penitentiary and that I'd ruined Eddie's career. Well, it seemed to me that Eddie was agreeing with him so I got desperate. I knew Eddie carried a small bottle of the capsules he was working on in his suitcase. While they were pouring drinks I made an excuse to slip into the bedroom and grabbed a couple of them. When I rejoined them in the lounge I offered to make more drinks while Eddie and Rhodes were discussing things. I honestly don't know now what I was thinking, but I put a capsule in each of their glasses. The capsules dissolved the second I dropped them in and they didn't notice."

She stopped abruptly. She looked kind of choked up again. I didn't say anything. After a moment or two, she took a deep breath and carried on.

"Okay, I did know what I was doing, but I just thought the drugs would knock them both out and that would give me time to get out of there. I never dreamt that it was going to affect Rhodes the way it did. He just started crying and babbling and then collapsed in the hallway. I tried to help but I had my hands full with Eddie. He was crawling around the floor in circles saying he wanted to get out to the pool. I had to hold him down as he kept heading for the back door. I had visions of him drowning, so I kind of lost my head. I should have called an ambulance but I was too scared. By the time Eddie passed out, Rhodes was dead. I called Joseph. He came over in a cab and we dragged Eddie out the back door, into his car and drove to the motel. I checked Eddie and me into a room and Joseph tried to make Eddie sick to get the drug out of his system. We stayed up all night with him and the next morning I realized I'd forgotten the documents, so I drove back to the house, and you know the rest."

It all sounded crazy enough to be true but it didn't explain why I'd ended up at the Sundowner with a bruise on my cheek and a lump on the top of my head. Justine must have read my mind because she reached out and held my hand.

"Johnny, you have to believe I didn't want you to get hurt. I thought that if I could get you out of the house for long enough I could go back and find the documents and that would be it. I was going to tell Joseph to keep you in the motel until I returned with the documents and then we'd have left you and Eddie there. I didn't know you were going to be such a tough guy."

That half-smile played on her lips again and I started figuring how quickly I could get her back to my apartment. But if everything she'd said was true, I had to get that flask back to Star Crest as soon as possible; once they had it and the documents, I figured Eddie wouldn't get into too much trouble. Justine was a different matter but I acted like I had all the answers.

"Okay. I need to talk to Joseph. Are you still in touch with him? We've got to get that flask back. If we don't, the Feds will put your face on the cover of every newspaper in the country."

"I haven't got a number for him but he's going to call me tonight around nine. I'm staying in a motel out near Inglewood. Here's the number. Oh, and by the way, I'm checked in under the name June Carson."

She handed me a matchbook for a place called the Star Lite Inn. *Modern, clean and reasonable, with whisper quiet rooms,* read the legend on the cover. I pocketed it, trying not to think of the number of times I'd written my number on a bar matchbook just like it and given it to some late night pick-up. Justine was looking at me expectantly. I didn't know if she was waiting for me to make a move on her or waiting for me to rescue her with a plan that would solve all our problems. I had no master plan either way, so instead I jotted down my home number on a paper napkin and passed it to her. It should have been an exciting moment.

"Okay," I said, "Either sort out a time and a place for Joseph to meet me or give him this number and get him to call me. And for God's sake explain that I'm trying to help. I'm not with the Feds, and getting this flask back will help everybody."

She nodded as I spoke and slipped my number into a clutch bag she had on the seat beside her. The shadows were getting longer on the street outside—the cocktail hour was approaching. It was time for me to hit the nearest bar. Alone. I put a couple of bills on the table.

"I've got to get going. Are you going to be okay? I hope you're not still driving Eddie's car."

She shook her head.

"No, of course not. I knew the police would be looking for it so I left it on a quiet side street in Glendale. I picked up a rental, that blue and white Pontiac, just over there."

She gestured towards the street.

"Did you use a false name?"

"Yes, of course." She sounded almost derisive as if it was something she did every day. Maybe she did. We left the diner, Angelo giving me a *you-sly-dog* smile as we passed by. Outside, the heat of the day was finally fading. Justine stood in front of me. I was still of two minds on my next move. She saved me from myself.

"I suppose you'd better go now, Johnny. You must have stuff to do but please call me later and don't forget, ask for Miss Carson, room 16."

"Sure, I'll remember. But don't *you* forget, Joseph's got to call me and, one last thing, that flask—did you ever get a look at it?"

"No, but Eddie told me it looks like one of those new thermos flasks for coffee. Shiny, aluminum, you know."

I nodded.

"Okay, Justine, I'll see you later. Take care of yourself."

"You, too. Don't do anything crazy." Her voice had a slight tremor in it when she spoke. She looked sad. As I started to turn away, she grabbed my arm.

"Thanks, Johnny. I'm glad you're on my side."

I didn't have time to answer before she leaned forward and kissed me on the cheek. I don't know how it happened but, for a moment, our lips touched. Another time, another place and we would have been in each other's arms. But in the bright, late afternoon sun outside the diner we stood, slightly awkward, our bodies inches apart. I should have grabbed her and really kissed her but before I could move, she turned, put her sunglasses on and trotted across the street. I watched as she reached her car, turned and gave me a little wave and then eased herself into the driver's seat. It was the craziest feeling. I was fifteen again. Frustrated, excited, nervous, happy and sad. As I drove slowly to my apartment I fought back a wave of guilt. Less than twenty-four hours after sleeping with Vicki I'd come within a heartbeat of starting an affair with Justine. And the worst thing was that I hadn't felt so alive in years.

Hollywood Twilight

The phone was ringing as I let myself into the apartment. It was Vicki calling from Palm Springs. She'd spent the whole afternoon since I'd left at Eddie's bedside, with various government agents keeping her company until her father arrived with his legal team. Once they showed up, the Feds were forced to wait outside the room and not in it. Eddie slept most of the time while Vicki, her father and his lawyers discussed the best way of getting him out of the mess he'd gotten into. She asked me if I'd made any headway in LA. For a split second I thought she was talking about Justine and I felt a pang of guilt. I told her I was chasing down leads, but she'd obviously heard something in my voice that shouldn't have been there. Twice she asked me if anything was wrong and twice I said that there wasn't. After another couple of minutes of aimless conversation we hung up. Even as she said goodbye I could still hear the suspicion in her voice.

I couldn't face any of my usual bar hangouts, so I mixed a couple of Martinis and tried to think what a real private eye would do. Somehow, all those hours as a kid, listening to Dick Tracy on the radio, weren't helping me any. By my second drink, the tension of the day slowly loosened its grip but my mind kept conjuring up images of Justine. Sitting in my apartment wrestling with my worn-out conscience wasn't solving anything, so I changed into a pair of beat-up penny loafers, Levi jeans, white T-shirt, and a navy blue zipper jacket. It was time to do some exploring in the wilds of LA.

Before I left the apartment, I thought about the album hidden under the Chevy's back seat. If the Feds were involved, hiding *Ritual of the Savage* in the apartment or the Chevy was inviting trouble. I had to hide it somewhere else. By the time I got the car into the flow of traffic heading west on Sunset, I'd figured on a potential "safe house" for the album. I made sure I wasn't tailed by switching in and out of lanes, running traffic lights on amber and generally driving like a madman. After twenty minutes of making myself the most hated driver in the city,

I doubled back and hit the quiet residential streets north of Melrose. I pulled over a couple of times and sat looking in my rear view mirror to make sure I hadn't been followed. Then, as the sun finally dipped behind the palms, I pulled up outside a modest little Spanish style bungalow, a few blocks east of La Brea Ave.

It was the home of the only one of my old Marine buddies who, like me, was still single and without kids. Gerry Mendez was a double bass player who made a living doing session work up at the Capitol Studios. Although his first love was jazz, Gerry wasn't precious about his art. He'd played on albums for snotty rock 'n' rollers, lounge crooners and even cornball country singers. Just lately he'd managed to wrangle his way onto the lucrative movie soundtrack circuit. Consequently he seemed to spend more time up at Warner Brothers' Burbank lot than he did at home. The music may have been schmaltz but the rewards were good; the money for the red and white '57 Corvette convertible sitting proudly in his driveway sure as hell didn't come from jazz gigs. I pulled the album out from under the back seat and walked quickly up to the front door. I just had time to notice that the wilting plants along the front of the house badly needed watering when Gerry appeared in the doorway before me.

Immaculate, as usual, in a red sports shirt and pleated dove grey slacks, he tugged gently on his trim goatee beard and looked at me without expression.

"Wow, that's what I call service. I didn't even have to knock…" was all I managed to say before he slammed the door in my face.

A second later it reopened and Gerry stood there smirking. He stuck out a hand and as we shook paws he gave me a playful punch on the shoulder.

"You know, I should have kept that door shut on you, man. Know how long it's been since you last bothered to show your face around here?"

"About two, three weeks" I replied lamely.

"Yeah, yeah. Try three months, you lazy bastard."

"Gerry, what can I say? I'm sorry, buddy, I've been tied up with work. Besides, I figured you'd be busting your hump over at Capitol or up at Warners."

"That's no excuse, man. I tried buzzing you a couple of times back in June."

"Yeah?"

"Yeah, I had a real sweet gig for ten days playing with a cool combo at Ciro's. I could have got you a front row table every night—and introduced you to two of the sexiest honeys that ever waited tables. Twin sisters, Johnny!"

"Don't tell me!"

"Two gorgeous chicas from south of the border, beautiful, big-eyed and innocent of our corrupt Americano ways. You could have helped me change all that…" he shrugged, "but I had to do it all on my lonesome."

He was smiling broadly but I knew that he was kind of pissed at me and I couldn't really blame him. We'd been best buddies in the Marines until that Jap shrapnel sliced me open back in '45. Although we were both Angelinos we probably would never had met if it hadn't been for the war. Gerry was second generation Mexican from down Orange County way while I was from the white hamlet of La Canada, up in the foothills. Out in the Pacific though it didn't really matter what our backgrounds were. We were both US Marines and that was all that mattered.

Gerry was one of those guys that you like the second you meet them, it's like, you have no real choice in the matter. You just can't help being friends. The kind of friends that you might not see for months, years even, but the minute you meet up again it's like you were with them only yesterday. Lately though, as Gerry's music career took off, I'd felt that he was leaving me behind. It seemed he was the one who'd finally made it to the big grown-up adult world. The world that I'd always shunned—the world that was now shunning me. His life was going somewhere while I was acting out a role I didn't believe in. I had no commitments, no schedules to meet, no routines… but here was Gerry clocking in every day and getting union overtime every night. It wasn't that I resented his success, more that I somehow felt like an intruder in it. Whichever way I cut it though, I'd been a lousy friend of late so I apologized as best I could. My apology turned into a recounting of all that had happened since I met Vicki at the Luau.

As I rambled on, Gerry ushered me into his lounge. The furniture was simple but expensive. Saarinen womb chairs, a Noguchi table, all the designers that Vicki had swooned over when we had our apartment back in the good old days. The matt red walls were decorated with African tribal masks and framed photos of the man himself with some of the band leaders he'd played for; Nelson Riddle, Duke Ellington, Count Basie. And, in pride of place along one whole wall, was his record collection. It stretched in neat shelves from floor to ceiling. Gerry had good friends at every record company in town and it showed. What he didn't know about music wasn't worth knowing so I wasn't surprised when he pulled the *Ritual of the Savage* from my hand and gave his verdict.

"Not my taste but not bad. If I had to go for Les Baxter it would be one of his percussion albums, like *Skins*. You know it?"

I shook my head. I'd never heard of it. Gerry reached up to a shelf and pulled out the album. Placing it on the hi-fi, he sat down and looked closely at the *Ritual* sleeve.

"So, you're telling me that these scribbles are young Eddie's formula for frying brains?"

"Not the way I'd put it, but in a nutshell, yes. The real McCoy though, is the formula *inside* the record sleeve, in the envelope."

"Jesus! Who'd have imagined that eager kid you brought to my gigs would end up involved in this kind of stuff?"

"Yep, from Chet Baker to brainwashing. Strange, huh?"

Gerry turned the album over a couple of times. Like he was looking for some detail he'd missed first time around. Then he handed it back to me.

"So, what the hell you gonna do? Shouldn't you just give this back to the Feds and let them deal with it?" He sounded concerned.

"That's what I ought to do, but the fact that those CIA guys didn't even mention the flask—or how dangerous this stuff is—makes me wonder. Eddie seemed pretty certain that no one should have this crap. Maybe he's right."

"Oh, no, buddy. Don't be the world's conscience. That's gonna get you a whole lot of trouble and very little thanks. You can't screw with the government."

As he spoke the massed congas, bongos and assorted drums of the *Skins* album began intruding on my powers of concentration. I winced and Gerry reached over and killed the volume.

He smiled "I guess you've got to be in the right mood for that kind of stuff."

"Yeah, I guess so. Anyway, the truth is I'm not sure what the hell I'm going do about all this. I just want to help Vicki and Eddie, in any way I can. But if the Feds start sniffing around me, I need this to be somewhere safe."

I held up *Ritual of the Savage*.

"Can you help me out? It's only going to be for a couple of days, three at the most. It's just while I try and make sense of things."

Gerry took the album from me and stood up.

"No problem, buddy. Come with me."

That's what I liked about the guy. When it came to favors, he didn't mess around. It was a straight yes or no. He went into his kitchen. A stack of used TV dinner trays and empty beer bottles lined the counter tops. The chrome table and matching chairs in the middle of the room were covered with Ritz cracker cartons and other snack food packaging. The musician's life was not a healthy one. Gerry caught me staring at the mess.

"That's the look my mom gives when she comes in here. I don't have time to eat properly, man. Some of these sessions start at four in the afternoon and go on 'til four the next morning. What can I do? Hey, I've got it, for this favor, you're treating me to a steak dinner at one of those swish restaurants you're always taking your dates to."

As I nodded agreement, he pulled the kitchen table to one side and carefully pried loose one of the big terracotta tiles that lay beneath it.

"Good thing about these old places," he grunted. "There's always somewhere to hide things."

With that, he pulled the tile clear of its surround to reveal an old wooden ammo box buried in the floor. Lifting its lid, he added the album to a couple of brown envelopes and a cluster of cigar boxes.

"You know I don't trust banks," he explained, "and the kind of thief we get round here just opens a couple of drawers, grabs a watch and then va-va-voom—gets out fast. No-one's gonna move a kitchen table and start checking for loose tiles. It ain't Fort Knox but, believe me, Johnny, it will do."

I wanted to believe him, so, I smiled and kept my doubts to myself.

"You might need this in case you need to pick the album up while I'm away," he mumbled as he gave me a spare key to his front door. He had an early call in the morning and after a couple of beers we agreed to meet the next evening at Sophie's, a little bar we both knew off Santa Monica Boulevard.

I prayed I wasn't getting Gerry into any trouble by dumping the album on him but he was the only guy in LA I trusted enough to look after it. As I drove north, towards the glitter of Hollywood, the streetlights gave an unearthly color to the grass and bushes lining the darkening sidewalks. The shadows made me think about Eddie's formula and what kind of strange breakthrough it was to be able to turn your waking moments into nightmares just by taking a pill. Jesus, my imagination was nightmarish enough without adding a man-made booster. The whole damned thing was like something out of *Amazing Stories* magazine. A liquid that could drive thousands insane and a whole flask of it was somewhere out there beneath the bright July moon.

I needed to call Justine and the Chevy needed fuel, so I swung east towards the Palladium and a gas station I knew that had a working payphone. I tipped the kid at the pumps fifty cents and asked him to clean the windshield and check the oil while he filled her up. I fished out a dime and called up the Star Lite Inn. A croaky old geezer answered and I wasted a good minute shouting down the receiver before he understood me.

"Miss Carson? Room 16? Okey-dokey, sir. I'll run and see if she's in."

From the sound of his voice, I figured it would take him a good half hour to reach Justine's room even at a run, so, I was surprised when I heard her voice just a few moments later. She sounded breathless. It wasn't an unpleasant sound.

"Hi, Johnny. Perfect timing. I've just spoken to Joseph. He's agreed to talk to you. He says for you to meet him tonight, one o'clock at Chalon's coffee shop, here in Inglewood. He says it's just off the Pacific Coast Highway. Do you know it?"

"Yeah, yeah. I've been past it a few times. How did he sound?"

"Well, if I didn't know him better, I'd say he was nervous. Listen, do you want me to be there tonight? Maybe I can help talk him around."

"No, Justine. Just stay put. Try to get a good night's rest and I'll call you first thing… we'll take it from there."

There was a moment's pause.

"Sure. But you will phone me? Promise?"

"Don't worry, I will. See you later."

I replaced the receiver, and for a second I thought of calling Vicki in Palm Springs. It seemed too weird though. To talk to her straight after talking to Justine felt like another act of betrayal.

I got back in the car and headed along Hollywood Boulevard. When my parents took me there as a kid, to show me the bright lights of the big city, I thought it was a magical place; the Chinese Theatre, the stars' hand prints on the sidewalk, the ritzy restaurants and the well-dressed citizens out enjoying the evening air. But, twenty-five years later, the magic had evaporated. Some of it was because I was older and more cynical but it wasn't just that. The impressive shops, restaurants and offices had moved out. Instead, there were cut-price places selling fake jewelry and novelties, cash-in merchants selling busts of James Dean and badly made rock 'n' roll clothes to spotty teenagers, dirty hamburger joints, and sidewalks littered with the human trash that such streets always attract. Hooray for Hollywood.

The Chevy crawled with the evening sightseeing traffic for a while, until I got too depressed. I hated that everything always seem to change for the worse. I should have been more like my Grandpa Davis. Just before he died, he told me that mine was the luckiest generation alive.

"You've won the biggest war in history and made America the greatest country on Earth. Reap the rewards, Johnny Boy. Reap the rewards. You're in the prime of your life and living in the kind of future my generation could only dream of…"

I figured I knew what he'd meant. That science and medicine and industry and everything had transformed our lives for the better. But all I could think was that he had been born during the Civil War. A war when cannon, muskets, and cavalry charges decided battles. Yet, in his lifetime, we'd moved on to tanks, jets, and atom bombs: from musket shots to thermonuclear war. That was some kind of progress. Before I got even more depressed, my stomach interrupted with a growl. "Eat, you bastard", it said," Eat. The end of the world can wait."

I decided to head for Tiny Naylor's on the corner of Sunset and La Brea and get myself a burger. The place was relatively quiet as I pulled into a parking bay under the main cantilevered roof. A carhop took my order, her eager little face shiny under the bright lights. Five minutes later, she delivered the food on a serving tray and something about the calm efficiency of the whole operation was reassuring. It was good to know that not everything in the modern world was as unpredictable as my life had become. There were a couple of cars pulled up near me, both with families seated inside eagerly chowing down on post cinema meals. And, opposite me on the other side of the serving island was a young couple in an aqua blue convertible. They were in their late teens, the guy with a perfect flat-top buzz cut, the girl all blonde hair and freckles. They were laughing and smiling at each other so damned much that I actually felt glad to be there, watching them. Knowing that similar scenes were being acted out from the Pacific to the Atlantic under that huge starlit continental American sky made me feel good. I ate my burger and fries, basked in the warm glow of the neon and felt at peace. It was an unusual feeling. I enjoyed it so much that it took me a while to get up the willpower to get rolling, but I finally managed and set off into the night.

Midnight in L.A.

It was almost midnight when I pulled up behind the Pacific Arts Supplies warehouse. The place was way out near the beach, in a grim little district filled with run-down factories and car repair shops. This was the side of Santa Monica that the picture postcards never showed, the perfect location for a nasty B-movie ending. The parking area behind the warehouse was empty. I waited in the car for ten minutes to make sure no one was around and then I got out into the night air. I could smell the tang of the ocean but it struggled against the odors of burnt metal and paint that crept over from the repair shops. I picked out a window behind a stack of garbage bins and jimmied it open. With a small flashlight tucked into the waistband of my Levi's, I climbed into the dark. Once inside I listened carefully. I couldn't imagine the place having a night watchman but there was no point in taking chances. Not hearing any sound except my own labored breathing, I flicked the flashlight on. Directly in front of me was a stack of sawed-off palm tree trunks. Next to them were a couple of big workbenches and racks of saws and other cutting tools. I moved the light farther along, until, suddenly, a giant face appeared out of the gloom. My heart skipped a beat and, for a second, I was ten years old again in the House Of Horrors at the carnival. It was a big, ugly, Tiki statue. The thing was seven foot high and carved out of a solid piece of wood, with a flat-topped head, demonic eyes and a down-turned grimacing mouth. Its body was squat and its disproportionately tiny legs were strangely bowed. Flashing the beam of light around, I noticed three other blocks of wood, each in a different stage of carved development from trunk to statue.

I made my way over to the four Tikis, my footsteps muffled by the inch thick covering of saw dust and wood chippings that lay on the cement floor. The most complete statue had a work docket taped to its back. The little beauty was apparently called Ku and he was bound for the Kon Tiki Restaurant in Phoenix. The docket also said he had been carved by Rudy and was one of a shipment of five due to leave for

Arizona in a couple of weeks' time. I still couldn't see what connection the Tikis had with Eddie and his magic formula except that Rudy was the name written on the back of the Pacific Arts Supplies business card. My only hope was that the flask had been hidden on the premises for some reason, so I checked every nook and cranny for anything that looked even vaguely like an aluminum flask. I found bamboo blinds, ugly carvings, glass fishermen's floats and all the other paraphernalia of Polynesian lounge bars, but no sign of a flask. The building's tiny office was no better. Maps of the Pacific, books on primitive South Seas art and a box full of shipping invoices lay on a battered teak desk. The invoices were for various carvings and Tiki statues that had gone out over the last month or so. It looked like Pacific Art Supplies were doing good business. There were deliveries to the Stardust in Vegas, the Luau Cocktail Lounge in San Diego, the Kaptain's Kabin in Reno and a shipment of Tikis to the Polynesian Pearl Bar in Honolulu. Looking at the names of those bars and breathing in the wood dust that hung in the air like very fine mist gave me a serious thirst.

I picked my way back across the workshop floor and climbed back out the window. The smell of wood chips gave way to the stink of garbage bins as I checked the lay of the land. Nothing was moving except a couple of rats foraging for an evening meal, so I headed back across the yard to the Chevy. Seated behind the wheel, I flipped open the glove compartment and pulled out a hip flask I kept for emergencies. The rum in it was strictly medicinal and after a couple of good gulps, the wood dust was gone. Joseph had wanted to meet at Chalon's coffee shop at 1:00 and it was pushing a quarter to. I didn't want to be too late so I stepped on the gas and sped down Highway One towards Inglewood.

I pulled up at the coffee shop at ten past. Joseph was still there. Wearing a narrow brimmed hat pulled low on his forehead, he was scrunched up in the booth nearest the fire exit at the back of the room. He was watching the entrance like a hawk and the second I noticed him he gave a barely perceptible nod in my direction. The place was surprisingly busy considering the hour. The usual late-night-diner mix of kids too wired to go home, grouchy old insomniacs and the kind of bizarre looking characters that seem to bloom in the dark, strange corners of all big cities. A couple of fat motorcycle cops were knocking back coffee at the counter, their butts not quite fitting on the narrow plastic seats that sat atop stands of shiny chrome tubing. Their presence was kind of comforting, though. There's nothing like a cop or two hanging out in a diner to make people behave. I slid into the booth, sitting opposite Joseph.

Seeing his face up close made me feel guilty. His lips were split and swollen and his nose was the size of a baseball. He looked like he was hurting. He also looked pretty nervous. That wasn't a good sign because I knew it wasn't me he was nervous about.

He glanced over my shoulder at the two cops and his voice dripped with suspicion when he spoke.

"I hope the coppers ain't your idea, big guy."

I smiled at him.

"You know, that attitude isn't going to help. Didn't Justine tell you I'm trying to sort things out? Besides, if I'd set this up, the cops would have nabbed you the second you walked in."

The simple logic of my argument seemed to appeal to him because he relaxed a little. He took a cigarette from the packet in front of him and lit up. He didn't offer me one. I wasn't too hurt.

"Okay. Okay. You got a point. So what's the angle, Mister Private Investigator?"

He said "private investigator" with a little bit more sarcasm than I think I deserved but not much more. I started to speak but he suddenly leaned forward and pointed a chubby nicotine stained finger at me.

"You know, I should be sore at you on account of how you messed up my face and kicked me in the guts. But then, I look at how I messed you up and I figure we're pretty even."

I'd almost forgotten the beatings I'd taken over the last few days and I couldn't be bothered telling Joe that most of the cuts and scrapes on my face were actually from a jealous boyfriend and his two punk buddies. If he wanted to think it was his doing, I wasn't going to spoil his fun. In fact, judging by his demeanor and the way he was dressed, in the same heavily creased red and black shirt as our first encounter in Palm Springs, fun was the last thing on Joe's mind right now. To help him relax more I handed over his flashy gold wallet. He started to check the contents.

"It's all right. Your twenty-six bucks is still in there, if that's what you're worried about."

He grunted, checked the money anyway, closed up the wallet and sat back in his seat.

"Justine said you wanted to talk to me, so get talking."

"Actually, Joe, I wanted you to do most of the talking. The more I know about this whole business the more I can try and help you guys out."

He snorted derisively.

"What the hell can you do to help me? You're just a private dick. You can't do nothing."

"Well, that's where you're wrong, Joe. You're forgetting that I'm connected to Eddie Hastings' family. They've got the best lawyers in the State. If you cooperate, I guarantee they'll help keep the heat off you."

I said it so convincingly that I actually believed it myself. I had no idea if the Hasting's lawyers would lift a finger to help Joseph, but as long as I was making progress I'd say anything. His red-rimmed eyes glared at me intently. I had his attention, at least.

"Look, I don't know how much Justine told you, Joey, but you've got to know that the Feds are on your trail. Yeah, you must know that, otherwise you would have been home to change by now."

As I spoke he tried to smooth out his shirtfront. He was one of those toughs who liked to look sharp. The poor guy was actually embarrassed about his appearance.

"The way I see it," I continued, "you can either try and help me get that flask back and get this thing settled, or you go on the run, trying to avoid a stretch in San Quentin."

There was a long silence and Joe looked deep in concentration. He lit up another cigarette from the dying embers of his previous one, took a hearty drag, paused for what I guess he figured was dramatic effect and started speaking.

"Okay, hotshot. This is what you get, but I'm only saying it once. I was out in Florida before I came to California. I did odd jobs for the boys in Miami but nothing crazy, you know. I roughed up bookies and looked after bars, that kind of stuff. Well, things got a bit out of control and the cops put the heat on so I shifted out here. I managed to fake some references, got a job at Star Crest and tried to keep my nose clean."

As he said that, he raised his hand to his battered conk and felt it gingerly. I tried not to smile as he continued talking.

"Anyhow, after a couple of months, I get a call from some guy named Fitch. Says he works for a couple of chemical firms back east. He tells me that one of the Miami boys recommended me. Asks if I want to make some real dough by doing some snooping around. He says all the big companies are doing it, poaching staff, tapping phones, lifting documents. Makes it sound like a legit side of business."

"It's called industrial espionage."

"Yeah, yeah, whatever. Anyway, all I hafta do is get hold of any Star Crest documents I can and he'll get it to the highest bidder. Well, I'm tempted, but I got no in's when it comes to the business shit. I'm just a goddamned night watchman. I sniff around and hear that Justine, who works in the research and development block, needs extra dough. She's a sweet kid, reminds me of my daughter—she's a nurse back in Miami, same age as her. Well, Justine tells me she needs dough real bad, so she's on board. Most of the documents we're copying early on was penny ante stuff—Fitch tells me it ain't too useful to his clients—but I'm still getting steady cash from him, so I'm happy."

"So, he kept paying? Even for the small stuff?"

"Yeah, sure. Then Justine starts getting me papers about this new drug that Hastings is messing around with in the lab and Fitch gets very interested. The money starts going up, but I'm getting nervous. I figure if this stuff is so important then someone's gonna catch us out. I told the girl to be real careful how she spent her cut of the dough—I told her—'don't make anyone suspicious, don't start wearing fur coats to the office'. She's a smart kid, she don't need telling twice. Anyhow, I'm making plans to cut out when the Hastings kid gives me this flask. He tells me it's the only lot of his special drug that's been made up. He wants me to look after it while he figures things out. I dunno what he's talking about but I see a chance to make some big money on this deal. That's all I wanted, make some real dough so I can get the hell out before the shit hits the fan. I tell Fitch I've got the flask and he gets real excited but the cheap bastard won't give me the big bucks until I've got the written instructions."

"What written instructions?"

He sighed before answering.

"The formula on how to create more of the damned stuff…"

I sat and quietly soaked it all up. The name Fitch was new to me but everything else Joey-boy told me tied in with Justine's story. I needed to know more about the flask, so, the second he paused for another puff on his cigarette, I threw in another question.

"So, you weren't worried what was in the flask or when Eddie might ask for it back?"

"Nah, why should I give a damn?"

"Eddie trusted you to look after it."

"Ha, don't give me that crap. I never said he could trust me. If it comes to that, how dumb is that kid? He might be a scientist but he knows nothing about people. What did he expect me to do with that goddamned thing? Put it in my own private bank vault?"

"Okay, Joe, keep calm. So, when did you give the flask to Fitch?"

"Fitch? I never gave it to Fitch. I've never even met the guy! He either calls me at home or there's a number I call when I've got something for him. No, I never give stuff to Fitch. It always goes to Rudy, at Pacific Arts. I give him documents, he gives me sealed envelopes with cash in. Every two, three weeks he either drives out to Fontana and I meet him in some bar or I go over to his workshop. He's the guy I gave the flask to. That was about a week ago."

I figured I was getting somewhere. But what the hell did a guy who carved Polynesian idols for a living have to do with industrial espionage? I put the question to Joseph who was now on his third cigarette. Blowing smoke from his nostrils he leaned forward again. His voice lowered to a harsh whisper.

"I thought you private eyes were supposed to be smart. Fitch obviously don't want me connected to him so he uses this Rudy as a go-between.

When you've mixed with the kind of company I have, you learn to do what the moneymen say. All I know is I took Rudy the flask six days ago. After that, I dunno what the hell happens to it. I don't wanna know what happens to it. The more you know the more life gets dangerous."

He was getting agitated and I wasn't sure why.

"Okay, Joe. Don't blow a fuse. I understand what you're saying, except that in the Marines we'd say that the less we knew, the safer we felt."

"The Marines! What the hell do you know about the Marines?"

"I was in the Fighting Fourth from January '44 until a chunk of shrapnel cut me up on Iwo Jima in March of '45."

He pushed his hat back off his forehead and stared at me with something approaching respect. When he finally spoke, his voice had lost its hard edge.

"I was in the 5th Division from '42 to '46. The Solomon Islands, Guadalcanal, every stinking step of the way. But Iwo Jima was something else. We were next to the Fourth for two months on that lousy piece of rock. I remember you guys took a helluva beating. Jesus, we all took a beating. I lost a lot of good buddies on Iwo Jima."

For a moment, his eyes glazed over. Like plenty of guys, I knew he probably didn't feel comfortable talking about the war. Iwo Jima wasn't something you wanted to think about too damned often. There were too many memories of suicidal Jap Banzai charges, of broken bodies, friends suddenly turned into hamburger meat in front of your eyes, freezing weather and sleepless nights. They were the nights when all you could think about was whether you'd be lucky enough to see the next sunrise. You can read about Iwo Jima in the history books and see it in the movies. You might even know the names, Hill 382, the Amphitheater, Suribachi, and the rest, but brother, if you weren't there you wouldn't ever understand. Every single foot of that Godforsaken chunk of dried lava was paid for in the blood of decent men. History will tell you how generals map out their strategies and their plans of attack, but what history won't tell you is that war is about one thing for the guys doing the fighting. For us, war was about exchanging real estate for lives. Fifty feet of open ground for twenty dead Marines, a rocky gorge for a hundred dead and maimed men, and thousands more for a whole island. So, Joseph sat with his memories for a moment or two before his gaze focused back on me. He stubbed out his latest smoke and extended his right hand over the table. We shook hands.

"No hard feelings, fella? You know, no hard feelings about Palm Springs?"

I shook my head in reply and then spoke to confirm the gesture.

"No, Joe. No hard feelings. But listen, about this Rudy. Is he someone you know real well?"

"You're kidding, ain't ya? The guy's a jerk and probably a draft-dodger. He looks like a frigging weirdo. Wears sandals all the time. Got a beard like a goddamned billy goat. Always wears these ratty black clothes covered in sawdust. Like I said, I'd give him an envelope and he'd give me one back. The only time we talked was when we were arranging the next meet."

"And Fitch? If you got the written formula how were you going to contact him?"

"I can't contact him. The number I had is dead now. Last time we spoke he said I had to arrange everything with Rudy."

"Okay, so how do I get to see this Rudy?"

"That's simple. Just go over to his workshop on Pico. Seems like he's there every frigging day, carving them dumb statues. But listen, I've gotta meet some people so I have to cut out."

I nodded.

"Okay, Joe. How can I get in touch with you again?"

"Listen, I hope you're on the level, fella, because I'm taking a helluva risk giving you this. It's the phone at the place I'm shacking up at for the next couple of days. You don't wanna come visit 'cos it's off Central Avenue in friggin' Mau Mau land."

He scrawled a number on a napkin and pushed it across the table to me.

"Well, it's over to you, Private Investigator. If I don't hear from you or the girl soon, I'm heading Mexico way. Tell you the truth, this whole crap shoot has got me jinxed. I gotta bad feeling about it. When the heat comes down, the men at the top like to tie up loose ends. We, my friend, are loose ends. Just keep an eye on Justine, will ya? She's a good kid. Well, Semper Fi, fella, Semper Fi…"

And with the Marine motto still on his lips, Joseph eased out of the booth and walked out into the dark Inglewood night. *Semper Fi.* Always faithful. Vicki would have smiled at that one. I sat there for five or ten minutes sipping coffee, my fatigued brain trying to tie up my own loose ends and failing miserably. I wondered how near the Star Lite Inn was and how Justine would react if I showed up at her motel room door at two in the morning. A small rabid beast inside of me slowly started stirring to life but this was one night when I had to keep it in check.

I paid and strolled over to the Chevy. As I opened the door, I heard the screech of tires and saw a black sedan disappearing around the corner across the street. Someone was late for something.

And then I noticed that five or six parking spaces along from mine, was a strangely familiar car. It was in semi-shadow but I could vaguely make out a figure in the driving seat. The person was facing my way and making no secret of the fact that they were looking straight at me.

I walked slowly towards the other car. Whoever was in there didn't seem to give a damn that I was approaching them. They just sat there, waiting. I got up close, my heart beating heavier than it should and waved at the driver.

"Come on, buddy. Don't be shy. Step out where I can see you."

There was no movement. No reaction. I stepped closer. The figure still didn't move, but I recognized the face as I bent forward and peered into the open passenger window. It was Joseph Safarini, one time US Marine. Poor Joe with the left side of his head splattered across the dashboard.

There was an entry wound by his right temple and thick, dark blood and gunk all over the passenger seat. Somehow his body had stayed upright, his head propped up against the side window. I was back on Iwo Jima again, and the guy next to me had brought it. Death was pretty arbitrary. The two of us had been talking a few minutes before and now one of us was dead.

Before I could unfreeze my thoughts, I heard the door of the coffee shop open behind me. It was the motorcycle cops. They were too busy chatting and pulling on their leather gauntlets to notice me. I stood rooted to the spot, holding my breath, as though that would somehow help make me invisible. They took a thousand years to walk the five yards to their Harleys.

I crouched down and moved slowly away from the scene of the crime and over to the Chevy. I opened the passenger-side door and, like a ghost, eased over behind the wheel. I turned the ignition on, flicked on the headlights and carefully backed out of the spot. As I swung the car towards the exit, the lights briefly lit up the cops and I had a glimpse of shiny black leather, white faces and motorcycle metal. Seconds later I was out on the street. I pulled up fifty yards away, behind a couple of trees and turned back to see what was happening. I heard engines kick into life and the lights on the motorbikes flashed on. The cops came swinging out of the coffee shop's lot and straight towards me. I ducked down as they changed gears, swept past me, and roared off in the direction of Hawthorne.

I sat numbly staring out of the windshield, and then without thinking I put the pedal to the metal and found myself driving down Pacific Coast Highway. It made sense to get as far away from the coffee shop as quickly as possible. Once Joe's body was found, I figured I'd be the prime suspect if anyone remembered me sitting with him. In the far distance, towards Hawthorne, I could see the glow of the construction crews' arc lights as they worked on the new International Airport. They were building a whole new world and I had a sneaking feeling I wouldn't live long enough to see it.

For the second time that night, I drove as though someone was on my tail. I'd spent enough time in the Pacific feeling like a human target and I didn't want to be one in my own goddamned country. When I was certain I wasn't being followed, I headed back into Inglewood. Before I even knew what I was doing I was parking the Chevy across the street from the Star Lite Inn. If they'd got Joseph, they might want Justine, too. Whoever they were.

I ran across the street to the motel's entrance. The first thing I noticed as I passed the front office was the absence of Justine's blue-and-white Pontiac rental. That wasn't good. I reached the door to room 16 and hammered on it. There was silence. I waited a moment and knocked again even louder. Someone, a couple of doors down, shouted at me to shut the hell up.

I knocked again. Lights started going on in several nearby rooms but darkness reigned in Justine's room. I was about to put my shoulder to the door when what I presumed to be the night manager came shuffling along. He looked half-frightened, half-angry. He looked how I felt. He was old enough to be my father but he acted tough.

"What the heck are you trying to do, buddy? This is a decent establishment. We don't want no trouble."

I didn't want trouble either and I was aware of faces peering out from behind the blinds in at least half a dozen rooms. A couple of disgruntled guests were even out of their rooms in their pajamas, intent on catching any excitement that might be going on. I held my hands out to the night manger to show I was unarmed, calm and not a threat. I spoke slowly but with feeling.

"Hey, sorry about the disturbance but I'm looking for someone. The girl who was here, Miss Carson, do you know where she is? I'm her uncle and it's real important I see her."

I heard someone behind me mutter something about the unlikelihood of my being Justine's uncle. I didn't take offence. If I'd just been woken up at two-thirty in the morning by some lunatic banging on a motel room door looking for a young woman I'd have muttered something as well. The night manager seemed calmed by my demeanor, though, and his voice lost its angry edge. I preferred the anger though to the irony that replaced it.

"You missed her, buddy. Your, ahem, "niece" checked out 'bout midnight. Said something about not being able to sleep and wanting to be on her way as soon as possible. I told her to drive careful, and off she went. Sweet young gal. I hope there's no family problems?"

I shook my head and, ignoring the stares of the woken guests, I walked back to the Chevy.

I got home around three. I parked, checked out the street and made it up to my apartment without getting my brains blown out. If Justine had been sitting seductively on my couch I wouldn't have been surprised, but she wasn't, so I bolted the front door, shut the blinds and staggered into the bedroom. I needed sleep. I carefully placed my .45 within reach, switched off the light, stripped and climbed into bed. My face was hurting, my legs ached and the rest of me was too tired to care. I shifted position just twice, and then I was out cold.

The Jive Hive

The intrusive clamor of the telephone woke me. It was about ten in the morning. I grabbed the receiver and mumbled what I hoped sounded like a greeting. The line was bad but under all the snap, crackle and pop of the static I recognized Justine's voice. I was glad to hear her for more reasons than I cared to admit. She sounded as tired as I felt.

"Johnny, it's me. I'm down here in Huntington Beach. I'm staying with an old friend from secretarial school. I know you said to stay in the motel but I got so scared and lonely I had to leave. I called you at your apartment around midnight but you weren't there. I thought of meeting you at that coffee shop with Joseph, but then I was worried you'd be angry if I showed up, so I just packed my things and drove here."

I tried to interrupt but she either didn't hear me or didn't want to listen. She said something about being safe and calling me later and that she was at a payphone and her money was about to run out. I shouted at her to stay on the line but that was it. The connection was dead.

I hit the shower to wake myself up fully, and little alarm bells began to go off in my head. Was it just coincidence that she'd checked out of the motel an hour or so before Joseph was shot? What if she had pulled the trigger? I didn't want to believe that she was capable of murder but there was already the ghost of poor, fat Rhodes haunting the desert in Palm Springs. Dropping a pill in a drink is one thing, though, putting a silencer to someone's head and blowing a hole through his skull is a whole different ballgame.

I rinsed off with cold water to feel more alive and then wrapped a towel around me and padded into the kitchen for my first coffee of the day. As I ate a bowl of stale Cornflakes, I pondered the mess I was getting myself into. In the Marines it was simple. You were given a job and you got on with it. You knew who your enemy was and who your friends were. This was different. This was just all wrong. Take Joe Safarini—he survives three years of hell, fighting for his country overseas—and ends up dying ignobly outside a suburban coffee shop. And why was he killed? Because someone was upset that he'd spoken to me? But they hadn't killed me yet. It had to be because they figured I might lead them to Eddie's formula.

I wandered into the bedroom and started getting dressed. Grabbing a short-sleeved shirt and a pair of slacks, both in black to match my mood, I returned to the kitchen. Perhaps now was the time to cry "uncle" and call in the Feds. Eddie would just have to face the music and admit that a flask of his chemical junk was loose in the world, but that would also mean letting Vicki down again and I'd done enough of that for one lifetime. No, I'd been dealt my hand and I was going to have to play it.

After a couple of mugs of java I called Pacific Arts Supplies again. With Joseph Safarini gone, this guy Rudy was my only lead to the flask. The phone rang twice and was answered by a voice that sounded like it came from a throat lined with gravel.

"Pacific Arts Supplies."

"Yes. Good morning. Could I speak to Rudy?"

"No, you can't. He ain't here. The lazy bastard didn't turn up for work—again. I got orders coming in by the bucket load and only two carvers working full-time. I'd can the jerk if he wasn't the best I'd got. Even so, if he don't show by the weekend he's out on his ear. Anyway, who the hell are you?"

"Me? I'm just an old friend of his, I'm trying…"

"Then, why the hell am I wasting time talking to you? I've got an order to finish by tomorrow morning. If you want the guy, you'll probably find him bumming around at that weirdo place on Sunset Strip."

"Which one?"

"If you're his friend, you'll know it—the Bee Hive or something dumb like that. If you see the asshole there, tell him if he ain't in by Friday he's fired!"

He slammed the phone down before I could say another word. He had to have meant the Jive Hive. I had to hand it to the late Mister Rhodes. He'd done some pretty good detective work in putting the *Ritual of the Savage*, Pacific Arts Supplies and the Jive Hive together. The Jive Hive was one of the places on his list. It was also one of the dives on the Strip where Gerry occasionally played. That was good. It gave me an "in" to check out the place later that evening. In the meantime, I had more calls to make. I tried Vicki, but she was out at the hospital seeing Eddie. Her father's secretary took the call and I told her to tell Vicki that things were going really well. If you're going to lie, lie big. Next was a groveling apology to the long-suffering Gladys down at my office.

She hadn't missed me a bit, but two potential clients had called and, more ominously, a couple of heavies had slouched into the office that morning asking my whereabouts. Dear, sweet, reliable Gladys had given them the usual "he's out of town on a job" spiel but she didn't think they were convinced. She was certain they wanted to take it further, but the building's janitor and the local fire inspector had been checking fire extinguishers at the time, so the unwanted guests left. She told me to be careful. I told her to take a week's paid leave. I didn't want her in the office if those two came snooping around again. This was my caper and there was no reason to put her in danger.

I finished the dregs of the coffee, left the apartment and stepped out into the sunshine. It was another sunny day in LA but it wasn't a good heat. It was sullen and resentful. Sitting in the Chevy, it suddenly felt too claustrophobic to stay in the city. So I decided to nix Angelo's and instead drove west towards the sea and the open sky.

I reached the beach just before noon. It was getting hot there, too, but the last tendrils of sea mist and the ocean breeze made the heat bearable. The sound of the ocean and the fresh salt air improved my mood so much that I decided to go for a swim. I always kept a swimsuit and a towel in the trunk of the Chevy for such occasions. When you live in LA you never know when you're going to be at the beach next, so it's best to grab the moment when you can. I still felt uncomfortable knowing that the two goons who visited the office might be tailing me, so I unclipped my .45 from inside the glove compartment, wrapped it in the towel and carried it down to the beach with me.

I found a spot that wasn't too crowded, changed and splashed into the waves. The cold water made me shiver at first, but I soon warmed up and swam and floated for half an hour or so until it felt like time to stretch out on the sand and soak up the sun's rays.

A hundred yards down the beach, a group of noisy kids were whooping it up, running in and out of the breakers, playing tag and generally having a ball. Their howls and shouts bothered me, but also reminded me of the years before Pearl Harbor. Those pre-war years when a gang of us kids from La Canada and Pasadena would drive down to Huntington Beach for the day, and we were the brats causing the commotion. Our gang hung out together almost every weekend back then. When we were real young, we used to hike along the bridle trails around La Canada with packed lunches our mothers had made us. With the slumbering San Gabriel Mountains behind us, we'd play cowboys and Indians amongst the oaks, brushwood and eucalyptus trees. When we got a bit older, we'd head into Glendale or Pasadena to drink sodas, tease girls, listen to Tommy Dorsey on jukeboxes, go bowling or watch Flash Gordon at the movies. And then we hit our sixteenth birthdays and automobiles changed our world. Every weekend it was a different beach, unless we went to the Mojave Desert to watch the speedsters dragging out on the salt flats. Summer vacations we'd spend weeks camping in Big Sur, Yosemite or San Clemente and wherever we went, it seemed a perfect, blue-sky world.

Even through the worst of the Depression years, when the last of the local orange groves were cut down, and some of our neighbors were getting handouts from the Community Chest, life for us kids was one big adventure. Don't let anyone tell you differently, California was a great place to grow up. Probably still is, I guess, despite the smog and the traffic jams. If Vicki and I had had children this would have been the place to raise them. It had just never seemed the right time for us, though. Crazy to think about it, but if we'd had a kid when we first got married he'd be six years old. He'd be running up and down a beach like the one I was on, maybe with a brother and sister, all blonde hair, laughter and freckles. We would have made sure he was the first kid on the block to have a Davy Crocket cap, a pair of Roy Rogers pajamas, a Slinky, the best train-set money could buy, and at least three trips a year to Disneyland. Instead of which, I was lying alone on the sand with a loaded gun hidden in my towel, watching other people's kids running wild and wishing they'd shut the hell up. I stayed on the beach until about three, and then I drove a short way to a small roadside diner. The place wasn't too busy so I sat at a table with a sea view window and ordered a steak followed by a slice of apple pie. As I ate I worried some more about missed opportunities. I thought about Vicki. I thought about Justine. Then I decided to drive back to town and face whatever fate was going to throw my way that evening.

Sophie's is one of those old-time bars that's been around since the sepia days when the silent movie was king. It stands on the corner of Santa Monica and La Brea, and looks like an abandoned set from a Phillip Marlowe film with its white walls, black beams, gabled windows, and a liberal covering of creeping ivy. It's probably best seen at night in the rain, when you can imagine Bogart striding out into a downpour with his raincoat collar up and hat brim down.

Inside the place, the decor is all oak-paneling, high-backed leather booths and deep red drapes. A cursory glance would make you think you were in an exclusive country club. But once you get accustomed to the subdued lighting and the blue-grey clouds of cigarette smoke, it's hard to miss the fact that the place has seen better days. The bar stools are badly frayed at the edges, the leather seats of the booths have splits and cracks that show their age, the carpet boasts stains that will never come out, and the drapes needed cleaning back when FDR was still president.

Amongst all the pastel-colored, streamlined newness that is modern Los Angeles though, Sophie's faded grandeur has an appeal that keeps its bartenders busy every night of the week. I got there early, while the place was half-filled with junior executives on their "two dry Martinis and then home to the wife and kids" early evening routine. The real heavy drinkers, who ran monthly tabs and knew the bartenders by their first names, didn't turn up until eight or nine. Head-man, Jimmie, was serving me my third drink when Gerry came in. A morning session at Warners had overrun, but with union overtime, he wasn't too upset. He pulled up a stool and ordered a whiskey sour.

"Well, Johnny, what's shaking in the big, bad city?"

"My nerves, if I had any damned sense. The night watchman I told you about, Joe Safarini, had his head blown off last night about five minutes after I spoke to him. We were at a coffee shop up in Inglewood;

we spoke for a while, he left, and boom! Someone shot him while he was sitting in his car."

Gerry put down his drink.

"Shit! This is getting too serious, man. It's time you called the Feds. Vicki will understand. I'm sure she doesn't expect you to get yourself killed over this."

"I know she doesn't but…" my voice trailed off as I searched for the real reason, "this isn't something I can just walk away from, Gerry. For a start, there's my little removal act with Rhodes' body."

"I'd still come clean if I were you, losing your license is better than losing your life."

"Yeah, you're right—but I still have to see this through to the end. I'm taking this personally. And it's not like I've got anything else hollering for my attention."

Gerry shook his head.

"If you say so… I'm just wondering, though, if doing all this *is* gonna help Vicki."

He had a point. But I couldn't really tell him that my life had become so meaningless that some delinquent part of me actually welcomed danger or that the thought of Justine made me feel alive again. Instead I explained that as Justine had skipped town, my only contact for solving the case was Rudy, the carver from Pacific Arts. If me and Gerry could track him down at the Jive Hive, I might be able to fill in a couple more pieces from the jigsaw. Gerry finished his drink and offered to drive us over to Sunset. I was feeling pretty fuzzy from the booze, so I was more than happy to let him deal with the Friday night rush hour.

As usual, at the start of the weekend, Sunset Strip was crawling with humanity. Gerry edged the Corvette carefully through the bumper-to-bumper snakes of traffic that choked the Strip from Crescent Heights to Doheny Drive, and back again. The trails of red brake lights curved away east and west as kids in hotrods, incognito Hollywood stars in foreign sports cars, and ordinary Joes in ordinary autos all contributed to the Sunset Crawl. Everyone was looking for some kind of action, even the foot-weary Beatnik patrons of the "legendary" Jive Hive. Just a block west of Ciro's, the Jive Hive—in contrast to the neon glare of its classy neighbors—seemed a dreary, almost grim place for finding any kicks. In front of its black-painted exterior were a few parked motorcycles and about fifty kids, all crowded around a roped-off entrance. Beneath an unobtrusive neon sign featuring a cartoon bee wearing a beret, a tiny teenage girl, who looked like a teen version of the French singer Juliette Greco, stood behind the rope, flanked by two burly doormen.

The girl seemed to be taking a sadistic delight in picking out who should and who shouldn't be let into the hallowed doors of Sunset's own little patch of beat Bohemia. She'd point at one or two kids and the doormen would open up the ropes to let them in while the others in the crowd stood there grumbling quietly. The lucky ones chosen to get past the rope didn't seem too excited to be gaining admittance to the place though. They slouched through the entrance as though they could take it or leave it. Unbridled enthusiasm was, obviously, considered uncool by the Jive Hive set.

As we gently pushed our way to the front of the waiting throng, I saw that little Miss Greco had noticed us and her porcelain white face was puckering in ill-concealed disgust. I wasn't surprised. We were two guys the wrong side of thirty, mixing with kids at least ten years younger than us, and I envisioned some kind of run-in with the witch of the rope. But, as we reached the front of the crowd, the bigger of the two doormen nodded a greeting to Gerry, ignored a comment from the witch and waved us in. I guess musicians are pretty respected on the nightclub circuit.

Inside, the Jive Hive was more like a normal teenage coffee bar than the dark, gloomy space I'd been expecting. A jukebox stood at one end of a long narrow room lined on both sides by a series of booths. The clientele were mainly teenagers but here and there were some older characters, mainly local crazies who looked bizarre enough to fit in with this younger crowd. Everyone sat around drinking coffee or cokes and tapping their feet to the jukebox. In one booth, a gang of blonde haired kids were fooling around on an acoustic guitar and a couple of sets of bongos, the must-have instrument for Beatsville, USA.

While I was absorbing the scenery, Gerry steered me to the side of the serving counter and down some concrete steps to the basement. Darker and larger than the room above it, this was obviously the focal point of the Hive. Groups of kids stood gossiping earnestly, others congregated at the dozen or so tables and booths that were arranged along one wall and in a couple of candlelit alcoves. A couple of snotty punks in leather jackets and greasy Elvis pompadours glared at us, but otherwise no one paid us any mind. There must have been another jukebox in the basement, because the amplified wail of a guitar bounced off the low ceiling and poster-plastered walls around us.

Tucked in next to a crummy-looking service bar was a small stage, empty of performers, but with a dozen or so onlookers waiting for the next show. Gerry spoke to one of the hassled-looking waitresses and she pointed out a booth that was still empty. We sat, ordered root beers and took in the buzz of the Hive. Gerry had played here a couple of times before but I could tell the place made him uneasy. He wasn't alone. If the squalor of the Hive was de rigueur for the so-called "Beat Generation" then I was glad I grew up before the war. The place was more dingy, and a lot more popular, than old Angelo's had been in its Beatnik phase. That was just a coffee shop with rough wooden tables and nightly poetry readings. The Jive Hive was the real McCoy, Beatnik central. Watching the fuzzy faced, scruffy kids in that grimy, bare-bricked basement, I thought of that Kerouac *On The Road* crap that *Playboy* kept publicizing. I'd tried reading it a couple of times but couldn't get past the first chapter. Those endless, rambling descriptions were too much for me. Murderers serving time at Alcatraz had shorter sentences.

Me, I preferred writers like Ray Bradbury. Bradbury's America, whether it was a past, present or future one, was something I could identify with. The America Kerouac conjured up, with its junkies and goof-offs, just filled me with disgust. It wasn't a place where I wanted to spend time. Much like the Jive Hive in fact. I tried to control my prejudices but it was difficult. The beatnik kids kind of got under my skin. I guess I couldn't understand why they had to dress like bums and gather like trolls in the dark. But I was there for a reason, so I kept my thoughts to myself and just watched the passing faces. Gerry was sure that Saul, the Jive Hive's owner, would be able to point Rudy out to us. Saul wasn't in the club but was expected shortly. Meantime, we watched and waited.

As we sat scanning the room, something caught my eye. Over in a corner booth, a bunch of kids were staring in silent awe at a guy who looked like the king of the hobos. He had long hair down to his shoulders, a bearded, weather-beaten face and was dressed in tattered denim. A colorful Navajo Indian blanket draped over his shoulders completed the whole bizarre picture. Sitting there, sipping a glass of water, he gently nodded his head to the beat of the bongos. He seemed like one very serene guy. Gerry caught my gaze and leaned over to me.

"That's the Hermit."

"Who the hell is the Hermit?"

"His real name's Eden Ahbez. He was beat when these kids were in diapers. Rumor has it he lives on nuts and berries, and sleeps up in the canyons. He's supposedly a real cool cat. But get this, the best bit of it is, he's the guy who wrote 'Nature Boy'."

"Nat King Cole's 'Nature Boy'?"

"The very same."

"You're kidding me?"

"Nope, this is the guy who helped Nat sell over a million discs, and yet he owns nothing and wants nothing, either, from what they say."

I was genuinely shocked. "Nature Boy" had to be one of the biggest records of all time. The first time I'd heard it was a couple of years after the war ended. I was passing a record store on Beverly and noticed a crowd gathered around the shop's doorway. Everyone just stood there, silently listening to that amazing song. Each time it ended, people would tell the record store guy to play it again. I stayed there for twenty minutes and heard it six times. I felt almost hypnotized. Something in its delivery had a sad, wistful quality, like it was a lament for all those lives lost in the war. It was like no other music I'd heard before, or since. Whatever it was, something about it got to a lot of people, because for months that song was played everywhere. Anyway, I'd always imagined that the composer was one of those hot-shot Jewish song-writers from the Brill Building in New York. *Life* magazine had run a piece on them, and it seemed like five or six of those whizz-kids had written every corny rock 'n' roll song that I'd ever heard. But Ahbez was nothing like them. He looked like an extra who'd just wandered off the set of Paramount's latest Bible epic. I was about to ask Gerry more about him when two beatnik babes slid in next to us.

They both had the regulation heavy black eyeliner, dyed black hair and pale lipstick, and were dressed in black jeans and black sweaters. They were cute, though, and were both as high as kites. The one nearest me put her hand under the table and squeezed my leg. As she squeezed, she spoke. The way her hand was working on my leg made me pay attention to what she was saying.

"Hey, big daddy. You don't mind if we share a booth with you, do you? We just gotta cool our jets somewhere."

I tried not to laugh at the corny dialogue. She couldn't have been more than eighteen and probably didn't know any better. She was just a little rich kid slumming it on the Strip, trying to shock mummy and daddy by going beat. I kept a straight face as I answered her.

"Hell, no. The more the merrier. That's what I always say, isn't it, Gerry?"

Gerry grunted back. I could tell he wasn't taken with our two little intruders. All the black clothes and dingy beatnik lifestyle made his blood run cold. Besides, his big thing was Latino chicks. He lived for his bass and pouty, voluptuous girls from south of the border. He never kept them long, though. They wanted commitment and he didn't even know how to spell the word.

The second of the beat girls took a liking to him though. She leaned across the table and smiled at him.

"You know, guys with brown eyes really send me. What's your name?"

Gerry groaned. He patted my leg, the one that wasn't being massaged, and levered himself out of the booth.

"Jesus Christ! I'm gonna circulate. See you later, *alligator*."

As he wandered off, the girl who liked brown eyes whispered something to her friend and got up. She followed Gerry into the darkness leaving me alone with her anxious-to-please buddy. The hand on my leg was slowly working its way higher. I tried not to mind too much.

"My name's Valerie. What's yours, daddy-o?"

"My friends call me Johnny."

"I'd like to be your friend, Johnny," she said softly and her hand began massaging the top of my thigh.

I put my hand over hers. I didn't dislike what she was doing, but business had to come before pleasure. She seemed slightly disappointed that I'd stopped her hand from reaching its intended target, and gave me a quizzical look.

"What's the matter?" she purred, "don't you want us to be friends?"

"Sure, I do," I purred back, "but I'm new on the scene so maybe you could fill me in on who's who in here?"

"New on the scene, new on the scene," she said it like she'd never heard the words before, but that now she'd heard them, she liked the sound of them. Nuzzling closer up to me, she repeated my little phrase twice more before adding her own dialogue.

"I knew I hadn't seen you before, daddy-o. I would have noticed you. You're not like the other cats who hang around here. They're either old and creepy or young and skinny. Like strictly dullsville. I kinda dig big guys like you. That caveman style really sends me."

With that, she squeezed my leg really hard.

"I'm not a teaser like these other chicks, I'll wow you, Johnny."

I didn't doubt for a second that she could, but I tried to be professional.

"Listen, Valerie. Before we get too friendly, could I ask you about someone I want to meet up with? It's a guy called Rudy, Rudy the Carver. You heard of him?"

"No. And I don't wanna gas about anyone else. We could swing the most, Johnny. Let me show you how. Like I said, I could really wow you."

I couldn't argue with her because her hand had suddenly reached its target. I was wowed. What she was doing was not the kind of romancing they show on the silver screen, not even in French movies.

Another couple minutes of that treatment and I would have dragged her out to the Chevy and gladly forgotten all about finding Rudy for another half-hour, or so. I guess that shows I'm just a savage. A guy who, just because a high school drop-out gets his blood rushing from his brain to his groin, forgets that his ex-wife is counting on him, or that a flask, full of nightmare visions was floating around as a corporation's answer to Pandora's box. I needed help and luckily, I got it. Gerry suddenly reappeared out of the gloom and banged on the table with his fist.

"Let's roll, lover boy. I've found your man."

I grabbed Valerie's expert little hand and reluctantly pried it off me. I couldn't stand up straightaway without embarrassing myself so I slid around the table and took my time finishing off my lukewarm root beer. Valerie wasn't happy with me.

"That's not cool, daddy-o. We could have had a blast. Why do you have to be such a square?"

"You know, Valerie, that's a question I ask myself a hundred times a day and I never get a straight answer. Maybe we can get together another time and discuss it."

"Drop dead, creep."

Gerry grabbed me and hauled me to my feet. He wasn't happy with me, either.

"Jesus, Johnny. Can't you ever stop? You told me this was important. I've found that Rudy creep you're after, so let's go get him, okay?"

"Okay, okay. Where is he? How do you know it's him?"

"I told you. Saul, the owner of the place knows him. He said he's in here a lot but the last few days he's been spreading greenbacks around like they're going out of fashion. He's exactly like you described him, right down to the sawdust on his sweater. He's sitting on the stage with a few hangers-on."

Gerry guided me through the throng. The Jive Hive was getting pretty busy. The stench of marijuana mingled with body odor and a fog of cigarette smoke that made my eyes water. I felt unclean just being there.

The area before the stage was crowded and, by the time we'd shoved our way to the front, our man was standing off to one side with a couple of mean-looking kids in grimy sweatshirts, jeans and sneakers. As we edged towards him, a spotlight shone onto the stage. People clapped half-heartedly, and a ridiculously tall guy, unshaven, wearing the tightest black trousers I'd ever seen, a white polo-necked sweater and a fake shrunken-head hanging from a black string necklace, stepped into the circle of light. He grabbed a microphone from somewhere and introduced the night's entertainment. Apparently, the act we were about to see was in the school of Kenneth Patchen. Not knowing Kenneth Patchen, I managed to keep my excitement in check.

As tight trousers spoke, a scrawny kid in a black beret climbed onto the stage, picked up a big double bass, and started plucking out a slow, steady rhythm. An equally scruffy character with a page-boy haircut also appeared from the gloom. He carried a set of bongos and sat cross-legged next to the bass player. He placed the bongos between his knees, rubbed his hands together for a few seconds and then started patting out a beat in time with the deep, walking rhythm of the bass.

A moment later, another kid, this one wearing an oversized grey sweatshirt and a pair of white jeans, slouched out of the darkness and stood in the spotlight. He spoke into the microphone and the audience quickly became silent. The kid had a high, nasal voice but something in his delivery seemed to grab the crowd. I listened.

"Last week I went to the San Diego zoo. The zoo! The zoo, where they keep the wild animals *locked up* so the citizens can stare at them. And I thought how society keeps us all in a cage and it made me write this poem. I call it 'Jaguar'… and it's for the wild things…"

He paused for a few seconds and the bongo and bass players gently raised the volume until he started speaking again.

Jaguar. You move in shadows. Always waiting, always waiting, while time unheeded, drifts on by.

Jaguar. You're locked in a dream world, uncomprehending as the moon waxes and wanes in an alien sky.

Jaguar. You gaze at phantoms, disbelieving, while the stone-faced watchers pass you by.

Oh, Jaguar, if hope was enough you would walk through walls.

Yes, if hope was enough you would walk through walls.

You try to remember, your memory shifting

but the cold bars of steel blot out your past

Another lonely night and the breeze slowly stirring

Tugs at the strings of your untamed heart…"

I glanced around the faces nearest me, and I noticed several of the girls and a couple of guys had tears running down their faces. I also noticed that Rudy was on his own, and absorbed by the poetry. I nodded to Gerry, who moved like a shadow through the audience and took up a position just behind the carver. I edged towards Rudy a step at a time. I was worried he might notice me but he kept his gaze fixed on the stage. The poet carried on… and on… and soon I was close enough to lean conspiratorially over to Rudy and whisper in his ear.

"Hey, Rudy. Listen carefully. You don't know me, but Fitch sent me to give you a message."

The guy's only reaction was to turn his head and stare at my face. Close up, I could see he was probably only twenty or so, younger than I first thought. He had bad acne scars on his cheeks and a sad, wispy, half-assed attempt at a beard. His eyes were bloodshot as hell, and I could tell he had trouble focusing on me. He rubbed the hairs on his chin and stepped back. I kept right with him and grabbed his arm in case he decided to bolt. The puzzled expression on his face intensified and he whispered back at me.

"What does he want this time? He told me there was nothing else right now."

As he spoke, I kept nudging him towards a door marked "Rear Exit". Gerry stuck close in case of trouble but no one paid us any attention. Rudy wasn't in a fit state to complain. He stank of marijuana fumes and seemed to find walking difficult. Gerry pushed open the rear door and the three of us stepped into the alleyway behind the club. It was like every alleyway behind every club in the world. It stank of urine, stale beer and cooking fat. It was ugly and oppressive. A place where bad things could happen and no one would ever know. Rudy seemed to sense the mood of the place and he suddenly became very edgy.

"Who are you guys? Fitch never mentioned you. What do you want?"

He made a brief, fruitless attempt to push past me and return to the club. Gerry effortlessly grabbed his arms and pinned them behind his back. The kid had a muscular build but whatever he'd been inhaling had sapped his strength. His nervousness set the tone of my answer. I decided to play it tough. I unhitched the .45 from the waistband of my Levis and pushed the barrel against his cheek. I was Alan Ladd, Humphrey Bogart and every other screen detective I'd ever watched over the years.

"You don't know us, Rudy, but we've been watching you. We know about your meetings with Joe Safarini, we know you were given a flask. What we don't know is what you've done with that flask. All we want from you is to find out where it is. Once you've told us that, you're free as a bird. You can rejoin your friends in the club there and you'll never see us again. On the other hand you can make things difficult for us, and your friends might never see *you* again."

Rudy looked at me appalled. He seemed so shocked by my threat and the gun in his face that I felt some pity for the guy. Even so, I had to keep the pressure on so I snarled at him again.

"You're not saying anything, Rudy and this isn't a good time to play dumb. Where's that flask?"

From his expression it looked like the carver's drug-addled mind was having difficulty in distinguishing reality from nightmare. And then the words poured out in a torrent.

"Listen, guys, I ain't done nothing wrong. I just took care of that flask and all that other stuff like Fitch told me. I didn't keep none of it. Everything went out on time, like it was supposed to and—"

"So where's the flask?"

"I put the flask in Ku and it got shipped like Fitch said. I don't know what happens to stuff after it leaves the work-shop, I just make sure it's hidden for the trip. Ku and the others were going to Honolulu. They shipped two days ago, maybe three—no, two, two days ago. Ku's got the flask. I know that for sure."

The words were coming out so fast that I had to shout at him to slow down. When that didn't work Gerry twisted his arm a little and the pain concentrated his mind long enough for him to catch his breath.

"You gotta believe me. I never took anything that I wasn't supposed to. Fitch gave me the money and I passed on the envelopes to that Safarini guy. I never opened them, I just took whatever Safarini gave me and put them in the Tikis."

I interrupted, "Say that again, Rudy. What do mean you put them in the Tikis? I'm not reading you. You're not bull-shitting me, are you?"

"I swear I'm telling you the honest truth, man. I carve a hole in the bottom of the Tiki, put whatever Safarini gives me into the hole, and then

115

I seal it up good so you wouldn't know it was in there. Ku is one of the Tiki Gods we're always carving down at Pacific Arts. The flask is in a Ku I did for a place called the Polynesian Pearl Bar in Honolulu, like I told you. Me and the other guys at Pacific Arts carved three pieces for them."

"Yeah? And then?"

"Then the truck picked them up Monday to take them to the docks… down in Long Beach."

"And then what, Rudy?"

"I think the freighter left there on Wednesday. The statues won't arrive in Honolulu until Sunday or Monday. I know that much. If the weather's good a ship can cross to Hawaii in four days flat. If there's a storm though it could be a week. Dig?"

He gave me the last bit of knowledge as though it was some big secret that only he was in on. The smell of the alley was getting to me and I was worried some kid would wander into our little man-to-man talk and scream blue murder at the sight of me shoving a gun into Rudy's face.

"Okay, Rudy, you've been very co-operative. Just a couple more questions and you're on your way. What other stuff did Safarini give you to hide, and where did that go?"

"Oh man, I already told you. It went to the Polynesian Pearl in Honolulu. I must have carved little hidey-holes in about a dozen Tikis and they all had shipping dockets to the Pearl. That place loves their Tikis, man!"

"And your boss at Pacific Arts, he doesn't mind you doing this?"

"Old man Connor? He don't know nothing about any of this. Mister Fitch seems to know when there's an order for Honolulu and that's when I meet up with Safarini. Up until this flask, everything else was in an envelope. Just lots of papers, I guess… look, Fitch pays me good dough to do it and I can't see the harm, so what the hell, I do it. Now can I go? I don't feel so good out here, I wanna get back inside. This scene is strictly for the birds."

His eyes were fixed, staring down at the gun.

"Yeah, sure Rudy, but how come this Polynesian Pearl buys carvings from a workshop in LA? Why don't they just order them locally on the islands?"

"Because no one on the Islands can make Tikis, anymore. The Hawaiians think all the Tiki stuff is embarrassing. They want to be in the super-modern atomic age. But the tourists want the Tikis, so they have to import them from guys like us. Look, I'm feeling pretty bad, can I go now?"

"Sure, Rudy, you can go. But just tell me about Fitch. What does he look like and where can I find him?"

"I don't know where you can find him. I only met the guy a few times. He always calls me. I never call him. He's got an answering service number but I ain't got it with me. Anyhow, I don't need to see him. He sends me money and stuff in the mail, regular as clockwork. If he's got an office any place, it'd be down in Chinatown."

"Why Chinatown, Rudy? Did he show you a business card?"

"No, no. Nothing like that, dad. Fitch is a Chinese guy. Crazy, huh? A Chinese guy called Fitch, ain't that something else? Anyways, I need to split."

As he spoke the fire door behind us swung open with a groan and a waft of pungent air swept over us. Two scrawny kids, a boy and a girl, stood blinking in the doorway. They were coming out back either to get fresh with each other or to light up a reefer.

Either way, I felt I was doing them a favor by shouting at them to get back inside. They started shuffling back into the club, but the distraction gave Rudy the energy to suddenly break free and dive towards the light. We didn't try to stop him. His sudden burst of movement obviously made him more confident because he stopped in the doorway and pointed at us. In his own stoned, comic way, he was trying to look indignant.

"You, you shouldn't have asked me all those questions. Fitch ain't gonna be happy when I tell him 'bout tonight. He's gotta couple of real tough guys who work for him. You're gonna be real sorry, man."

As he spoke he pointed at me in what he probably thought was a threatening manner. One good threat deserves another, so I gave him something to chew on before he slipped back into the subterranean world of the Jive Hive.

"Listen, Rudy. You got off light tonight."

"Yeah?"

"Yeah, Joe Safarini got himself killed yesterday and I'm guessing your Mister Fitch was responsible. You know too much, Rudy, and the crap you smoke will make it hard for you to keep quiet. You should get out of town for a bit—Greenwich Village or San Francisco might be your speed. But wherever you go—and I'd go soon if I were you—I wouldn't talk to Fitch again, otherwise the next statue you carve will be for St Peter at the Pearly Gates. Dig, man?"

Rudy just stood there, mouth open, framed by the red light oozing from the club through the still-open fire door. The light gave him a slightly demonic aura, like a poor, confused sinner at the gates of hell. I slipped the .45 back under my T-shirt as Gerry grabbed my arm.

"C'mon, Johnny. This place is giving me the dry heaves. Let's get out of here. I need a drink."

I didn't need telling twice. I kicked the door shut and we walked out of the alleyway and back to civilization.

Back at Sophie's I nursed an Irish coffee while Gerry savored a malt whiskey. I wasn't happy. As fast as one door opened, another slammed firmly in my face. I'd finally found Rudy but the damned flask was supposedly already heading for Honolulu. I had no reason to disbelieve the kid because he was too hopped up to lie. In fact, everything he told me made sense in a crazy, twisted way. The whole caper was a pretty slick routine. What customs official in Honolulu is going to start sawing up wooden statues from LA to check for stolen documents? It was so simple it was almost laughable. What wasn't laughable though, was this character Fitch and the final destination of the Star Crest documents. If there was mob involvement in this racket, how come they were sending the stuff to Hawaii? It didn't make sense. Something told me this wasn't a case of domestic industrial espionage gone too far. No, this was political and international. If the Red Chinese wanted a conduit out of the States for any secrets they'd stolen, then the trans-Pacific route to Hong Kong via Honolulu was as good as any. A little slow perhaps, but not easily detected. Hawaii was virtually part of the Union. From there to Hong Kong and on to the People's Republic might be a little harder but still relatively trouble-free. It sounded like Fitch or his comrades had thought of everything. I explained my thinking to Gerry and he tried again to convince me to call in the Feds.

"Hey, this is too big for you now. If you're right and the Commies are behind this, the government should know. Those Reds are pretty smart cookies, man. If they get hold of this formula they could jazz it up and create something even more lethal."

I knocked back the last of the Irish coffee. I still couldn't admit to him that I was starting to enjoy the case or the idea of feeling useful again. And then, of course, there was Justine. I swung off the stool and patted him on the shoulder.

"Gerry, buddy, I've got a hunch I can get that flask back without the Feds", he raised a skeptical eyebrow but I ploughed on, "I'll make a deal with you, I'm going to be out of touch for a couple of days. It's Friday night tonight. Give me the weekend and if you've heard nothing by Monday evening, send the album to Vicki's father down in Palm Springs. He'll do the right thing."

I scribbled down the address and passed it to Gerry. He placed it carefully in his wallet. Then he left a couple of bucks for the drinks and stood up.

"Okay, man. I hope you know what you're doing… is there anything else I can do?"

"Gerry, what you've done already has been above and beyond the call of duty. I'll be okay, but if things go wrong and I need help, I know who to call."

He smiled. "Thanks for the endorsement, but just call the Feds. They're equipped for this kinda thing."

We left Sophie's and stood for a moment outside on the sidewalk. Although the day had been hot, the night had a chill edge to it. I told Gerry to watch his back. He wished me luck. We shook hands, walked in opposite directions to our cars and then I drove back to North Formosa.

The second I turned into the street from Sunset, I knew something was wrong. A black-and-white prowl car sat out front of the apartment buildings, its red roof light sending out lazy, revolving flashes of color around the street. As I pulled up in the last parking space on the block,

I noticed a little knot of people clustered around the entrance to my apartment building. I strode briskly up and pushed through the half dozen chattering onlookers and into the lobby. Standing there were two uniformed cops, and talking to them in a very agitated manner were two of my neighbors and Karl Lanski, the super of the building. As they led me excitedly up to the second floor landing where my apartment was, Karl filled me in on what had happened.

Two guys had broken into my apartment sometime after eight and had turned the place upside down. My neighbor across the hall had gotten suspicious at the noise and called the cops. The intruders left moments before the police arrived, Karl actually passing them in the lobby as he returned home from a night at the bowling alley. The grey-haired super tried his damnedest to sound sympathetic as he gave me the facts, but the way his vivid blue eyes were twinkling, it was obvious this was the most excitement he'd had on the job for a long time. He and the cops followed me up into the apartment and stood there making tut-tut noises as I surveyed the damage.

While I'd been digging the scene with the Beatniks down at the Jive Hive, someone had gone through my apartment like Sherman through Georgia. The bastards had smashed my two hundred dollar hi-fi, thrown my *Playboy* and *Esquire* collections across the lounge floor, emptied my LPs out of their sleeves, torn my Haitian voodoo masks from the wall and ripped the stuffing out of my sofa. Oh, and just in case I hadn't noticed any of this, they'd dumped books, papers and photo frames everywhere.

The cops asked me a few questions as I numbly wandered through to the bedroom and I answered in grunts while I stepped over piles of clothes and bed linen. My bedside tables were lying sideways next to my overturned mattress and the metal trunk—the one I kept stowed under my bed—had been broken open, its contents scattered across the carpet.

That trunk held my life in its narrow, rectangular confines and that life now lay ripped and torn before me. Jesus, there wasn't much there. The main attractions were framed photos of Vicki and me on our wedding day and the Mark Twain signed copy of *The Adventures of Huckleberry Finn* that grandfather Davis had given me on my twelfth birthday. That was it, aside from my Marine dog-tags, some photos of Mom and Dad, a couple of track medals from John Muir High School, and a bunch of old letters and postcards.

My neat and orderly bachelor pad had been turned into a slum. Of course, I knew what the intruders had been looking for but I was surprised at how strong my emotions were. For an uncomfortable few moments I could imagine how someone else would see my place if I had died and all I'd left behind was what was in those few rooms. The clothes, books, music and mementoes that I valued so highly, would just be so much junk to them—the kind of stuff that would end up on the shelves of a neighborhood thrift store. Not for the first time since that fateful meeting with Vicki at the Luau, I almost felt sorry for myself. But if the war taught me nothing else, it was that self-pity achieved nothing. It was just an indulgence that wasted time and forestalled action.

After a few more questions and a belated offer of assistance, the cops left me alone to begin clearing up. I started with the upturned trunk of my personal effects. Putting all those bits and pieces of my past back in order actually changed my mood and, by the time I got around to restacking my books and records in the lounge, any lingering shreds of self-pity were replaced by a deep, growing anger. Anger at this Fitch character and his hoods and the way they'd invaded my territory. They'd trashed my place, given me my own little Pearl Harbor. I placed the broken bits of my hi-fi system on the coffee table and plotted revenge.

After downing a pot of strong coffee, I packed a suitcase with light-weight summer clothes. There was a blue-grey hint of dawn in the sky as I left the building and walked down to the Chevy. North Formosa was deserted, and down on Sunset only the occasional delivery truck broke the morning quiet. The small rectangles of lawn between the sidewalks and the buildings glistened with dew. I took a big lung-full of Los Angeles air and, at that time in the morning, it almost felt healthy.

Once in the car, I switched on the radio and drove out to the airport. United Airlines had a daily early morning flight to Honolulu and I paid cash for an open-ended return ticket. I hunkered down in a phone booth while I was waiting for the flight to be called and telephoned Vicki in Palm Springs.

She sounded slightly groggy from just waking up and I felt a stab of remorse that I wasn't with her.

"Did you hear about that night watchman you told me you fought with in Palm Springs? He was killed the other night. The police are certain it's connected to the Rhodes man's death because they were both at Star Crest. Dad said I should never have called you in on this, but I knew you'd be able to help us. I don't want you getting killed or hurt, though. Where are you now? What else do you have to do?"

"Honey, relax. I know about the night watchman being murdered and it isn't going to stop me sorting this thing out. Look, I'll be careful and what I'm doing now will help get Eddie off the hook. By the way, how is he? Still in the hospital?"

"Yes, he's still there but only until next week. The doctors say he'll be fit enough to leave on Tuesday or Wednesday. And the lawyers have done a deal with the FBI—he can leave Palm Springs and come home with us, but he can't leave the States without permission. They've interviewed the poor dear three times in the last two days but he isn't saying much. He just keeps asking about that girl, Justine… have you seen her lately?"

There was no mistaking the edge in her voice this time. I couldn't blame her for not trusting me, but what I couldn't understand was why she thought there was anything between Justine and me. The cold truth was that there was nothing between us. I'd only met the girl twice and the only thing I had to feel guilty about was my imagination. There must have been something in my voice when I'd first mentioned her, something that had alerted Vicki's sixth sense. Once again, though, just the mention of Justine's name had put me on the defensive. I tried to sound as normal as possible when I spoke.

"No, no. I haven't seen her. She's keeping a pretty low profile but I'm making progress without her." I should have shut up then but I burbled on, "Besides, I'm sure the Feds will pick her up any day now."

"Yes, they probably will. They think she might have been involved with the murder the other night. They found Eddie's car yesterday. She'd left it in Glendale."

"Yeah, I know."

"How do you know?" The suspicion was so thick in her voice it was like molasses. "The police haven't contacted you, have they?"

I was digging myself a hole deep enough to climb into. It was *Justine* who'd told me about dumping the car not the police.

Before I could say anything, the operator saved me by cutting in on the line and demanding twenty cents more for the next three minutes. I took my time putting the coins in and then spoke immediately, before Vicki could catch me off guard again.

"Listen, honey, I've got to go now. I'm catching a flight out of the State. I can't tell you where just now, because you never know who's listening. Two things before I go though. First up, I might need you to wire me some money before the weekend is out—I'll let you know where to send it. Is that okay?"

"Oh, J.D., of course that's all right. You're doing this for the family, aren't you? Just let me know how much and where to send it."

"Thanks…"

"That was the first thing… what was the other?"

"I'm really sorry about everything that happened between us. I was an idiot, but I want you to know that I love you, Vicki." I couldn't help myself. Right then I really *did* love her.

"Oh, I love you, too, Johnny, but why do you always have to make things so confusing?"

I didn't really have an answer to that so I just threw her another apology.

"Honey, I'm sorry I'm such a screw-up… but we'll get Eddie out of this, don't worry. Okay, I have to go, they're calling my flight. I'll call tonight if I can. Take care now."

Her voice was resigned in reply. Resigned and concerned.

"Look after yourself and please be careful."

I replaced the receiver before she could say anything else. I hated farewells. I shouldn't have told her I loved her. I wasn't lying, but I didn't want her to think I was keen about giving our marriage a second try. Not because I didn't want to, but because I still didn't know if I could trust myself. Trust myself, hell! Five minutes later, I was in the United Airlines lobby waiting to board the plane. While I waited, I couldn't take my eyes off the stockinged legs and rear-end curves of the stewardesses as they swayed out of the lobby ahead of us and out to the plane.

Then it was the passengers turn to follow them out to the runway. We walked out to the shiny, silver Stratocruiser that sat poised and gleaming in the morning sun. The check-in girl had said that the flight only took nine hours to reach Honolulu. Nine hours! The last time I'd been to Hawaii was in 1951—Vicki and I had gone on a Matson passenger liner that took over five *days* to cross the ocean. No doubt about it, the world was shrinking, and thanks to the Russians and their little Sputnik, it now seemed smaller than ever. Space and the future were the only great unknowns now. Our world was fast running out of mysterious places. I thought of Eddie's albums with the cover art featuring exotic women in exotic places. Did those kinds of places exist anymore? I mean, sure the places *existed* but not in the way the album sleeves portrayed them. According to photos I've seen in *Life* magazine, people all over the world dress just like ordinary Americans. Yet on the covers of those albums, all Africans wear loincloths and war paint, Japanese women wear those fussy little geisha outfits and Hawaiian girls only wear grass skirts and smiles. The only time I'd seen Hawaiian girls in grass skirts was at those big luaus they put on strictly for tourists. On the streets of Honolulu, the girls wore skirts, dresses, hi-heels and slacks exactly like the women in LA, but without having to try quite so hard.

Somewhere Beyond the Sea

As the Stratocruiser lumbered down the runway before lifting off into the clear morning sky, I gripped hard onto the seat rests. I hated flying. That's why God gave us General Motors and ships, so we could travel by road and sea and not defy nature by taking to the sky in unwieldy metal birds. I'd flown in transports a few times during the war and on every single occasion I'd thanked God I wasn't in an Airborne Division. Give me the roll and pitch of the ocean any day. But flying was the only sure-fire way I'd arrive in Honolulu before my wooden friend Ku.

Once we were at cruising altitude, I knocked back a couple of Martinis and tried to sleep. The stewardess serving the drinks was a haughty brunette with a twinkle in her eye. As all the other passengers seemed to be married couples or families, she probably felt sorry for me sitting there all on my lonesome. We made a half-assed attempt at flirting but I don't think either of our hearts was in it. I was tired, so I propped my arm on the seat rest, leaned my head on my hand and, before I knew it, I was in dreamland.

Maybe it was the altitude, but my dreams were pretty vivid. I was back in the Marines, in San Francisco, on leave. I was in full combat dress and I was desperately trying to find a bus that would take me to LA, but the driver only took me as far as San Jose where he dropped me off in the middle of nowhere. Wandering around lost, I ended up walking a tree-lined drive to a big antebellum mansion like they have down in Mississippi. People were strolling all around it, admiring the hell out of the view. Then, somehow, I'd mysteriously become a guide to the house and I was showing Justine around. She was very nervous and sweet; then suddenly Vicki appeared and stood next to us with a sneer on her face. I felt pity for Justine, angry with Vicki and confused as hell. Both girls then walked away from me, and the house had become a tram stop. I waited until a tram to La Canada pulled up. All I knew was that I had to get home to Mom and Dad. But the tram was too damned slow so I jumped off and ran over to a phone booth. I tried to call my folks but the line was dead. Angry and frustrated, I walked out of the phone booth and found I was on the bridle trail leading to our house. All our old neighbors passed me on the trail, but no one recognized me because I was in uniform. I thought everyone would know I was the Davis kid, but then I realized all they saw was a 33 year old stranger dressed as a Marine—a Marine who was out of place and out of time. The longer the dream went on the deeper my sense of unease grew, so I was relieved when a patch of turbulence bumped me awake, halfway to Hawaii.

I was trying to work out which was real, the plane or the dream, when one of the stewardesses brought me back to reality by bringing me a tray-load of food.

She gave me a smile.

"You slept through the breakfast service so I bet you're going to want some lunch?"

She was right. I ate everything on the tray and finished off a half bottle of wine to help me get some more shuteye. Since Vicki left me, alcohol was virtually the only thing that guaranteed I could sleep nights. Too many guilt-ridden hours counting sheep had convinced me that booze was my best passport to a well-deserved rest. A white-haired old lady across the aisle from me lent me a week old Saturday Evening Post. I read half of it before the wine had the desired effect and I drifted off again. I don't remember much of the dreams I had the second time around, except that at some point I was making out with a United Airlines stewardess in a swanky hotel room. She was still wearing her white blouse and dove-grey cap but from the waist down all she was wearing were hi-heels, black stockings and suspenders. The rest of the dream was a blur, but by the time I awoke again we were beginning our final descent into Honolulu International.

As we made our way down the steps from the plane to the tarmac, the beautiful, half-remembered balmy Hawaiian air swept over me. Even the tang of gasoline couldn't spoil the way the sunshine and the cool ocean breeze combined to create that perfect island atmosphere. There was even a handful of local girls greeting the excited passengers with leis as they placed their feet on Hawaiian soil. It wasn't quite the same as the welcome Vicki and I had as disembarking passengers on the SS Lurline back in '51. Back then, we had a chorus line of gyrating Hula girls, the Royal Hawaiian band playing "Song Of The Islands", clouds of colored streamers and crowds shouting Alohas at the top of their lungs. At the airport, it was just five averagely cute girls in flowered dresses giving hurried kisses and forced aloha smiles. Still, it was the friendliest greeting I'd had in days so I wasn't about to start complaining.

As the taxi taking me to Waikiki drove past the docks, there seemed to be a lot more construction going on than when Vicki and I had been on Oahu, seven years earlier. The first thing I recognized was the old Aloha Tower and then, minutes later, we were at the start of Waikiki Beach. I thought the Hawaiian Village Hotel would be an easy place to get a room because it was one of the biggest places on the beach but I was wrong. All the rooms in the big new main building had gone. The only accommodation they had available was one of the chi-chi bungalows down amongst the palm trees in the hotel's grounds. Naturally, they were more expensive than the rooms and at thirty-five bucks a night I had a sneaking feeling that I'd be wiring Vicki for money sooner than I expected. Once I'd checked in, I was given another lei, a bellboy took my suitcase, and led me though the gardens to my bungalow.

The place was a very upscale Hawaiian hut with a palm thatched roof, furnished with rattan screens, modern bamboo furniture, and flower-print fabrics. With its open-plan lounge and kitchenette, double bedroom and en suite bathroom, it was bigger than I needed; but after all the crap I'd been through, I figured I deserved a touch of luxury. I tipped the bellboy, unpacked my suitcase and got into the shower. After washing away the grime of the day's travel, I shaved and pulled on the white slacks and black aloha shirt decorated with a print of white pineapples I'd taken from the case. Feeling rejuvenated, I opened the blinds on the windows to check out my surroundings. Just outside the cottage was a low wall of impossibly green, spiky, big-leaved plants intermingled with fire red flowers. Beyond that, a cluster of plumeria trees stood on a small, well-manicured lawn that led invitingly down to an aqua blue swimming pool. There were maybe a dozen or so people in and around the water. Seven of them were women. Five were in bikinis. Two were something special. But they would have to keep. I reluctantly dragged myself from the window and picked up the phone. I got the hotel operator and asked her for a Honolulu number.

I was trying to reach Scott Lopaka, an old buddy who ran a fishing boat and guided tour business from an office on Kalakaua Avenue. Scott was a half Hawaiian, quarter English, quarter Swedish kid who'd spent two months in the bed next to mine in the military hospital at Schofield Barracks, during that endless spring of 1945. Scott was in the 420th Field Artillery Group headed for Okinawa when a kamikaze plane slammed into the transport ship he was on. The ensuing explosion peppered him with chunks of flying metal, and he ended up pumped full of morphine and covered in bandages back on the island of his birth. And I was lucky enough to be berthed next to him. Not only was he one of the funniest guys I've ever met, but his family, who visited him almost every day, adopted me as one of their own. Whilst we were convalescing, the Lopaka clan took us to luaus and picnics all over the islands. I even dated one of Scott's sister's friends a couple of times, and didn't exactly turn cartwheels when I was declared fit for active service and shipped back to the mainland.

By the time Vicki and I took our honeymoon on Oahu, six years later, Scott had started his fishing business; taking wealthy tourists out to catch tuna and swordfish. The last postcard I received from him, sometime in May, announced business was doing so well that he was branching out into running tourist excursions to the neighboring islands. Scott was my only local contact in Hawaii and I was counting on his advice before making my next move. The operator finally got me connected to Scott's office, but his secretary had bad news for me.

It turned out that the man was over on Kauai for two weeks, organizing sightseeing trips for a movie crew. Scott being away for so long was going to make things that much tougher for me. I asked the girl if there was any way of reaching him.

"Well, he's officially staying at the Coco Palms but he'll be spending a lot of time on the North Shore and he hasn't given me a phone number for the accommodation he'll be using up there. But, if you give me the number where you're staying, I can get him to call you if he calls the office."

"Okay. Tell him that Johnny Davis really needs some help and I'm at the Hawaiian Village in cottage number eight."

She must have picked up the hint of desperation in my voice because instead of just taking my message she threw me a lifeline.

"Oh, the Hawaiian Village. Well, you know that's where Mr. Lopaka's brother works don't you? He's one of the investigators for Hawaiian Eye. I'm sure he could give you the help you need. And as you're a guest you'll probably get some kind of discount."

"He's an investigator? What exactly is this Hawaiian Eye he works for?"

"They're the hotel's detective agency. Tom Lopaka is a hotel detective there. You really should speak to him—if you can. In the meantime, I'll pass your message on to Scott if he calls from Kauai. Is there anything else I can do for you, Mister Davis? If you want to go fishing over the weekend we have one or two places still available on our regular excursions or I can arrange a private trip for you with one of our top line boats?"

Fishing was the last thing on my mind but I thanked her anyway, hung up and tried to dig Tom Lopaka out of the dim recesses of my memory. He was just 14 or 15 when I last saw him. He'd visit Scott at the hospital and tell us about the surfboard riding he'd been doing instead of going to school. He was a real beach bum, spending all his time flunking classes and getting into trouble. Scott had mentioned him briefly last time we met, and I got the distinct impression that he'd become the black sheep of the family. And yet, here he was, six years later, working as a private detective. I just hoped to hell he was better at his job than I'd been at mine for the last two years.

I left the cottage and strolled through the lush gardens back to the lobby. The winding path took me past another clump of plumeria trees, their white and yellow flowers scattered like confetti across the grass. On an impulse, I knelt and scooped up a handful of the freshest looking blooms. I cupped my hand and held the flowers to my nose. Inhaling deeply as I walked, I let the fragrance send my memory drifting. Scott's mother used to bring leis of the white and yellow flowers into our ward. Their sweet smell was a welcome respite from the hospital's disinfectant stench. After a couple of days, the leis would wilt and the nurses would throw them out, but I always managed to keep a flower or two by my bed. Their lingering scent helped take the edge off the constant headaches I got from the medication they'd pumped into me. It also reminded me that just beyond the walls of the hospital lay beautiful Hawaii. Thirteen years later, the petals in my hand smelled as good as ever, but my thoughts didn't get any clearer.

At the entrance to the main hotel building, I dropped the flowers and stepped into the air-conditioned cool of the lobby. The place was busy with guests checking in and checking out, but I managed to grab a bellboy and asked him for the Hawaiian Eye office. It was right next to the hotel's main entrance. Dodging through a crowd of loud retirees who'd decided to hold an impromptu get-together just outside the lobby; I opened a glass door that proclaimed it was the home of Hawaiian Eye. Just inside the doorway was an ugly Tiki statue. Next to that was a desk and a rubber plant; behind the desk was a very cute blonde. She was flicking through a magazine, but put it down on the desktop when she saw me. A pair of inquisitive green eyes gave me the once over. Her voice was businesslike but not unfriendly.

"Good afternoon. Can I help you, sir?"

"Yes. I wanted to go surfing. Maybe you could show me how it's done?"

That threw her. She stammered a reply.

"I'm s-s-sorry. I think you've come to the wrong place."

"Oh. It's just that I noticed you were looking at those surfing photos in your magazine there, so I figured you might know something about it."

She knew from my grin I was just teasing her and she gave me a real Hawaiian smile in return.

"I love watching it but I just can't do it. I'm not really the athletic type and I'm not much of a swimmer."

It was my turn to smile.

"Well, nature has a way of compensating, usually by being generous in other areas."

She blushed a little, and folded her arms on the desk in front of her not inconsiderable bust. Before I could apologize for throwing her such a lousy line, another voice cut in from behind me.

"Tut-tut, Linda. All it takes is one corny line and you're speechless. You should be used to these tourist pickups by now."

Tom Lopaka lacked his older brother's tall muscular build but the facial similarities were striking. The boyish tanned face, snub nose, and strong chin were almost carbon copies of Scott's features. Dressed in an Ivy-styled, silver mohair suit, crisp white shirt and narrow black tie, Tom appeared more like a young Madison Avenue executive than any private dick I'd met before.

I stuck out my hand.

"Tom Lopaka, I presume?"

"None other. And you must be the legendary Johnny Davis?"

"Guilty! But how the hell did you know who I was? The last time I saw you was in May of 1945."

"I'd like to say it was my photographic memory but the truth is little Laura, from Scott's office, called me five minutes ago to tell me you were here."

"Wow. Word travels fast in the islands."

"Yeah. Best coconut telegraph in the Pacific! Anyway, she said you had something important to do this weekend and that you wanted Scott's help. Is it anything I can help you with?"

"Well, it might be, but I don't want to cut in on your own schedule. I mean if there's hotel business you need to be getting on with."

Tom gave me a pearly white Lopaka smile and threw his hand in a sweep around the office.

"Does it look like we're busy?"

"Well, now you mention it…"

"Okay, then. We'll have a drink and you can tell me what's on your mind. Come on in, this is where our real office begins."

The inner office was a large lanai, the open side leading to a sun-drenched patio complete with a small, sparkling blue swimming pool. Beyond the pool was a high bamboo fence separating the patio from the hotel gardens.

I was impressed.

"Some office you got here. So what is Hawaiian Eye? A security service for the Hawaiian Village?"

"That's the way it started out but we've kind of diversified lately. Now we take on business that isn't strictly related to the hotel. Most of our work has to do with the hotel of course—and they've got first call on our services—but we've even started to get inquiries from the neighboring islands."

"Really? What kind of work is it?"

"A lot of it is insurance fraud. It's amazing the number of rich people who bring all their most valuable jewelry to Hawaii, and then claim it was lost at a luau or in their rooms."

"Hard to believe that people could be so crooked," I laughed.

"Isn't it? But I'm guessing you didn't come to the islands to hear about our problems. I remember Scott telling me that you're a private investigator in LA. Is that what brings you to Honolulu? You're on a case?"

The younger Lopaka was just like his brother. No beating around the bush, just straight to the point. It was an approach that suited me, though. If Tom couldn't help me, it would be better to find out sooner than later. He gestured to a chair and asked if I'd like a drink. The Martini was cold and it was dry. I took a couple of sips and waited until he'd seated himself on the edge of his expensive looking desk before I began.

"Yep, I'm on a case. It's a smuggling racket. Someone's been taking industrial secrets and selling them to the highest bidder. It seems like that bidder is here in Honolulu. I've been told that the latest shipment of these secrets is supposed to arrive here some time tomorrow."

"Do you know how it's coming in?"

"By freighter. My problem is intercepting that shipment before the bidder gets hold of them."

Tom smiled.

"You're playing your cards pretty close to your chest, Johnny. Secrets. Bidders. Smuggling rackets. It sounds like a plot from a paperback novel. I understand you're probably worried about client confidentiality but if I'm going to help, I'm going to need names. Look, any friend of Scott's is a friend of mine. Now, you obviously don't want the police involved or you'd be down at headquarters right now. I've got time on my hands and, if I can help, I will. If it's out of my league I won't waste your time. Fair enough?"

"Okay. Thanks… this thing has made me pretty cagey, I guess. Anyway, here it is… the company involved is the Star Crest Corporation. You know, the pharmaceutical people?"

Tom nodded. Everyone knew Star Crest. I carried on, taking care to avoid mentioning Vicki, Eddie and the exact nature of the contents of the flask. I also kept Justine to myself, for reasons more complex than I wanted to admit to.

"Well, Star Crest has been losing a lot of company secrets. At first it seemed like a bad case of industrial espionage but it's starting to look more serious than that."

"More serious?"

"Yep, I managed to track down two of the people involved. They told me that the Star Crest documents were being smuggled out to Hawaii. They've been hidden in carved Tikis and sent as decor to a place called The Polynesian Pearl."

"Yeah, yeah, it's a restaurant."

"You've got it. Anyway, the latest shipment contains a flask of some new chemical. I was told that the ship left LA on Wednesday. The weather's been fine so it should reach Honolulu tomorrow. I'm afraid I didn't get the name of the ship. But the guy who's organized it all is a Chinese character called Fitch. That, plus the fact that they're aiming to take it out of the States completely, made me think Red China. I could be wrong about that but I doubt it. Either way, I have to get that shipment, Tom. I have to get that flask back."

"You're right. It doesn't make sense that an organized crime syndicate would bring this stuff to Hawaii—not unless it was going to a foreign buyer. As for Red Chinese activity on the islands, well that's a different matter. Like the mainland, most Chinese on the Islands are seriously anti-communist. We know about a few communist sympathizers, but I haven't heard anything concrete about Red spies operating out of Honolulu. The un-American Activity boys sent a task force out here back in '52. I always got the impression that they did a pretty thorough job, but they say rust never sleeps, so who knows?"

I nodded agreement.

"Yeah, how many of their neighbors would ever have guessed the Rosenbergs were working for the Russians?"

"Exactly. Okay, I'll tell you what I'll do right now. I'll make some calls down to the docks—I've got a couple of contacts in the harbor-master's office—they can check which Honolulu-bound ships left LA on Wednesday and when they're due to arrive here. The Polynesian Pearl, however, I can tell you about right now. It's always had a pretty bad reputation."

"As what?"

"As being a front for a narcotics ring. The Honolulu Police Department raided the place about nine months ago but found nothing. Also, there have been rumors about the owners being involved in the vice trade. You know, supplying call-girls for business tourists who've left the wife back home while they attend some conference…"

"Hmm… married men and call-girls. That's a nice little match if you're interested in secrets or blackmail."

I finished my Martini and carefully placed the glass on the hardwood coffee table at my side. From the outer office I could hear Linda's voice engaged in a phone conversation, while from beyond the pool's bamboo fence surround, the afternoon breeze rustled the big leaves high on the palm trees in the hotel's grounds. Noticing that my glass was empty, Tom offered me another drink. I reluctantly declined.

"I'll take a rain check on that, thanks. It's just a little bit too early for cocktail hour for me."

"Well, I won't push you but you should know that, officially, every hour is cocktail hour out here."

As he spoke, the phone rang in the outer office and Linda called out that Tracey Steele was on the line. Tom grimaced.

"I'm going have to take this, Johnny, but listen, I've got to take care of some hotel business first, so let's meet in a couple of hours, in the Tapa Room bar here in the hotel."

He glanced down at his watch and confirmed the meeting for seven thirty. We shook hands and I strolled back through to the outer office as Tom picked up the receiver on his desk. Linda was deep in conversation on the phone as I left but she gave me a little wave as I passed by. A certain something in her eyes had me thinking about taking some R&R in Honolulu after I'd sorted out the problem of Eddie and his damned formula. I'd only been in the islands for a couple of hours, and I already felt ten years younger. Forget Laguna, maybe the Territory of Hawaii was the place for me. The air was clean, the weather was great, the sea was warm, they more or less spoke the same language and the women were beautiful. It was something to think about.

The long line waiting for cabs outside the lobby convinced me that it wouldn't be a good idea to rely on taxis for the next few days, especially if circumstances took me outside the city limits. The concierge was busy with a couple of bewildered old folks who were waving around handfuls of maps and brochures, so I strolled over to the reception desk to book a car. A ten minute wait and a couple of phone calls later, the receptionist had me a confirmation for a '57 Oldsmobile coupe at seven bucks a day plus gas. The car wouldn't be available until the morning, though. I put the rental agreement in my pocket and headed back to my "hut." As I walked in the door, the phone rang from reception.

"Hi, Mister Davis. We have a message for you. It's from someone called Justine. The message says; 'Have to meet you tonight in the Bora Bora Lounge at Don the Beachcomber's. Please be there at eight. This is very important.' And that's it, that's all it says."

I couldn't believe it, what the hell was she doing in Honolulu? Had she tailed me when I left for the airport? And how did she know which hotel I was staying in?

The receptionist seemed perturbed by my silence.

"Is everything okay, Mister Davis?"

"Yeah, yeah. Sure. Can you tell me exactly where Don the Beachcomber's is?"

"Oh, it's really near. It's in the International Market Place, which is just ten minutes' walk from the Hotel—or I can call a taxi for you, if you wish?"

"No, no, that's fine, I'll walk it."

"Is there anything else?"

"Yeah, can you connect me to the Hawaiian Eye office please? I need to speak to Tom Lopaka."

Moments later, I was talking to Linda. Tom had already left the office and wasn't due back until just before eight. Well, I couldn't be in two places at once so I told Linda to make my apologies and to tell Tom I'd call later. After that, I changed into my lightweight cream suit and headed down to the beach. They say you haven't really been to Honolulu until you've seen the sun set on Waikiki Beach. Vicki used to cry at the sheer beauty of it when we watched it on our honeymoon and for sentimental reasons I wanted to witness it once more.

As I reached the beginning of the sand, I realized that I wouldn't be alone with my memories. I obviously had the same idea as half the guests in the hotel, as tourists thronged the beach; "oohing" and "ahhing" as the big red sun sank slowly beyond the horizon. For a few moments, red, orange and purple shafts of color lit the sky, as the day reluctantly ended and another tropical night began. As the sun's last rays shone despairingly above the ocean, and the clouds over the distant Pacific swell turned pink, hotel employees dressed as ancient Hawaiians appeared, seemingly from nowhere, and began igniting the dozens of luau torches that marked the boundaries between the hotel and the sands of Waikiki Beach. Trying to ignore the sudden sense of empathy I had with the sinking sun, I turned my back on the glory of nature's eternal cycle and walked briskly towards my rendezvous with Justine.

Night of the Tiki

The shops and stalls of the International Market Place were busy with crowds of tourists looking for souvenirs and excitement as I made my way over to the arched bamboo bridge that led to Don the Beachcomber's. The place was filling up fast. Guys, in bright Hawaiian shirts they'd never dream of wearing back on the mainland, sucked up rum cocktails and ogled the cute Hawaiian waitresses, while their wives smiled indulgently, politely sipped Mai Tai's and got quietly soused. A petite, high-cheeked cutie showed me to a table and handed me a drinks menu. I ordered a Zombie and told her I'd run a tab. My corner table gave me a grand-stand view, so I scanned the room for Justine but she wasn't there yet. I settled back to take in the atmosphere. The decor was similar to the Luau back in LA. Bamboo tables, chairs, and paneling were everywhere. Displays of tropical flowers adorned the tables, and wooden Tiki statues of various sizes were dotted around the walls. Those grimacing wooden idols were a nasty reminder of why the hell I was there in the first place and I suddenly felt uneasy. The freighter carrying Rudy's carvings was supposed to dock the next morning. I had to come up with something pretty damned quick.

The Zombie arrived and tasted really great. Before I knew it, the glass was empty and I'd started on my second. The place was starting to buzz. People were seated, crowded around tables, shouting, laughing and generally whooping it up. Back on the mainland, most of them were probably upright pillars of their communities, but here, with leis around their necks and demon rum in their blood, their reserve was fast heading south. Just a few feet away, a striking blonde at a table of women who looked like a tour group of middle-aged librarians from Iowa was giving me a come-hither look. She was in her late thirties and although I generally preferred my women younger, something about the way she carried herself roused my interest.

Her face was more handsome than beautiful but the way she smiled was pure sex. She was wearing a tight red dress and her lei of pink and white flowers did nothing to hide a cleavage that Jane Russell would have killed for. Her tanned, nicely muscled legs were slim and firm and I'm damned sure it was no accident that the way she crossed and uncrossed them meant the hem of her dress had ridden halfway up her thigh. I smiled back at her and her eyes flashed an invitation that was damned near unmistakable. Half of me wondered where the hell Justine had gotten to, but the other half was wondering what color panties Blondie was wearing, and if the rest of her body was as smooth and tanned as her legs.

I checked my watch. Justine was thirty minutes late. I decided to give her another ten minutes and then to hell with it. I tried to keep my eyes away from Blondie for those ten minutes but gave up after about thirty seconds. Oh, she knew how to flirt! The second I looked over at her, she turned and talked to her friends. She chatted with them for a while as if she wasn't that interested in me and then she very casually looked back and tilted her head imperceptibly in my direction, flashed her eyes and made with a coy smile. Then she turned back to her friends as though I wasn't there. This little performance went on for the next few minutes, with ever longer eye contact and ever more flirtatious smiles. Finally, I figured that Justine wasn't going to show and I should just grab some fun.

I was about to get out of my chair and get myself into trouble when, without warning, the lights in the bar suddenly dimmed. A hush descended on the merrymakers. A waiter lit a couple of flaming torches at the side of the stage and a slick-looking guy in a white tuxedo stepped jauntily before us and grabbed a microphone.

"Aloha, ladies and gentlemen! Welcome to the exclusive Bora Bora Lounge at Don the Beachcomber's, in the world-famous International Market Place right here in beautiful Honolulu. I have great pleasure, ladies and gentlemen, in introducing to you someone who is a Capitol Records recording artist and the musical sensation of the Islands. Please put your hands together for Martin Denny and his band!"

A huge wave of applause swept the club. As the clapping died down, spotlights went up on a combo of musicians wearing white tropical shirts decorated with a print of a little brown Tiki. A guy I took to be Martin Denny—his shirt was different from the others—raised his hands to bring the clapping to a gentle finish. Blond hair, and built like a quarter back for Notre Dame, he smiled at the audience, nodded to the band and then began tapping out a melody on a big wooden xylophone. After eight bars the rest of the group joined in. It was, basically, just a smooth Latin rhythm, but something about the instruments the musicians were playing gave the music a more Hawaiian feel. It was pleasant enough. In all honesty, I was just grateful it wasn't the usual ukulele crap about "Lovely Hula Hands" or "My Little Gal from Manekolou Bay" that they always throw at you on the Islands. Jesus, back in '51 Vicki and I had been driven half-crazy hearing the same cornball tunes at every bar across Oahu. Sure, some people go for that stuff in a big way when they're over from the mainland but not me. The style this Denny guy was playing was more modern, more relaxing, more my speed.

On the second number the band started adding bird noises to the music. For a second, I imagined I was back in the Marines, wading through a lagoon with parrots squawking at us from the coconut tops and heading towards deep jungle, deep trouble… boy, the alcohol was really starting to kick in. The music sounded more intense. A little louder and a little faster, and I'd want to dance.

After the third number, Mister Denny took the applause and then announced that the band was about to play a song that had sold over a million copies world-wide.

"Ladies and gentlemen. We give you *Quiet Village!*"

I recognized the song. I'd heard it dozens of times on the radio. It was a very popular tune. It was during the slow, moody opening of the song, as all the musicians were making birdcalls and other jungle noises that I started to feel kind of queasy. Perhaps I wasn't used to the fresh, clean Pacific air or perhaps the nine-hour flight was catching up on me. Either way, I decided to leave the rest of my Zombie in its glass. I figured it was safer there. What I needed was water.

I was trying to grab a waitress's attention when something grabbed mine. The blonde from the next table was swaying over to me. From the way she moved she looked as drunk as I felt. She pulled up the chair next to me, sat and gave me a big, big smile. For some reason that struck me as sort of funny. I gave her a huge smile back. She waved a cigarette in my face and asked me for a light. I wanted to say something witty and seductive to her, something to impress, but the words came out crude and cheap.

"Well, now, if I give you a light maybe we could dance. I could really use some exercise right now—if you get my drift."

And then I gave her a big, leery wink. I knew I was being a jerk, but I couldn't help myself. I kept on smiling. Blondie looked a tad taken aback. Her face held a mixture of disappointment and contempt—two expressions Vicki had taught me a lot about. I was still smiling when beautiful Blondie stood up and jabbed the still unlit cigarette towards me.

"The only exercise you'll be getting, mister, is jumping to conclusions."

With that, she strutted back to her table. Jesus, her behind was magnificent. I couldn't understand why I'd come on to her so crudely. We could have had a fun time together. I thought about what she'd just said and, the more I thought about it, the more I thought it was the funniest thing I'd ever heard. Jumping to conclusions! What a line! Before I knew it, I was laughing out loud. So loud that Mister Martin Denny glanced up from his xylophone to see what the fuss was. I could sense people around me weren't happy with my laughing but I couldn't seem to stop. The guy on percussion was peering at me, too, whilst his hands beat out a rhythm on the congas. It looked like his goddamned hands had a life of their own, as though his body couldn't control them. As I watched, little ripples of air bounced away from the surface of the congas and spread across the room. I could actually see the air moving! Now that *was* really something. I couldn't help laughing because it was so crazy.

There was a big old wooden Tiki idol directly behind the drummer and, as the shock waves of the conga beat washed over it, it slowly began to move. It was like watching Disney's "Fantasia" when I was a kid. The idol was doing an obscene parody of a hula, its solid hips rolled with the rhythm and its giant, ugly head rocked stiffly from side to side. As I looked on—amused, fascinated and a little frightened—sound waves from the other musical instruments started to make the bamboo walls shimmer as well. I wanted to get up and touch the sound waves because they looked so damned pretty, but my feet were like lead. I looked down at them and they seemed a million miles away. Were they even *my* feet? With a real effort, I glanced back up. The Tiki was starting to move towards me. The carved ridges on its wooden face and body were glowing like the luminous tubes that run down the side of big jukeboxes and its sightless eyes were fixed on me. Suddenly, it wasn't so funny anymore. It wasn't funny at all. Something told me that if only the music would stop, then maybe the damned thing would stop dancing and the ripples of air would vanish. But the music kept on and the bird calls began to get all twisted up and ended up sounding like screams. The musical waves undulated over the ashtray on my table and its edges sparkled like lines of diamonds. The diamonds were the shards of a million broken Martini glasses. A thousand and one wasted nights.

While I stared at the ashtray, the music seemed to get louder. All the instruments just blurred into each other. I needed to hear something else. I wanted Gene Krupa's "Drum Boogie". I wanted Louis Jordan's "Choo Choo Ch'Boogie". I wanted the music I used to dance to when I was twenty. I wanted the music I knew when I was still a war hero. I didn't want the damned birdcalls and the exotic percussion anymore. And, as those thoughts raced through my head, I suddenly had the crazy notion that I was actually thinking out loud. I didn't want people to know what was going on in my mind, but it was too late. The Tiki had heard me. His face was frowning and his dancing was like the lurching of Frankenstein's monster and the damned thing was closing in on me. My mood suddenly shifted from awe and bewilderment to fear. What in God's name was happening to me?

I turned to ask Blondie to help me but she was pointing at me and laughing. Her friends were laughing too. Then I got it! Everyone in the room thought I was a sideshow geek, the freak attraction at the carnival. I had to get away. Carnival madness! I tried standing up again, but clumsily knocked my Zombie to the floor. The glass smashed with a sound like thunder and I could hear each individual splinter echo endlessly off into eternity. A pool of red and orange alcohol and fruit juices spread around the shattered glass. To my horror I saw that it too was beginning to undulate to the rhythm of the music. The way the liquid moved one way and then the other made me feel seasick. And still that goddamned percussive beat went on and on. I tried humming the Andrews Sisters' "Bounce Me Brother With A Solid Four" to ward off the primitive evil of the music that was all around me. Sing the song, Johnny, sing the song.

"Say, what kind of beat is that? Man, that really spins my hat. Does it sound like boogie-woogie."

For a vivid moment a memory flashed across my mind. I was in uniform. I was dancing. The Sisters were singing up a storm before a ballroom sea of jitterbugging khaki uniforms and girls in their evening best.

"Seems to us that it's in four. Let us hear it just once more. Can you latch on to that rhythm 'cos the solid four's my meat."

But no, the Sisters couldn't drown out the music or stop the Tiki. His coarse face had twisted into a hideous rictus of hate and more of the wooden monsters were swaying through the orange gloop towards me. I finally managed to stand. I was cold and shivering, and I couldn't understand what was going on, but I stood. Sheer terror clawed up from my gut and my brain yelled at me to get out of there. I was vaguely aware that someone was next to me telling me to sit down but the red and orange waves of my spilled Zombie were now lapping at my feet. And it wasn't just the Zombie in the spilled liquid. There was blood in there too, thick red blood. I looked up and around—Blondie was smiling but half her face was blown away. Behind her, all the other tourists were in a similar nightmare state—casually sipping drinks and looking at me coldly as blood oozed from jagged, raw wounds. They must have been in on the first wave—when the Japanese artillery was shelling the beach—because some of them were missing legs and arms. I had to move. I had to escape the sickness, escape the slaughterhouse. There was a doorway with an exit sign above it. I started splashing through the blood that was rapidly spreading itself before me. It was like running through quicksand. This was how it had felt wading through the freezing sea water as we landed on Iwo Jima. Maybe I was back there, maybe I'd never left...

I could hear the bird noises. I was behind the radio operator. *Quiet Village* was drifting from his transmitter. We were on dawn patrol in the jungle. I was there, I was really *there*. I could even smell the eucalyptus scent of the mosquito repellent we were wearing. One minute we were in a narrow clearing at the foot of a gorge and then, suddenly I was out of the gorge and in a dark corridor. The walls were vibrating. I thought I heard someone calling my name and I turned. Two snarling Jap soldiers were bearing down on me. I had no idea where they'd come from and, before I could react, one of them raised a fist that glinted like steel and punched me in the face. Streams of electric colors poured like a rainbow across my eyes. Out of nowhere, I took another blow, this time in the stomach. I staggered and then, oh, so slowly, I sank forward and hit the floor. I was in trouble; I knew I had to get back to the hotel. I knew I had to get back to *the present*. I knew I needed help. I hoped that if I closed my eyes the whole stinking house of horrors would disappear so I kept my eyelids shut tight. So tight it hurt. I prayed to God Almighty to get me out of there. Stretcher bearers! Then there was a pain in my side. Someone had kicked me. Hard. Another kick followed and waves of impossibly bright neon colors, frightening in their intensity, swirled behind my eyes. I endured the Technicolor fallout for as long as I could. Seconds, minutes, hours, who knew?

Finally I opened my eyes again. I stared in disbelief at my out stretched hands. Tiny green bamboo shoots were sprouting between my fingers. I could feel the sharp points of other shoots pressing against my palms. I had to get up before they grew through me! Before I could move, though, another thought struck me like a sledgehammer. What if the plants weren't growing? What if it was me that was sinking down into the ground? My own body weight was going to impale me on the bamboo! A surge of panic gave me enough strength to struggle up and I managed to drag myself onto all fours. I lifted one hand from the bamboo pincushion that was the floor and tried to grab on to the wall. Maybe I was going to make it! My hand found a door handle and grabbed on to it like it was a lifeline. As I did so, I was aware of a shadow looming over me. I started to turn and then, it felt like the back of my head had been hit by a grenade. I plunged, screaming, into a blood red pool. Toppling over and over into darkness. Man down. Over and out. Goodnight.

Birds of Paradise

My head felt like it was filled with cotton wool. I couldn't move my arms or my legs, but I tried not to panic. I'd been locked in an unending sequence of nightmares for God knows how long, but now I was awake. At least, it felt like I was awake. Slowly, painfully slowly, my vision cleared. The panic was still there hovering at the edge of my mind but at last I was almost making sense of my surroundings. There were tropical flowers everywhere and two dark, blurry figures looming in front of me. Was I on Iwo Jima again? I dimly remembered two Japanese soldiers coming at me. Where the hell was my rifle? Why did my mouth taste of rum and sour fruit?

I struggled to focus on the shapes. For a bad moment I thought the figures were the dancing idols again but then a voice seemed to explode out of nowhere. As I shook my head to clear the fog, the voice became quieter, more natural sounding. It had come from the bigger of the two dark shapes. I forced my eyes to concentrate. There were two people standing there. One was a Chinese man, middle-aged and wearing a white, linen suit. The other was Justine. She looked frightened and very tired. What was she doing there?

The air stank of fertilizer and vegetation and for a moment I thought I was going to puke. I controlled myself, though, and focused on my surroundings. We were in a large conservatory filled with huge red and orange blooms. Reed matting was arranged under most of the glass roof but here and there bright sunlight shone down in shafts onto the lush vegetation. I was on a high-backed chair, my hands tied behind me and my feet bound together. The rope was tight and I could feel my fingers starting to tingle as the blood supply was slowly choked off. The last thing I remembered was the band playing *Quiet Village*, and the feeling of nausea as the ground beneath me turned into a lake of blood, rum and fruit juice.

Then the thick jungle vegetation that was choking my mind developed a clearing. The damned Zombie had been spiked, and judging from the nightmare I'd been through I'd been drugged with a dose of Eddie's formula. Jesus, how did he expect the stuff to help people? Opening the doors of perception? More like cracking open the gateway to hell. But before I could take that train of thought any farther, the Chinese guy in the white suit spoke to me. Surprisingly, his accent was pure Californian with no hint of the Orient. His face also had more than a hint of European in it. It had to be Fitch.

"And how are you feeling now, Mister Davis? Not too ill, I hope?"

Justine stood there nervously, her face showing concern. Even with my mind short-circuiting and my head ringing with pain, I noticed she was wearing an aqua blue dress that did nothing to hide her shape. Familiar stirrings flickered to life deep inside me, but then Fitch spoke again. For some reason I found myself staring at a cluster of vivid orange flowers that exploded from a row of lush green plants on the table behind him. I'd never seen anything so intensely orange before in my life. They were the beak-like flowers called Birds Of Paradise. In California I'd taken them for granted, but at that moment they possessed a strange mysterious beauty that seemed overwhelming.

"Mister Davis. Are you with us? I trust the after-effects of your over-indulgence last night will soon wear off. I have many questions to ask you and I'm sure you have questions you'd like to ask me?"

I couldn't sort my mind out so I played dumb. I didn't have to try too hard.

"Yeah. I have one question…" I could barely manage the words as my tongue felt so thick, "…why does a guy who spends so much on plants have such a lousy tailor?"

Okay, so it wasn't Jackie Gleason but Fitch smiled anyway.

"I do like humor, Mister Davis… but not at my expense."

The words were barely out of his mouth before his hand lashed out at me. It was so fast I didn't see it coming. I damned well felt it though. My head jerked to one side and I felt blood ooze from my cheek. He was wearing a couple of chunky rings on his fingers and they cut. My head was still pounding when I made out Justine's voice.

"For God's sake, Johnny, don't be stupid. Just tell him what you know about Eddie's formula and you won't get hurt. They'll just keep you hidden for a couple of weeks and then, when everything's been cleared up, they'll let you go."

There was a note of concern in there somewhere, but I didn't know what good it was going to do me. I also had to wonder if she really believed what she was saying. Whatever happened, I was going to get hurt real bad. And there was no way they were going to give me free board and lodging for a couple of weeks followed by a friendly goodbye. She was either more naive than Snow White or was indulging in wishful thinking.

"Yes, Mister Davis. Just tell us what we require and I'll see you're well looked after." His voice was so smug and self-assured that I opened my big mouth before I had time to think.

"I don't know what the hell you're talking about, fella, and as for you…" I turned to Justine but didn't get the chance to finish my sentence. I was half-expecting the blow second time around but it still hurt. What the hell was wrong with me? Why couldn't I keep my big mouth shut? Ever?

"Oh, dear," Fitch smarmed, "look what you made me do. This is such a waste of time and energy. Don't you understand what's happening to you? It's all very simple. You were getting involved in something very important to us and it was vital you were stopped, as much for your own sake as anything else. Too much knowledge can be a terrible burden."

I nodded dumbly as he continued.

"You *must* talk to me. You've already caused us a fair degree of trouble and we need to know whom you've spoken to and what you know of our operation. We also need to know the whereabouts of Eddie Hastings' documents. They were in that record sleeve that was taken by you in Palm Springs. Where are they now?"

I ignored him and turned to Justine. "Nice people you got yourself mixed up with, baby. I hope they paid you real well for this little caper."

Fitch raised his hand again. I tried to prepare myself for the blow. It didn't come. Instead he forced his face into a grin.

"You know, you really should keep a civil tongue in your head. Maybe then things wouldn't be so bad for you."

"Maybe you're right, but what does the lady think?"

Justine had tears in her eyes. She looked very confused, and her voice trembled as she spoke.

"Please, Johnny, just tell him what he wants to know. It doesn't have to be like this."

Fitch pushed her to one side.

"Enough of this. My patience is at an end. Miss Moore convinced me that you had the formula. She almost convinced me that she alone could get it from you. I think my methods will get the desired results."

He clapped his hands loudly and a few moments later a smaller Chinese guy wearing wire frame glasses and a starched white laboratory coat, appeared from somewhere behind me. He had a nurse trailing in his wake. She looked like an Oriental Natalie Wood, while my befuddled brain thought he was a Chinese version of Peter Lorre. That struck me as kind of amusing until I made out what he was doing. He was pushing a bulky metal and wood trolley contraption that appeared to have two car batteries strapped to its surface. The new guy said something in Chinese and Fitch nodded back at him. Then he turned to me.

"Meet my comrade, Zhao, he is very good at prying the truth from stubborn people. He perfected his technique on some of your countrymen when you fought us in Korea. I believe the GI prisoners called him Sparky."

He spoke again to Sparky and the bespectacled man smiled. It wasn't a nice smile and I could feel my guts start to tighten. I thought of Vicki and how I'd loused up our marriage. I thought of Mom and Dad, waving me off in my brand new Marine uniform in '43 on a foggy winter morning in San Francisco. I thought how good it would be to celebrate Christmas again. I opened my mouth to speak, but I couldn't get my lips to form the words. I watched as Sparky unraveled a couple of thick black wires that were tipped with shiny metal crocodile clips. He fiddled with the apparatus on the trolley and an ominous low electrical hum started to throb from the machine. Seconds later he held the two crocodile clips an inch apart and a bright blue spark flashed between them. I could hear Justine in the background begging Fitch to give me another chance. She even used his name, real respectful like. But I guess it was no go because Sparky whispered something to the nurse and she stepped behind me, pushed my sleeves up and smeared Vaseline on my hands. Then Sparky slowly approached me with the crocodile clips. He was smiling again and his glasses reflected my own face back at me. Damn, I looked scared. Reaching behind me he stuck a clip on each of my hands. I tried straining against the ropes but nothing was giving.

I found my voice then.

"You lousy stinking bastards. We should have bombed your Commie hell-hole to kingdom come when we had the chance instead of letting you try to breed us off the planet!"

I realized I was shouting like a madman and then Sparky flipped a dial. The juice hit me all at once. It was like the 4th of July and Iwo Jima rolled into one! I felt like my body was ripped apart. I heard someone screaming really loud. A single rational brain cell deep inside my skull knew who it was. Every muscle in my body was jumping and suddenly I felt the rope around my wrists give way. The sheer violence of the jolt my body had taken had forced my hands apart and the rope had loosened. As quickly as it started the pain subsided. That's to say it went from pure hell to mere agony. My body was still shaking as Fitch stepped forward.

"I'm most impressed. Most people black out when the dial is set so high. I've also known an unfortunate few to bite clean through their own tongues. But how much more do you really think you can take. I can ask Comrade Zhao to lessen the voltage. The pain is surprisingly more agonizing if applied slowly, I've heard. I hate to say it but by this evening you'll be begging for death. Can't you see the all too obvious hopelessness of your position? For several reasons, our current operations here and in California are being terminated. Within a week, our network will have disappeared. We have gained some very useful knowledge from our contacts with your West Coast pharmaceutical industry, but I'd really like to tie up one or two loose ends before my departure. The Huxley Project papers that you have are one of those loose ends."

As he spoke I could feel that my hands were now unbound. Because everyone was standing in front of me, no one had noticed the rope unraveling. I just needed a little time and, unwittingly, Justine gave it to me. She began shouting at Fitch. I couldn't make out the words because of the static buzzing in my head. Whatever she said must have upset

148

him though because he strode away from me and slapped her hard. She held her face in her hands and staggered backwards. By the time he got back to me my hands were completely free. I had to time things just right. I prayed and shook my head like I was coming out of a trance. I whispered, pretending that my voice was gone. Fitch pushed the trolley away from me, and Zhao and his assistant turned their backs to us and started readjusting dials on the black boxes. Fitch bent down to hear me. I whispered again, mentioning the CIA and Eddie. He put his ear a couple of inches from my face.

"Speak up, Davis. I need information on the whereabouts of the Huxley Project papers and then we'll take care of your pain."

His face was so close I could smell his cologne. With all the strength I had left, I lurched forward in the chair. My teeth grabbed his ear and I bit hard. Really hard. Now it was Fitch's turn to scream and he tried to pull away from me. I swung my hand up and grabbed the lapel of his jacket pulling him back towards me. I kept biting down and felt something crack. While his hands were flailing at me, I shoved my other hand up between his legs. I grabbed hard and felt something soft and round in the crotch of his pants. I squeezed with everything I had and twisted my grip as far as I could. Fitch didn't take pain too well, because the second I took my teeth from his ear he slumped to the floor.

I'd moved so fast that Zhao, the nurse and Justine were frozen in shocked disbelief. I still had my feet tied though and as I tried to stand I realized my legs were numb. As I fell back onto the chair Zhao reacted first, fumbling in his lab coat for a squat snub-nosed .45. As he pulled it free from his pocket Justine lunged at him. She was lucky and her hand knocked the gun to the floor. He grabbed at her and in the melee she managed to kick the gun over to me. I leaned over Fitch's still prostrate body and picked it up. The feel of it in my hand was strangely soothing. Zhao broke free of Justine and stepped towards me. He was too far away and too slow. By the time he'd gotten within six foot of me I had the .45 leveled at his chest. He stopped in his tracks and raised his hands over his head. He wasn't smiling anymore. I tried a smile of my own and squeezed the trigger. I aimed at his left knee and I hit it. There was a sound of wet, splintering bone and he keeled over with a screech. The nurse didn't utter a sound, she just backed up until she was against a flower-laden table. And then she stood there, her face a mask of fear while I kept the gun leveled at her.

Justine ran to me and untied the rope around my ankles. As she finished, I noticed Fitch was stirring so I ground my heel hard into the bloody mess that was his ear. He went out with a loud groan. Justine was tugging at me and I struggled to understand what the hell she was saying.

"We've got to get out of here. There're about a dozen men working in the main house and the gardens. They'll have heard the shot; they'll be here in minutes. Johnny, we have to go."

I realized she was screaming at me.

I shouted back at her

"Okay, okay, where do we go?"

She pointed through the rows of plant-covered trestle tables to a door twenty yards behind where I'd been seated.

I pushed her in front of me.

"Get going. I'll catch up with you."

As she took off down the walkway between the plants, I reached in to Zhao's lab coat and found two more clips of ammo for the snub-nose. The man himself was moaning and clutching at his shattered knee. I crouched over him, careful to avoid slipping in the small pool of blood that was forming about his legs. I held his face in my hands. His glasses fell away. The eyes behind them were wide in pain and fear.

"You son-of-a-bitch. This is going to be too quick for you but I haven't got time to waste." He was whimpering at me. I hoped he was begging for his life. I put the gun to his mouth and pulled the trigger. A fine spray of blood misted my hand and my sleeve. I didn't look at the damage I'd done but scrambled over to Fitch and put a bullet through his head as well. It was a reflex action. Maybe I wasn't really there and maybe they weren't really dead. Maybe I shouldn't have done it. Maybe I was thinking of Fitch slapping Justine. Maybe I was thinking of my trashed apartment. I can't remember. They were the first men I'd killed since 1944. I felt sick, empty, and tired.

I turned away from the bodies and realized the nurse was still standing against the table, a look of horror distorting her pretty face.

For a moment, we stared at each other and I saw something in her eyes I can't really describe. Whatever it was—her soul maybe—I felt a surge of empathy for her. My finger was on the trigger but I couldn't do it—I couldn't shoot her. I lowered the gun and moved backwards. She slumped to the floor, whether in shock or relief, I'll never know. I turned to go and almost passed out. I clutched at the edge of the nearest table to keep from falling. As I clung to the table's edge, my face was inches from a large cluster of Birds of Paradise. The spiky orange flowers that crowned the stems seemed to be diseased. There were tiny, deep red spots scattered across them. It seemed a shame. I reached up and gently brushed the flowers with my fingers. The red spots blurred. The plants were bleeding. I couldn't understand what was happening, but then Justine's voice, urgently calling my name, snapped me back to reality. I lurched from the table and staggered towards her. By the time I caught up with her, she was at the glass door at the back of the building.

"What was that shooting?" She asked as I stumbled up to her.

"I thought I saw someone coming after us. They were warning shots." I lied.

Even as I spoke she noticed the bloodstains on me and she looked at me as though I were an alien let loose from a science fiction movie. I was beyond caring, because I was sure none of it was real anyway. Justine turned from me and wildly pushed open the door and pointed across a wide expanse of lawn to a line of short, squat palm trees. For a second I thought they were a row of giant Tikis until I squinted at them and they became trees again. Hidden behind their bulbous trunks was a low-roofed, white walled building. It couldn't have been more than fifty yards away.

"That's the garage. I'm sure there're a couple of cars in there."

I didn't need to hear more. I grabbed her hand and started running. From somewhere back in the plant nursery I could hear shouts. I pulled Justine along even faster. As we neared the palm trees I felt my legs growing heavier and heavier. I was conscious of the fact that as soon as any of Fitch's goons reached the door of the nursery we would be clear targets until we had reached the palms. The sweat was pouring off me as I half pulled, half dragged Justine behind me. We reached the shade of the palms as I heard a bullet whistle past us and ricochet off the wall a yard from our faces. I pushed Justine ahead of me and, dropping to one knee, I turned and fired at two men who had just run onto the lawn behind us. I was too tired to fire straight and I missed them by a mile. It didn't matter though because at the sound of the gun they threw themselves to the ground. That gave us valuable seconds to round the corner of the building and get into the open entrance.

Justine had been wrong about there being two cars parked in the garage. There was only one, but it was enough. It was a beautiful cream-colored Buick convertible. A late 1940's model but looking like it had just rolled off the assembly line. I wrenched open the driver's door and checked the ignition. Someone up there was on my side because the keys were in the slot just waiting. Justine slid in next to me and I caught a glimpse of tanned skin above a stocking top. I knew I had to stay alive just a little longer. With shaking hands I switched on the ignition and started the engine. It growled to life and I thanked God for Detroit workmanship. I slammed the pedal to the floor and swung the beast onto a gravel track that led away from the main house. Where the hell we were headed I didn't care. I just wanted to be moving. I heard the crack of a revolver behind us but the guy was a lousy shot. Justine clung to my shoulder as we slewed and skidded along a track that twisted and turned more than a burlesque dancer on payday. Lush green vegetation slapped at the windscreen as I fought to keep from plowing into the bushes. We must have gone almost half a mile when suddenly the track widened up and, around the corner, were a pair of wrought iron gates flanked by moss-covered stone walls. I started pumping the brakes, sending a spray of gravel into the bushes. But, even as I did so, the gates started opening inward of their own accord. The Buick must have activated some electronic signal in them and we squeezed through the still moving gates with an inch to spare on either side.

Once through the gates we were on a decent sized road. I had a choice. Left or right. Justine read my mind and told me to go left.

"This way takes us down to Diamond Head and around to Honolulu. The other way just goes back into the mountains."

I had to believe her and I saw no reason why she would lie now. As we headed downhill with the Pacific filling the horizon ahead of us, I kept checking the rear-view mirror and drove like a bat out of hell for a couple of miles but after almost coming off the road one too many times I eased off and slowed to a crawl. I was finding it impossible to concentrate and Justine, whose shouted interventions had kept me from veering off the road more than once, finally convinced me to stop.

"You have to let me drive, Johnny. You don't know what you're doing. Move over to the passenger side and please use this to wipe that blood off your face. I can't stand seeing it, you look awful."

I pulled the Buick over and glanced in the rear-view mirror at the apparition that used to be me. I took the handkerchief she'd pulled from her handbag and wiped the bloodstains from my forehead and cheeks. There was nothing I could do about the bloodshot eyes though. Then, as Justine ran around to the driver's side, I hoisted myself across to the passenger seat. I felt a thousand years old. I wanted a bath, a good night's sleep, food and water to drink. I slumped back in the comfort of the leather seat as Justine edged the Buick back onto the road. As the road gently curved southwards towards Diamond Head, we found ourselves facing the setting sun. It was only then I realized it was late afternoon. There was little other traffic on the road and we drove in silence until Justine glanced over at me and spoke in a voice tinged with sorrow.

"You killed them, didn't you?"

I nodded. I wanted to say I'd spared the nurse but nodding was all I was capable of. Justine seemed to realize that, and she kept her thoughts to herself and just drove. The sun's rays were so low that they flickered like a strobe light between the shadows of the bushes and the trees along the roadside. I had a thousand and one questions for Justine, but no energy to begin asking them. I sat exhausted, halfway between consciousness and oblivion. For a while, I dreamt I was with Vicki back in '51. She was driving us to our hotel in Waikiki after a luau where I'd drunk too much. She was humming "Sentimental Journey" and I rested one hand on her warm, bare thigh as she steered our rental car along the coastal road from the North Shore. We didn't have a care in the world, just the two of us in paradise. And that time dissolved into another time. I was ten. I was dozing in the back of Dad's Packard as we went home from a week's vacation in Yosemite. The radio was playing quietly. Dance music, live from some hotel in Bakersfield. Mom and Dad were chatting about the things they had to do when we got back to La Canada. Just the three of us, safe and snug in our little metal cocoon. Soft, comforting voices, the steady purr of the engine, and dappled sunlight playing on my eyes.

I woke to the sounds of a woman's voice and surf breaking gently on the shore.

"Johnny? Are you awake? Are you okay?"

At first I thought it was Vicki. I forced my eyes open. It was almost night and the sky was dark with just a smudge of red on the horizon to show the sun's recent departure. I was in a nice, cream-colored automobile, on the passenger's side, and a beautiful girl was in the driver's seat, an anxious look on her face. Not Vicki. Justine.

"How are you feeling? I stopped because I didn't know where we should head to next. We're at the start of the beach at Waikiki."

My mind was not a functioning machine. There were too many loose connections. I made a hesitant attempt at speech. I sounded like a lush.

"Um. Give me a second? I need to think. What time is it? How long have I been out?"

"God, you sound awful. It's around six-thirty. You nodded off about twenty minutes ago."

"Yeah?" I mumbled, still feeling blurred.

"Look, I can't take you to the Hawaiian Village because Fitch's men know you're staying there. It might be better to get a room somewhere else, at least for tonight."

Smart girl. I couldn't fault her logic. She wasn't to know about Tom Lopaka and the Hawaiian Eye set-up. I was positive Tom could sort out some kind of security service that would scare off Fitch's hired goons. But I was still confused. The concept of time seemed completely alien to me.

"I was at the International Market Place, wasn't I? When was that? Last night, two nights ago? Was it you who slipped me one of those lousy capsules?"

"No, no, that wasn't me. I swear to you. A couple of Fitch's men work there. They only slipped half a capsule into your drink. They didn't want you completely crazy in case you couldn't answer Fitch's questions. But I can explain all that later. Let's just get off the street in case they come looking for us."

She was right. The cream Buick stood out way too much on the quiet evening streets of Honolulu. I needed to call Tom Lopaka and then we could head for The Hawaiian Village. Before hunkering down in a hotel room though, I needed food. Not a room service platter but a big, juicy steak, medium rare with a baked potato. I was faint from hunger. Justine was looking at me intently. I realized it was my turn to speak.

"Okay, here's what we do. I have to eat. Find us a good place to chow down. Then I can think about the other stuff."

She nodded. She drove along the beach road for a few minutes and then swung off inland towards the lights of the eastern residential area of Honolulu. The first food joint we came to was a fancy restaurant called Kane's Kitchen. The place had the obligatory A-framed roof and luau torches burning out front, and the sign promised the best food in Honolulu. We parked around back, out of sight of passing traffic. Before we got out of the car, Justine used my handkerchief to tenderly pat the bloody cuts on my face, until the bleeding stopped. Once out of the car, she helped steer me to the front door. I managed to walk in unaided and only yawned twice while we waited for a waiter to show us to a table. The place wasn't busy yet, and the only occupied tables were a few nearest the entrance. The waiter tried to seat us at a small table bang in the middle of the room. It wasn't what I wanted: too exposed, too noisy, and too bright. I wanted one of the darker, more private booths towards the back of the restaurant. I pointed to them. The waiter shook his head.

"I'm sorry, sir. We don't open the booth area until later."

I kept my reply polite, but it wasn't easy.

"Nevertheless, that's where we're going to sit. Let's all just pretend that it's later than it is."

And with that, I led Justine to the farthest booth and sat down. The guy didn't say anything, just brought us a couple of menus. I guess someone with a bloodstained suit and cuts and bruises on his unshaven mug wasn't someone he wanted to upset. After I chugged down a couple of glasses of water, we ordered two New York steaks with salad and baked potatoes, cheesecake, and plenty of strong coffee. As we were waiting for the food, I dug out some change from my pockets and found a public telephone out by the restrooms. While Justine went in to powder her nose, I asked the operator to connect me to Hawaiian Eye and prayed someone would still be in the office. Whoever was watching over me must have gone off duty at almost the same time as the Hawaiian Eye staff, because the phone rang unanswered. Well, it looked like it was going to be another night before I finally was able to sleep in that thirty-five bucks a night plus tax bungalow at the Hawaiian Village.

I ambled back to the booth and slumped down in my seat as Justine returned and the salads arrived. We were still picking at those when the real food came. It wasn't the best steak I'd ever had but it was the most welcome. Neither Justine nor I said a word as we concentrated on our meals. We were on our second coffee each before either of us could be bothered to start a conversation. For the moment I was content to just sit and soak up the image of Justine, her face and shoulders gently lit by the amber glow of the Japanese lantern that hung above our booth. Her cat-like eyes stared back at me for a few seconds until she leaned forward and grabbed my hands. I thought she was going to say something meaningful or deep. I needn't have worried. She was a practical girl.

"Johnny, I hate to bring this up but you do realize that they took your wallet away back at the flower farm. How do you feel about a woman buying you dinner and paying for your hotel room? I hope you don't mind being a kept man for one night."

She raised her eyebrows as she said it and gave me a little half-smile that played havoc with my nerves. At any other time I would have pounced on the all too obvious sexual connotations of what she'd just said, but my safari through the doors of perception was catching up with me fast. I managed to mumble something about being in no position to refuse her generous offer and left it at that. Justine got our check, tipped the waiter and ordered a cab. We decided to leave the Buick where it was over night just in case Fitch's people were searching for it. The cab took us to the nearest hotel and five minutes later we pulled up at a place called the Castaways.

Its entrance was set back from the road and shielded from passing traffic by a line of giant birds of paradise plants. The bellboy who opened the taxi door for us tried to hide his surprise at our lack of luggage but failed miserably. As we walked up the stone steps to the lobby, I could see that the moon was big and bright over the distinctive volcanic ridge of Diamond Head. I stared at it too long and I stumbled into the Castaways' lobby. My less than graceful entrance startled a young couple who were just going out as we came in. The guy wrapped his arm protectively around his girl and they both gave me a very wide berth. I couldn't blame them. My once immaculate cream suit was discolored and crumpled, I had burn marks on my hands from the electric shock treatment I'd been given and cuts on my cheeks. I just hoped there wasn't going to be any unpleasantness at the front desk. I needn't have worried; Justine linked arms with me and strode right up to the counter like she owned the place. The two young Hawaiian girls behind the counter greeted us politely enough, but I got the distinct impression that if I'd made a wrong move they would have had the cops there in a second.

Justine must have realized that people had me down for a violent drunk who'd been in a bar room brawl because she edged in front of me and brightly began talking a mile a minute.

"Hi, there! My husband and I *desperately* need a double room for the night. We've had the most *awful* day. We're staying with friends on the North Shore and this afternoon we drove down to the beach by Chinaman's Hat and got ourselves completely lost."

One of the reception girls still had an eyebrow raised but the other seemed to be buying it as Justine rambled on.

"Well, I'm not a good navigator and by the time we got ourselves sorted out it was dark. Then a darned dog ran out in front of our car and we ended up in a ditch. My hero here managed to push us out but, of course, the engine *wouldn't* start. We walked for miles until we found a store and they called a garage for us. Turns out they can't tow us until morning, so we got a taxi here as it's closer than going all the way up North again. *Please* say you've got a room. We really need a good bath and a comfortable bed…"

What a girl! Her story was perfect for explaining my appearance—and our lack of luggage. I was also pleased at our new marital status. Both girls ended up listening to Justine's tale with open mouths. The second she finished they flew into action finding us a room. Five minutes later we were led through the Castaways' impressive lobby, with its tall vaulted ceiling hung with a full-size outrigger canoe, and up to a third floor suite looking out over the Pacific. Through the panoramic windows, we had moonlit Diamond Head to the left of our view while the lights of Honolulu twinkled on our right. The room had two queen-sized beds. I flopped down on the nearest one. I meant to find out what Justine was doing in Hawaii and why she'd been out at the flower farm. I vaguely remember asking her something, but she said she needed a shower before she could do anything else. I heard the water running in the bathroom and the surf breaking languidly on the shore below. Somewhere down on the beach, a girl was singing. The three coffees I'd had earlier couldn't delay the inevitable. I closed my eyes for a moment and after that, I didn't have a care in the world.

Morning at the Castaways

I slept long and deep but woke up with a start. I had no idea where I was. My head ached, my body ached and I was totally confused. A pattern was starting to emerge in my life and I didn't like the way it was going. Two things I knew. It was daylight and I'd spent the night sleeping still fully dressed. If there was one thing I hated, it was falling asleep in my clothes. I'd had to do that too many times in the Marines to like doing it in civilian life.

I sat up on the bed. As I rubbed my unshaven face, I stared out at the world and struggled for answers. Then gradually, like nickels dropping into a jukebox, all the little pieces of information that made up reality fell into place. I switched my vacant gaze from the blue sky beyond the window to the bed where Justine should have been. The bed had been slept in but there was no girl in it. I got up and pushed open the bathroom door. The bathroom was empty, too. She'd done another disappearing act. I slammed my open hand against the wall in anger and strode back into the bedroom. At that moment, the door swung open and in she walked. She was dressed in a powder blue and white striped summer dress and had her damp hair pulled back in a pony-tail. She looked fresh and glowing and good enough to eat.

"Aloha, sleepy head. So, you're finally awake. Good, because I popped down to that shop in the lobby and picked you up a few things."

With that, she handed me a carrier bag that bore the logo, "Castaway's Cabin—Island Shopping In Style!" Inside the bag were a pair of white slacks and a pale blue Aloha shirt decorated with a print of orange and grey koi fish. It was a beautiful shirt. The girl had taste. She had a practical side as well, because she'd also bought me a razor, shaving cream, toothpaste and a toothbrush.

"I think the clothes are your size. The shirt is extra-large, the slacks have a medium waist, long leg. And everything only came to thirty dollars. That leaves plenty for the room and a taxi."

As she spoke, I wandered into the bathroom and made use of the tooth brush and paste. The simple act of cleaning my teeth made me feel slightly more human again. Justine had carried on talking while I was catching up on my dental hygiene and I'd obviously missed something she'd just said. She frowned at me as I emerged from the bathroom.

"Well, tell me!"

I was confused.

"Tell you what?"

In answer, she sashayed past me to the full-length mirror that stood beside the chest of drawers. Standing in front of the mirror, she admired her new dress for a moment before doing a little spin.

"Well, what do you think? Does it look good on me?"

She turned her head, glanced at me over her shoulder and flashed a cheeky smile. In that moment, I forgot about Fitch, the flask and my drugged-induced walk on the wild side. There was something so cute and so girlish about the way Justine looked, right then, that all I could think was how gorgeous she was.

She turned fully around to face me. I didn't need to answer her questions. My eyes told her all she needed to know. Right then, I didn't care whether she'd set me up or what was going to happen later. I just knew what was going to happen next. I grabbed the soft, warm skin of her bare shoulders and pulled her against me. Then we were kissing. Only then, as our mouths pressed together, did I realize how much I'd wanted her all along. I don't know how long the kiss lasted, but at some point I found the zipper on the back of her dress. She didn't resist as I tugged it down but dug her fingers into my shoulder blades so hard that it hurt.

As the top half of the dress fell from her shoulders, I moved my mouth from her lips and began kissing her neck, her shoulders, and the gentle swell of her breasts. I was fast losing control. I could hear her moaning gently as my hands impatiently slid the dress over her hips and onto the floor. Her bra and panties followed. She was grinding against me so hard that I lost my balance. We fell, but as we fell, I twisted her body beneath me and we ended up entwined on one of the beds. As I took my weight off her first with one arm then the other, she helped me tear my clothes off until I was naked, too. Then she was like a wildcat writhing under me. It took every last ounce of my concentration to keep up with her.

It wasn't lovemaking. It was just pure, uncorrupted animal passion. Almost as though both of us sensed that if we paused or took things slowly, we'd wake from the moment. Conscience. Morality. Consequences. None of them existed. All that mattered was her mouth, her eyes, her stomach, her hips, her legs, her breasts. My mind was blank but my body loyally and automatically performed a ritual it knew very well. Justine's moans grew louder. Her back began arching beneath me, her limbs suddenly taut. I hung on to control for as long as I could. Eventually, we gently untangled ourselves and lay side by side. After my breathing slowly became more regular, and my heart no longer felt it was going to beat its way out of my chest, I couldn't resist leaning over her again and kissing that beautiful tanned flesh. As she lay there, with her eyes closed and a sheen of perspiration giving her passive body a golden glow, my mouth began nibbling her neck until she giggled and turned her head to me.

"Hey, easy. Let a girl catch her breath."

And with those words, she became human again. Still gorgeous, still desirable, but no longer the sensuous, almost unreal, almost supernatural creature with whom I'd just had sex. She was merely Justine again. And once she was Justine again, the spell seemed broken. She must have seen something change in my eyes because she suddenly became attentive. Her voice almost sounded apologetic as she snuggled up to me.

"Johnny. I don't mean I don't like it. I'm just exhausted is all."

She kissed me on the cheek and rested her head on my shoulder. I said nothing, just wrapped an arm around her and held her tightly. It didn't matter what she had said of course. Lust had departed as inexplicably as it had arrived, and uncomfortable reality had barged in to take its place. I gently draped my left arm over her and as I did so, I stole a glance at my watch. It was almost ten. What day was it, though? I tried to arrange my thoughts in an orderly fashion but it wasn't easy. Vicki. Eddie. Fitch. Tom Lopaka. Don the Beachcomber's. Ku. The flask. Yes, the flask. The ship that carried the Tiki that carried the flask that carried Eddie's liquid nightmare… the ship was supposed to have docked twenty-four hours ago. Don't laugh, Vicki, I thought to myself. I did it again. I screwed up.

But what was done, was done. I couldn't change the past. I just had to try and get back in the race. I needed to call Tom Lopaka. Find out what had been happening while my mind had gone AWOL. I patted Justine's beautiful backside and whispered in her ear.

"Hey, gorgeous. We have to get up. We've got stuff to do."

She didn't reply right away and for a moment I thought she'd gone to sleep. I was about to repeat myself when she slowly stirred. She twisted her face to mine and kissed me on the lips. After the kiss ended she gingerly touched her fingertips to the faint rash my stubble had left on the delicate skin around her mouth.

"You're right. I need a shower and you definitely need a shave. But I feel so lazy right now."

I thought I detected an air of resignation in her voice. I hoped she wasn't going to be too determined to keep us where we were. The ennui and sense of depression I always got immediately after sex was fast wearing off. I was becoming increasingly aware of the pressure of Justine's breast against my chest. I realized my hand was beginning, unconsciously, to stroke the soft, baby-smooth skin of her rear. If I didn't get clear now I knew we could easily spend the whole day in bed. Even knowing that, I was more disappointed than relieved when she gave my cheek a quick kiss and eased herself off me. Strangely modest all of a sudden, she picked up one of the sheets that had come off the bed and wrapped it around her nude body. She retrieved her discarded underwear from the floor and strode purposefully into the bathroom. As she passed me, she trailed a finger along my chest.

"Okay. I'm going to hit the shower first. I won't be long and I promise to leave you some hot water."

I waited until I heard the shower running and then I grabbed the bedside phone. I got the operator to connect me to the Hawaiian Eye office. The phone only rang twice before Tom Lopaka himself picked up.

"Hey, Tom, it's me, Johnny. Listen, I'm sorry as hell I've not contacted you before, but my hands were kind of tied."

Thinking of where I was the day before I figured that a truer word had never been spoken.

"Johnny! Where in hell have you been? The hotel said you didn't get back to your room at all last night or the night before. What happened?"

"It's a long story. I got shanghaied Saturday evening at Don the Beachcomber's. I woke up at a flower farm north of Diamond Head; the guest at a torture party thrown by that guy Fitch. I managed to get out and now I'm on the other side of Waikiki. I've got a nasty feeling, though, that Fitch's buddies might be out looking for me. How's security at the hotel? Should I come back? I'm only asking because I have it on good authority that they know where I was staying."

"Wow, Johnny. You certainly bring the party with you! Is this how you live on the mainland? Look, you don't need to worry about security at the hotel. Get yourself back here and I'll have you shifted into one of the penthouse suites. We can put a couple of uniformed men outside your door. But listen, where exactly are you now? Do you need me to pick you up?"

"Yes. That would be good. We're at a hotel on the beach called the Castaways. Do you know it?"

"Yeah, sure I know it—I'll be there in an hour. That'll give me time to sort out your accommodation with the hotel. Hey, hold it a minute, did you just say 'we'?"

"I did. There's a girl with me. But I'll explain all that later. More importantly, Tom, did you get the docking details on that freighter out of LA? Has it arrived yet?"

"Yeah, it arrived yesterday morning and unloaded its cargo in the afternoon."

A sinking feeling dragged at my innards. Once the Commies got the Ku statue and laid their hands on that flask it would be almost impossible to track down. It didn't matter that I'd killed Fitch, the man who organized it all. The bastards had gotten what they were after. While I was cursing my luck, Tom's voice cut in on my inner turmoil.

"Johnny? Johnny? Did you hear what I said? I said you don't have to worry. I've got some good friends at the Customs building. For some strange reason they've decided that some wooden statues destined for The

Polynesian Pearl had traces of woodworm. So, the Tikis are impounded in the Customs shed until they can be thoroughly checked out by pest control."

"Tom, you're a genius. How long can they be kept impounded?"

"Well, the pest control people are busy men with a lot of imports to check through. It might be another 24 hours until they get around to them. But listen, I can give you more details later. It's ten-twenty now, I'll be there around eleven-fifteen. What room number are you?"

I groped under the bed for the room key that Justine had dropped when I first grabbed her.

"It's room 315. We're checked in under the name Smith."

"That figures. You've got some explaining to do, my friend. See you soon."

I hung up and lay back on the bed. I could still hear the water running in the shower. I reluctantly swung myself out of bed and pushed open the bathroom door. It was like a sauna. There was so much steam I couldn't see myself in the mirror and I could barely make out the dark curvaceous shape of Justine behind the plastic shower curtain. I called out to let her know I was in the room and waited for her to turn off the water. Instead, the shower curtain was pulled back and there she was. Even Esther Williams never looked so good wet. She reached out a hand to me and tugged me towards her. I stepped into the bath. The sharp spray of the shower water felt good on my tired skin. She placed my hand against the flat of her stomach. Five minutes later, we were on the bath mat. Ten minutes after that we were toweling ourselves dry. Water was everywhere. I was tired and hurting but everything except my conscience was clean.

Justine's Story

As Justine dressed, I quickly shaved, cutting myself only three or four times. The cuts weren't too bad, far smaller than the cuts that Fitch's rings had etched into my cheeks. What worried me was the fact that my hands were shaking so much. I dried my face, patted the blood with tissue, and put on the new clothes that Justine had bought me earlier. My bouts with Justine had left me feeling drained of energy and urgently needing food and coffee. She, on the other hand, was flitting around the bedroom, straightening the bed linen, opening the windows to let in the sea breeze and generally making me feel old before my time. It was bizarre. She was acting as though we were on holiday, without a care in the world. I tried to bring her back to what I considered reality by asking a question I'd meant to ask her the day before.

"I have to know something. How the hell did you manage to get here? Three days ago, you told me that you were staying with some friend in Huntington Beach. Said you were scared stiff. Yet, here you are in Honolulu. You ask to meet up, you don't show and then you're with Fitch and his Commie friends in that flower farm. Care to explain any of that?"

As I spoke, she just stared out of the open window at the surfers and swimmers enjoying themselves on the morning waves. Without looking at me, she started speaking in a slow, deliberate tone.

"I can explain everything if you're prepared to understand. I really like you, Johnny. I like you too much, in fact. That's why I'm here. I didn't tell you everything back in LA. I know that if I tell you everything now you probably won't understand and you'll end up hating me."

"Why don't you try me? Just give me the truth. I won't hate you. I honestly don't think I could."

They seemed the right words to say. I'm pretty sure I meant them. Justine took a deep breath, seeming to savor the warm air that blew in from the sea.

"Okay, here it is. I told you that Joseph Safarini approached me about stealing Star Crest's confidential files. I don't know what you spoke to

Joseph about at the coffee shop, but I'm guessing he told you more or less the same thing. Well, he was telling the truth as he saw it, but it wasn't the whole truth. The man you killed back at the flower farm, Fitch, he contacted me before he contacted Joseph. He told me that I could make money from giving Star Crest's secrets to other companies. I just didn't know how to get the relevant information off the premises. Maybe I was too scared to do it myself, I don't know. Anyhow, I saw Joseph's job application form and had a feeling some of his references were bogus. I passed that information on to Fitch. He called Joseph and I had to pretend to be surprised when Joseph contacted me."

I was shocked. I'd tried to convince myself that Justine was an innocent caught up in an intrigue beyond her control. Now that argument was shot to pieces. I moved across the room and stood a couple of feet from her at the window. Her profile was framed by the silhouette of Diamond Head. She looked like a still from a movie. But I had a gut feeling she wasn't acting. I asked what I thought was the obvious question, although I knew I probably wouldn't like the answer.

"How did you meet Fitch in the first place?"

She carried on staring out to the ocean. The breeze caught a loose strand of her hair and blew it down across her cheek. She brushed it back behind her ear and spoke softly.

"When I moved to Fontana, a girl at work told me about a bar where wealthy men would go to meet younger women. I was alone in the town. I was poor and I didn't want to be. Star Crest's money wasn't enough for what I needed. I knew men found me attractive so I went with this girl to see what would happen. I tried to tell myself that I would just be keeping these men company. That all I'd have to do was flirt with them. Sit and listen to them moan about their jobs, their shareholders and their wives. But I realized that if I wanted more than a few free Martinis or a fancy dinner I would have to do more than just laugh at their stupid jokes."

She paused. I could tell it wasn't easy for her, and it sure as hell wasn't easy for me, either. She glanced at me to see my expression. My face was a mask. She carried on.

"Well, I took the next step. I told myself it wasn't really me. I pretended it was all some crazy movie that I was in, but afterwards I hated myself.

What I didn't hate though, was the fifty dollars I came home with. I had a few more horrible experiences and realized that if this carried on I'd go mad. That's when Lee Fitch turned up. He was different. He didn't act like an over-sexed wolf, like so many of those so-called gentlemen. He asked me about my life. About my family and my work. He listened to my problems and then… and then he offered me a solution." She paused.

"Okay," I said "what was the solution?"

"His solution was that he paid me for spending time with him…"

"Oh, Jeez," I blurted it out before I could stop myself.

"It's not what you think, Johnny. He just wanted to look at me."

Like a dope, I woodenly repeated her last phrase back at her.

"He just wanted to look at you?"

"Yes. Look at me. He'd drive me to a motel, switch on the TV with the sound off, pull the curtains and turn off the lights. Then I would strip for him. And he'd just sit, fully clothed on the bed and watch me. He just wanted me to walk around the bed as he sat there and stared at me. I always had to wear high heels and he didn't want me to talk. Just to walk up and down. Sometimes he'd get me to bring different outfits along and I'd have to change from one to the next while he watched me."

I had a sudden vision of Justine's lithe, young body bathed in the flickering blue light of a cheap motel room's TV. I couldn't cut the vision off before the leering face of Fitch appeared in it. I wanted to go back and shoot the bastard all over again. It seemed insane to be hearing this confession while holidaymakers innocently splashed in the surf yards from our window. And still she spoke.

"He never touched me. Not once. And the money was unbelievable, a hundred dollars a night, once a week. Just for one hour or so in a motel room. It only lasted for a few weeks though. One evening he mentioned the idea he'd had of me copying Star Crest documents and passing them on to him. I knew it was dangerous but it sounded a hell of a lot better than posing in a motel room. I honestly didn't think I was hurting anyone by passing on company information. They all do it, anyway. Steal each other's staff and ideas. It was better than the hurt I'd have gone through the other way."

It all sounded so incredible. I asked the first question that came into my head.

"Wasn't it strange that of all the girls he could have met, Fitch met up with you? Someone who could give him all those secrets he wanted. Isn't that one hell of a coincidence?"

"I think that's all it was, one big coincidence. I realize, now, that he was probably trawling the bars, trying to meet someone like me who worked for a big company. You can't miss, in Fontana. There's the Kaiser Steel Works, there's Star Crest, and all the other corporate research plants. He would have found someone useful sooner or later. People always need money. I was his lucky strike. With me, he could indulge his perversion, or whatever you want to call it, and still get what his government wanted. While I thought he was being charming, asking me about my work and all, he was just seeing if I was suitable. I know I was being used, but I had to do it. Does any of this make sense to you?"

I wasn't sure what to say or how to sound. I tried to keep my voice level.

"Why did you need money so badly? Other people get by without having to turn to…"

The words failed me but Justine turned to me, her eyes wet, her mouth a grim line.

"Oh, you can say it. It's not as though I haven't said it to myself. Yes, I know others scrape by without becoming whores, but *I* couldn't. Okay? I needed that money like you can't imagine. Eddie told me you're not short of a buck or two, so don't judge me."

"Jesus, Justine, you're a smart girl. Didn't you realize that all this information you were stealing from Star Crest was going to the Reds? Eddie's formula was being researched by the military, so you must have known there was a good chance you were selling classified material to the enemy. Didn't you care what would happen if Red China got its hands on Eddie's lousy formula?"

I was getting angry now and I didn't want to be. I could have kidded myself it was the communist involvement that upset me, but it was that image of Justine in the motel room that really soured things. Her almond eyes flashed angrily as she responded to me.

"What difference does it make who gets the formula? And please don't use that patriotic line on me! I don't owe America anything. America killed my father!"

"What in hell are you talking about? Who killed your father?"

"They all did, McCarthy and the rest of them. They destroyed him. Big deal, so he wrote a documentary about Joe Hill and the IWW, and he raised funds for the farm worker unions! They killed him for that!"

"What do you mean "killed him"? Someone shot him?"

"Oh, Johnny. You don't need a gun to destroy a man's life. Someone started a rumor that he was a Red agitator, so they called him in. He refused to name names at the House Un-American Activities Committee and they blacklisted him. After that, he couldn't get work at any studio in Hollywood. People he'd been friends with all his life crossed the street rather than talk to him. It was as though he had the plague. Do you know what it's like to see a man you love reduced to begging people on the phone for odd jobs? He lost everything. He was so ashamed that he couldn't look after us that he killed himself. We came back from visiting my grandmother one afternoon and there he was in the garage…"

The tears came but her voice held steady.

"And people were so hateful. On the day of the funeral a man rung the house and told my mother he was glad that 'the dirty Commie' was dead. And father wasn't even a communist! He hated Stalin! He was just pro-labor, but that was enough to get him in trouble."

I nodded glumly, maybe it was true, maybe it wasn't. I kept listening.

"My aunt tried to help out, but mother was so in love with dad that she couldn't cope without him. She started wandering off, almost getting hit by traffic, sitting on park benches in the pouring rain. I was only fourteen, Johnny, what could I do? So I lost my mother too. She was there in body but her mind just retreated to a different place."

She paused, took a deep breath and went on: "After a few months they had to put her in a home. My aunt looked after me and took me to see mother there and it was awful. It was a horrible state-run place that was more like a prison than a nursing home. I couldn't bear seeing my beautiful mother in that place."

She shuddered at the memory as she spoke.

"A place that always stank of disinfectant and where there were bars on the windows. I swore that as soon as I could, I'd get enough money and put her in a sanatorium that actually cared about their patients. A private nursing home where she would have her own room, where there were beautiful gardens, where they put fresh flowers in the dining room every day, somewhere she could be content."

The tears were flowing faster now and she finally let her emotions take over completely. Her body shook as her crying overwhelmed her. I held on to her shoulders and pulled her close. Her arms wrapped around me and the girl wept. Now it was my turn to stare out to sea. After a few minutes, the sobs grew less intense so I spoke gently to her.

"So that was why you needed the money? Hospital bills?"

She nodded her head. Her eyes were red and puffy from crying and her face was streaked from the mascara that had run with the tears. And yet somehow she looked more beautiful than ever. It would have been so easy to kiss the wetness from her cheeks but it would have been wrong. She was too vulnerable. Instead, I gave her my handkerchief and she dabbed her face dry.

"As soon as I got the job at Star Crest I managed to scrape enough money together to get her moved to a nice little place up near Santa Barbara. But as the bills kept coming, I got desperate. That's when I started going to that awful bar and met Fitch. The money I made from him gave me enough to pay mother's bills a year in advance. For the first time since I was fourteen, Johnny, I actually felt I could relax. I had a life again."

She made it sound like she was using a wrong to make a right. Part of me felt sorry for her but, whichever way you cut it, she was still a thief and a prostitute. She'd stolen secrets from a company that had trusted her and had paid her wages, and she didn't give a damn where those secrets went.

"Justine. I'm real sorry for everything that's happened but can't you see that by selling those documents to Fitch you've betrayed your country?" She didn't answer me and, although I knew I should shut up, I kept right on going.

"Sure, it was terrible what happened to your father but is what you've done going to change that? The McCarthy trials ended, didn't they?

People saw that it had gone too far and it was stopped. In wartime, innocent people get hurt and, like it or not, we're at war with the Communists, whether they're Koreans, Russians or Chinese. At least in the States we can admit mistakes were made and that the wrong people got hurt. And most of them got new jobs or carried on with their lives someplace else. But what chance do the Reds give their victims? How many thousands in China have been taken out and executed after a show trial? No chance of apologizing to them later on. Look at those poor bastards in Tibet, monks beheaded and whole villages butchered. And you're comparing us to them? The way I see it, you did what you thought you had to, to help your mother. Don't try and turn it into some crusade against the whole country."

I don't know if any of it sank in. Justine's face betrayed no emotion except sadness. Maybe I wasn't the right guy to start giving lectures about morality. Neither of us spoke. My words just hung there, like a storm cloud on the edge of a golden summer's day. The longer the silence lasted, the more my conviction that I was right wavered. I looked at my watch, there wasn't much time left before Tom Lopaka arrived and there was still plenty I needed to know. I spoke quietly but my voice still sounded too loud after the long silence.

"And what about Eddie? You know he loves you, don't you? All he could talk about in Palm Springs was how he was worried he was losing you. Did you ever think about him, and how much trouble he'll get into if that flask isn't returned?"

"I told you before, I really liked Eddie, but it wasn't the same for me as it was for him. And he changed—how he changed…"

Something in her tone should have made me pay attention to what she'd just said but I was too obsessed with getting all my questions out.

"Okay, but you still haven't told me how you ended up out here. What were you doing with Fitch at the farm? Did they kidnap you in California?"

At first, she didn't answer. I began to think she was sulking, angry with me for questioning her motives. But then she moved from the window and sat on the edge of the bed, her back turned to me, her arms folded defensively across her chest.

"Why do you have to know everything, Johnny? Isn't it enough that you have the formula and we're here now? Would knowing everything change anything? Would it make you happier? Are you hoping I'll tell you things that'll make you hate me even more?"

I couldn't answer any of those questions except the last one. I knelt in front of her and brushed back the stray strands of hair that hung in front of her face. I placed my hand under her chin and raised her face to look up at me.

"I don't hate you. I've no reason to hate you. I want to help you. That's why I need to know these things. Can't you see that?"

I was being honest but for some reason I felt like I was acting out a part. All I was aware of was Justine's eyes staring deep into mine. As I stared back into them, I felt something strange happening to me. For a second I worried I was about to take my second journey through the doors of perception. But it wasn't that. No, thank God, it wasn't that. But, like my experience with Eddie's magic potion, this, too, was something I had only experienced once before in my lifetime. It was almost ten years ago in the small hours of an aimless Friday night in the heart of LA, under the florescent lights of Canter's Deli. She had a blonde ponytail and blue-green eyes flecked with gold. She smelled of summer. Her table didn't have sugar, mine did.

But even as Vicki's image from that night flashed across my subconscious, I found myself leaning in closer to Justine's tear-streaked face. Her lips were slightly open and waiting, her eyes still staring into mine. I knew when we kissed this time it would be more than just lust. I leaned closer. She closed her eyes. It would have been so easy to lean forward those last few inches, but I didn't do it. Call it guilt, call it cowardice, but I couldn't do it. Instead, I gently kissed her forehead and stood up.

For a moment, I felt dizzy. Everything that had happened since we got to the Castaways seemed a dream. Perhaps the drug in my system was altering my state of mind. What had Eddie said about people taking his formula never being the same again? Justine looked up at me. I knew I should speak but I couldn't find the words. It was she who finally broke the silence.

"I was at the flower farm because Fitch wanted to help me get away from the mainland. I called him from the motel in Inglewood, told him the FBI was after me. I asked him for some money so I could buy a ticket to somewhere, like Brazil. He convinced me to fly to Honolulu. He said he'd meet me out here and give me enough money for a new identity. When I called you that morning I wasn't in Huntington Beach, I was at the airport. I was nervous about coming out here but I had no choice. I didn't know what you and Joseph were going to work out. Part of me was scared you'd turn me in."

The mention of Joseph jarred me. Because of that, I probably sounded harsher than I meant to when I interrupted her. It didn't help that it was the third version of events that she'd given me. Her stories were like those Russian dolls that have smaller and smaller ones hidden inside them. Just when you think there can't be anymore, out pops another.

"So, Fitch decides you should live, and he tells you to come to Hawaii, but Joe Safarini isn't young and pretty so he gets rubbed out. Is that how it was?"

Suddenly her face was a mask of bewilderment. She stuttered a reply to my question while her eyes filled with tears again.

"What do you mean rubbed out? What happened to Joseph? Tell me!"

"Five minutes after we spoke in the coffee shop, I walked out to the parking lot to find someone had blown his brains out. And now you're telling me you knew nothing about it?"

"Oh, God, no! Not Joseph. I had no idea. How can you even think that I knew anything about it? Joseph was always straight with me. He used to tell me about his daughter in Florida. Oh, why did they have to do that?"

She was either a better actress than Garbo, or she was on the level. Either way I answered her question.

"They murdered Joseph because Fitch and his kind don't care about individuals. Their so-called ideals are more important than mere people. Maybe Fitch had an ounce of normal human feeling left in him, so he tried to save you, or maybe he figured on setting up home in Hong Kong with his pretty California girl."

Justine gave me a glare of contempt but let my comment ride. I realized I was sounding like a jealous lover, but my mouth went on working faster than my brain.

"But once you arrived here, what happened then? How did you know I was staying at the Hawaiian Village? Why didn't you show up at The Beachcomber's after you arranged to meet me?"

"God, Johnny. You don't give me time to think. Question after question. Firstly, I didn't know you were here until Fitch told me. He told me they were going to grab you in LA, but instead they tailed you to the airport. They expected you because that character Rudy disappeared and they figured you'd got to him and found out about the Hawaii connection. But when Fitch told me you were here, I tried to convince him that they didn't have to hurt you, that I could persuade you to hand over that damned album. I think he suspected my motives and... maybe he was jealous."

I was intrigued.

"What exactly did he have to be jealous of?"

There was the faintest coloring of her cheeks and then she carried on in a faltering voice.

"I told him that I thought you had a thing for me. That you were a womanizer whom I could, you know, convince to give me the album. He liked the idea of using me as bait, but I don't think he liked the idea of you actually being with me. He let me call the hotel and leave that message for you, but then he made me stay at the farm while a couple of his men grabbed you. I had one last capsule of Eddie's formula with me when I arrived. They took it from me to use on you."

The jangle of the bedside phone saved Justine from answering any more dumb questions from me. It was Lopaka. He was down in the lobby, waiting to drive us to the Hawaiian Village. I told him we'd be down in a minute and then I explained to Justine where we were going. We didn't exactly have much to pack. I left my ruined suit in the room and Justine put her old dress in the Castaways' Cabin shopping bag. We were downstairs in less than five minutes.

Ku's Secret

The drive back to the Hawaiian Village in Tom's silver Pontiac was uneventful. No masked Red Chinese gunmen tried to run us off the road and the only jarring note was the noncommittal, monosyllabic brush-off Justine gave to Tom's attempts to start a conversation with her. Back at the Hawaiian Village, an armed security guard escorted us to the Hawaiian Eye office. Tom offered us drinks. Justine asked for orange juice and plenty of ice, which sounded the healthy option. I took the same with a shot of vodka to steady my nerves.

As Tom made busy with bottles, glasses and ice, he explained that as the hotel was so full, Justine and I would have to share my little luxury cottage in the hotel grounds. He promised us that two uniformed men would be outside the door, on watch, the whole time. Despite his reassuring tone, Justine's silence made the atmosphere uneasy and I think Tom and I were both relieved when she said she had to get some rest. Before she went, Tom arranged for room service to have a breakfast tray for us sent over to the cottage. Once she'd gone, escorted by the same guard who'd met us earlier, Tom cleared his throat.

"Wow, she's quite a looker, Johnny. An old acquaintance or someone you met on the Island?"

There was an edge to his voice I didn't like. I took a sip from my drink while I prepared a suitable answer. For some reason I felt guilty as hell, but then guilt and I were old, old buddies.

I began giving an abridged version of the truth when the phone rang. The interruption saved me from going into too much detail about Justine. From the sour expression on Tom's face, the call looked like bad news. He nodded his head slowly then he hung up.

"Okay, we've got to move fast. My buddy down at the customs shed just received a call from some lawyer working for the Polynesian Pearl. They've got a letter from the DA's office allowing them to collect their impounded Tikis at one this afternoon. It doesn't give you much time to dig out that flask."

He was right, it gave me less than an hour and a half to get down to the docks and find Ku's guilty little secret. I was surprised that a restaurant with a reputation for dealing narcotics could get through to Honolulu's DA so easily. I asked Tom what the deal was. He gave a weary smile as he opened the door to the reception room.

"Honolulu is like anywhere else in the world. If you've got the bucks you can get action. The guys behind the Pearl can afford the best lawyer money can buy. They squawk to the DA, he passes the buck. My friend at Customs wants a quiet life—he's done me a favor but now he has to do what he's told. The only way we can stop them from picking those Tikis up now is by telling either Customs or the Police Department that there's a flask of smuggled narcotics involved. And if you do that, it becomes official business and you don't get to pick up the flask."

He was right. I didn't want the cops to get hold of the flask. I'd convinced myself that the best way to help Eddie, and Justine, for that matter, was to have Eddie hand back both it and his papers. That way, I was pretty certain, both Star Crest and the authorities would be more forgiving. Moments later, we were back in his Pontiac, driving west towards the docks. My guts growled a couple of times in protest at the breakfast I was missing, but the way Tom was driving made me kind of glad I had an empty stomach. As we headed down the busy side streets that led to the Customs sheds past the Aloha Tower, the clear blue sky of the morning rapidly gave way to a bank of ominous looking rain clouds. Sure enough, as we pulled up at the entrance to the block-long, two-story buildings that made up the storage section of the Customs facility, a sprinkling of huge raindrops began falling from the heavens.

As we trotted from our parking spot to the entrance of the building, the sprinkle turned into a tropical downpour. The rain didn't bother me too much, though. At least it was warm, almost like being under a shower. Once inside, Tom led the way through to the office we wanted. The two Customs officials were both around the same age as Tom, and he greeted them like long-lost brothers. After the briefest of introductions, one of them escorted us to an exit that opened onto the wharf. We were now on the harbor side of the Customs sheds and the rain was coming down in sheets. I guess the official protocol should have been that Tom's buddy escorted us to the warehouse, but he took one look at the weather and, leaning out into the deluge, pointed us in the right direction. The rain was so heavy he had to shout for us to hear him.

"Okay, guys. You want Shed C. It's three doors along. The shipment you're after is on the left hand side as you go in. The three statues are all still in their wooden boxes but the lids are open. If anyone asks what you're doing, show this pass. And you'd better hurry. You've got an hour and that's it. I still don't understand why having a look at those damned things is so important... anyway, there's a phone just next to the shutters. Call me if you need help but, in this rain, it'd better be for something serious."

With that, he patted Tom on the shoulder and ducked back into the shelter of the main building. We splashed our way through the puddles that were already forming on the concrete wharf and into the doorway of Shed C. Two guys were loitering just inside the entrance. One, a beefy Hawaiian dressed in faded overalls, looked like a longshoreman, the other, older, guy was in the uniform of the Customs service. They were both smoking and looked vaguely embarrassed at our arrival. They obviously figured no one would bother visiting the sheds during the downpour and had decided to take an unofficial cigarette break. Once they realized we weren't officials of any kind they relaxed and, after a cursory glance at the pass Tom's buddy had given us, they pointed us in the direction of the three, boxed Tikis.

The huge space of the shed was stacked full of wooden crates of various sizes waiting to be either checked or collected. The boxes we wanted were stored, side-by-side, behind a couple of small forklift trucks. All three had been tagged with Hawaiian Department of Agriculture warning notices. The yellow sheets of paper detailing the reason for the warning, in this case suspected woodworm infestation, were clearly stamped with big red letters saying *Approved for Collection*. Standing next to the three big boxes I felt apprehensive. What if the flask wasn't there after all? Trying to put that doubt to one side, I grabbed the lid of the nearest crate and swung it open. There, partially covered by packing straw, was a seven or eight foot carving. Although I could only make out part of its head and its peculiar little bent knees, I knew it wasn't the Ku figure I'd seen back in the Pacific Arts Supplies workshop in Santa Monica. This one had a kind of extended headdress rising from its shoulders and a different, but equally ugly, facial expression. Tom brushed the straw from the surface of the wood until the whole front of the statue was clearly visible. A tattered sheet of paper bearing the Pacific Arts Supplies logo and the single word "Lono" was stapled to its rounded belly. This definitely wasn't our guy but seeing the thing lying there had a strange effect on me. The nervousness I'd felt moments before hit me even harder. The last time I'd seen one of these monsters, it was shuffling after me at Don the Beachcomber's. Just thinking about that night made me feel nauseous. I was also aware of the fact that since I'd first seen Ku and his half-formed brothers, three men had died and I'd killed two of them. Something in my face must have shown what my mind was going through because Tom patted my arm.

"Hey, Johnny, are you okay? You don't look so good."

"No, I'm fine. It's just the lack of sleep and that missed breakfast catching up on me."

He nodded sympathetically and then pointed to "Lono".

"Is this our guy?"

"No, this isn't the one. We're looking for one called "Ku" but I think we should check its base anyway. Maybe there's other stuff they're trying to smuggle in."

We brushed the straw to either side of the box until the base of the thing was completely visible. Even in the less-than-bright overhead lighting of the shed it was obvious that the stand of this particular Tiki hadn't been tampered with. We replaced the straw and the lid and moved on to the next box. From the sound of the rain hammering on the shed's tin roof the downpour wasn't easing up any. The trouble was that neither was my feeling of anxiety. With shaking hands I dragged off the lid of the next box. This one was so covered with straw that we had no idea which end was which until I uncovered its face. It had the same gaping mouth as Lono but a different headdress and, of course, it wasn't Ku.

We examined its base, found nothing and then moved on to the last crate. The second we shifted the lid, I could see that this was the guy we wanted. Ku. Tom cleared away the packing around its base and we leaned closer for a better look. It wasn't the kind of thing that you would notice unless you were really looking for it. But we *were* looking for it and we found it. A slightly rough, circular line about twelve inches in diameter was visible in the middle of the bottom of the wooden base. I tapped the center of the circle and it had a hollow tone. Tom whistled.

"Well, well. We find the hidden treasure. But how do we get to it? Is there a secret technique to getting it open?"

It was a good question. The last thing I'd thought of was how I was going to get the flask out once I'd found Ku. The inner circle etched in the base looked like it had been glued in place and, without a hammer and chisel, there was no way we could loosen it. I glanced at my watch. It was twelve thirty five. We had less than half an hour to find the flask and get out of there before Fitch's pals from the Polynesian Pearl turned up to claim their Tikis. While Tom was tapping away at Ku's base I looked in desperation around me. Back at the entrance to the shed, the Customs guy and the longshoreman were still chatting, their silhouettes framed by the dark grey curtain of rain that was buffeting the docks. They would get suspicious if I asked for a hammer and chisel. We were supposed to be in there just checking on a shipment, not carving holes in it. And then I saw what we needed.

Next to the forklift trucks was a metal toolbox. Checking the guys on their cigarette break weren't looking in my direction I walked over and picked it up. I lugged it over to the packing case and opened the lid. The box was filled with a tangle of well-used spanners, screwdrivers, wrenches, chisels and at least two different sized hammers.

I asked Tom to keep an eye on the two smokers while I got to work. The rain beating down on the roof was so loud that any noise I made was going to be pretty muffled. But I didn't want to take any chances, so, I wrapped an oily rag around the top of the chisel to dampen the metallic clang when I hit it. Leaning into the box, I pressed the sharp end of the chisel against a spot on the glued circular outline and hit it with the hammer. There was just enough room between the bottom of the statue and the end of the wooden crate to allow me to chip freely away with the chisel.

After five minutes of continuous, careful work, the small inner circle on the base felt loose enough to pry open. I grabbed a screwdriver from the toolbox and began gently to lever the round wooden plug out of its hole. After a couple of attempts, the circle of wood popped free. Rudy, the carver, had done his job well. The three-inch thick wooden plug he'd cut out of the base fitted into its hole like a hand in a glove. With the plug resting on the floor of the packing case I could now see the cavity that had been dug into the lower half of Ku's wooden, squat body. The space was filled with more packing straw and clumps of scrunched-up paper. Tom came over to see what was happening.

"Well? You found anything, yet?"

"Damned right I found something. Look at this hole. With all this straw and paper packed in there, there has to be something hidden inside. How much time have we got left?"

"Not long, buddy. Maybe fifteen minutes if we're lucky. I don't want to get Danny or Mike into trouble by being here when the guys from the Pearl turn up. We need to step on it."

"Okay, okay. Just keep an eye on the entrance. I'll be quick."

With that, I started removing the packing from Ku's secret compartment, handful by handful. The stuff was really wedged in tight but, after about a dozen handfuls of straw and paper I touched something smooth, cold and metallic.

The flask was just as Justine had described it. About a foot high and five inches in diameter, it looked like a bulkier version of an aluminum thermos flask. It had *Star Crest* embossed on one side and on the other a stenciled batch number. As I held it, I had an almost overwhelming desire to remove the top to see what this damned liquid narcotic looked like. But, remembering what Justine had told me about its possible use as a vapor-borne weapon, I kept my curiosity in check. My trip through Eddie's so-called "Door of Perception" was going to be a strictly once-in-a-lifetime experience, if I had anything to do with it. I carefully placed the flask on the concrete floor and checked to see if Ku was carrying any other cargo. Sure enough he was. As I scooped out the last of the straw and paper, I discovered two bulky white envelopes crammed into the end of the hidey-hole. I stuffed them inside the waistband of my slacks and was grateful that Hawaiian shirts were loose-fitting enough to hide suspicious bulges. I called Tom over.

"That's it. Our work is done here. I've just got to repack all the straw and put this circle of wood back into place and we can vamoose."

Tom threw a glance back to the shed's doorway and stepped next to me. Reaching into the inside pocket of his jacket he produced two wallet-sized plastic bags. Each was full of a dirty white powder. He smiled at me.

"Not so fast, Johnny. I've got a little gift for our friends at the Pearl, two packets of heroin that a guest left under his mattress at the hotel a couple of weeks ago. I meant to hand them over to the Vice boys in the Police Department but forgot to get around to it. The Islands are magical my friend, the strangest things can happen here. I wouldn't be surprised if the Police didn't get a tip off from a concerned citizen about the presence of narcotics at the Pearl Restaurant the minute they unpack this baby."

I couldn't help laughing.

"You Hawaiians are a resourceful people, Mister Lopaka. If you ever move to the States the LAPD would give you a job in a second."

Shoving the bags into Ku's base, he helped me replace the packing material. Once we couldn't force anymore in, I positioned the wooden plug back into its hole and gave it a couple of swift blows with the hammer to make sure it was in tight. The sound of the rain was easing off as we rearranged the big clumps of straw around Ku's base. It took a few moments after that to return the tools to their box and the box to its original spot by the forklift trucks. Then we placed the lid back on Ku's packing case, Tom slipped the flask under his jacket, straightened his tie and we headed for the exit. As we approached the doorway the longshoreman wandered over. Stopping in front of us, he stubbed out his cigarette butt with his heel.

"You guys finished back there? I gotta get those lids nailed back down before the customer fella turns up to cart them outta here."

He headed over to the forklift trucks and we headed out onto the wharf. The rain had stopped and over in the direction of Waikiki a giant rainbow arched into the sky. Above us, the trailing, ragged ends of the rain clouds were moving slowly westward towards Pearl Harbor. Despite

181

the hunger pangs in my stomach I felt good. With the flask and Eddie's original written formula it was an even bet that the Hastings' family lawyers could get Eddie home free. But more than that, I'd done what I'd set out to do.

Back in the Pontiac I half-expected a truck from the Polynesian Pearl to screech to a halt in front of us, but we left the Customs area without incident. Once we'd put the docks behind us Tom handed me the flask.

"There you go, Johnny. You've got what you came for, so what's next?"

"Lunch and a Mai Tai. Then I'll be happy."

It was a flip answer but the question nagged at me. Maybe the hardest part of this caper was behind me but it was far from over. I had phone calls to make, as both Vicki and Gerry were probably wondering what the hell had happened to me. Then I had to get the flask to Eddie so he could hand it back to Star Crest or the Feds. And then, of course, there was Justine. If I convinced her to fly back to the States with me, what would happen to her? I didn't even want to start to analyze the way I felt about her or Vicki. No, I couldn't think that far ahead. So I carefully placed the flask between my feet and pulled out the two envelopes I'd removed from Ku's hidden chamber. The stiff, white envelopes were plain except for a couple of Chinese characters scrawled on them. Tom glanced down at the envelopes.

"Don't tell me our wooden friend had more than one secret stashed in his gut."

"He sure did. And I've got no idea what's in these packets. Only one way to find out."

I ripped open the bulkier of the two envelopes. As I pulled open the torn paper, I couldn't help but let out a low whistle. Packed side-by-side were five bundles of hundred dollar bills, each bundle held together by a strip of blue plastic and each must have contained at least five thousand dollars. My first thought was that they were counterfeit. I'd read in *Life* magazine that the Reds were trying to destabilize the economy by flooding South East Asia with fake US currency but, as I flicked through them, the little green beauties looked pretty much like the real McCoy to me. I figured it was Fitch's operational money. Cash that he was shipping back to China because his West Coast scam was shutting down. For me, it was the icing on the cake, I had a tax-free gift, courtesy of the Red Chinese. Tom was impressed enough by the money to pull over to the curb so he could get a better look. I held one of the bundles out to him.

"Here. Check this. Tell me they're for real. They look right. They feel right. Goddamn it, they even smell right."

He took the bundle, pulled a few bills out at random and looked them over. After a few seconds his face cracked into a smile.

"Well, well, Johnny. You've restored my faith in the old Hawaiian Gods. Our man Ku is supposed to be the God of good fortune. I'd call this good fortune. There's got to be at least twenty five thousand dollars there, maybe more. You going to keep it or are you going to hand it over to the police?"

"As far as I know the police don't even know this money exists. And I think I'm going to keep it that way. But if you've got any objections I'm always open to advice. Don't appeal to my conscience though because he's on permanent vacation."

"I wouldn't dream of troubling your conscience. If Ku decided you should have the money then so be it. From what you've been through, Johnny, I figure you deserve it. But what about that second envelope?"

The envelope didn't contain wads of cash. What it did contain though was possibly more valuable. There were a couple of dozen sheets of paper, each one covered in what I presumed to be Chinese printing and on almost every page were several addresses written in English. Most were in California but a few were in New York and Philly and at least two were in Washington DC. They could have meant anything; addresses of informants, of safe houses, of local hoods, of other Red spies even. However, whatever it was, this envelope was definitely going to the Feds. Tom agreed.

"The sooner you get that back to the mainland the better. In the meantime, I can get one of our hotel security boys to look it over. He's third generation Chinese but he's still fluent in Mandarin."

I nodded, but my stomach was telling me to get the hell out of the Pontiac and into a restaurant. I told Tom to keep the bundle of bills I'd given him and begged him to get me back to the Hawaiian Village and food. He thanked me and calmly slid the money back over to me.

"Johnny, you're a friend of Scott. I can't take this. It's too much. Just getting to plant that heroin in old Ku is reward enough for me."

With that, he turned the ignition and steered the Pontiac out into the Waikiki-bound traffic. I clutched the two envelopes and my stomach, gazed out at the locals and tourists going about their business, and tried not to think of Justine. At my feet, the flask of a thousand and one nightmares sat there innocently, just biding its time.

The Lure of the Tropics

Back at the hotel, I was tempted to go straight to the bungalow to check on Justine but I figured the Hawaiian Eye office was a better place to make some long overdue calls to the mainland. My first had to be to Vicki. She was probably worried sick that I hadn't called since I spoke to her at the airport. The operator put me through to her parent's house and, as the phone rang at the other end, two and a half thousand miles away in Beverley Hills, a keen sense of guilt crept up on me. What was I going to tell her? *Hi, darling. Guess what! I've think I've solved Eddie's problem but I've also had great sex with his ex-girlfriend.* Before I could get my mind straight, someone picked up the receiver. It was the family maid. Vicki was in the garden with her mother taking afternoon tea. Vicki's mother's grandparents had come over from England about a thousand years ago and mother was determined to keep her ancestral traditions alive. A liking for gin, sherry and afternoon tea were the three most important. The line hummed and crackled as I waited for the maid to get Vicki and then she was there, breathless and angry.

"J.D., where the hell have you been? I haven't heard from you in four days! I tried calling Gerry and that funny little Gladys woman who works for you but neither of them knew where you were. Why didn't you call me? I've been going out of my mind with worry."

"Honey, for God's sake calm down. Everything's OK. I'm sorry I didn't call before but I had my reasons. This is the first time that I could talk to you. I can't tell you where I am, but I'm coming home tomorrow. The main thing is I've got back all the stuff that belongs to Star Crest and that should be enough for the Feds to go easy on Eddie."

"Why is it that whenever I get angry with you, you always have an explanation that makes me feel guilty for being mad at you? It's wonderful news but why can't you tell me where you are? Oh, don't bother telling me, what difference would it make? The main thing is that you're okay. I had the worst dreams about you. I imagined you were lying injured somewhere and no one knew where you were. Thank God, you're safe.

Listen, I've got good news too. Eddie spoke to those two men from the CIA, Adams and Forester. He told them everything that had happened since that Moore girl met him at Star Crest. He didn't want to say it, but he knows now that she was just using him. Once she'd seduced him into an affair, she blackmailed him for information. She guessed that mother and father would be angry with Eddie for having an affair with an office girl. He knew he was being stupid but he was too infatuated with her to stop. The CIA men seemed very understanding. Agent Adams told father that Eddie's version of events confirmed things they already knew. It turns out that her father was a communist writer who was up before the House Un-American Activities Committee. They think she was selling Star Crest secrets to the Chinese and that she and an accomplice stole a flask of Eddie's formula."

"Hold on a second. Who was this accomplice, do they know?"

"Yes. It was that Safarini man from the Fontana plant. They were in it together but I think she betrayed him, too. She sounds so conniving. God, the way she used Eddie. I'd kill her if I ever got my hands on her."

I don't think I could have felt more guilt than I did at that moment. If Vicki knew I'd slept with Justine, I would be out of her life forever. At the same time though, it seemed Justine was getting a raw deal. Perhaps Eddie had done a deal with Adams and Forester. They wouldn't want to drag a son of one of the wealthiest families in the State into court. Better to pin the whole thing on the offspring of a Commie writer. Eddie would get a slap on the wrist and she'd be the scapegoat. With her family history it would easy to present her as a cold, calculating Red spy, using her feminine charms to seduce the naive young scientist from a good family. With Fitch and Safarini dead, it would be her word against Eddie's. In other words she didn't have a chance in hell.

"J.D. You're not saying anything, are you still there?"

"Yes, I'm still here. It's just a really bad line. So Eddie looks to be in the clear, huh?"

"Yes. And if you bring back the stolen documents and that flask, we can put this whole mess behind us. But be careful with that flask. Agent Rycroft finally mentioned it and told me it was highly dangerous."

As soon as she said Rycroft's name I felt my insides tighten.

"Don't worry about the flask. I know it's dangerous. But what was Rycroft doing talking to you? I thought the CIA men were dealing with this."

I knew I must have sounded jealous. So help me, I *was* jealous. Just the thought of that arrogant creep being near Vicki upset me.

"Look, I know you didn't like him in Palm Springs but he's been really helpful to us. He gets along with Eddie really well, and I think he was the main reason Eddie finally got everything off his chest. He's a sweet guy. He even took Eddie and me out for dinner on Monday evening."

I wasn't in a fit state to swear to it but she seemed to enjoy feeding me this tasty morsel of information.

"Well, I'm glad my tax dollars are paying for FBI agents to dine with my wife. Sweet guy! Jesus!"

"God, J.D.! Calm down. He just took us out for dinner. That was it. And in case you'd forgotten, we're no longer a married couple. If I want to go out for dinner with him or anyone else, it's no concern of yours!"

Okay, I'm not so stupid that I didn't realize I was the world's biggest hypocrite. Finally the swinger was getting swung. I'd just had sex with Justine, but I was angry because Vicki had gone out for dinner with Rycroft. Vicki had seen a couple of other men since our split. It wasn't that. It just bugged me because it was that arrogant Ivy League smart-ass.

Right then Tom strolled back into the lanai from the reception office. He looked at me questioningly. He'd obviously heard my agitated tone of voice. I smiled at him, took a deep breath and got back to Vicki. For the sake of appearances I was eating humble pie and it wasn't easy.

"Okay, honey, you're absolutely right. I guess I'm just a little overtired and underfed. Listen, I've got to go now. I'm aiming to get back to LA late tomorrow. I'll call you the minute I'm in town, okay? "

I think she was a little thrown by my change in attitude. There was a long pause.

"Sure. Please be careful. And J.D.," she paused, "I want you to know that the whole family is really grateful for everything you've done."

And then the line went dead. It seemed a fittingly abrupt end to an uncomfortable conversation. I dropped the receiver back in its cradle. Tom stretched out on the sofa in front of his desk.

"Everything okay?"

"Yeah. I guess so. I need to make one more call to the mainland if that's all right with you?"

"Be my guest. Oh, your tray from room service is here. You want me to bring it in or shall I have it sent over to the cottage?"

"This will be a quick call. Send it over to the cottage and I'll get out of your way."

Tom stepped back into the reception office. I could hear Linda laughing. Hearing her laugh made me think of Justine. I got that weird feeling again. It must have been hunger. I grabbed the phone, dialed the operator and placed a call to Gerry. He grunted hello and I got straight down to business.

"Hey, Gerry, it's me. Yeah, it's a bad line. I'm where I told you I was going to be but I'm aiming to get back tomorrow evening. Listen, did you send that package off to Vicki, yet?"

"Man, I am so damned sorry. I had a really crazy weekend. I only just got back to the pad last night. I could do it first thing tomorrow morning."

I could hear a girl giggling in the background. I envied the bastard, not a care in the goddamned world.

"Gerry, don't sweat it. Just hold on to it for me. I'll swing by when I get home and pick it up then."

"Sure thing. I don't know if I'll be here though. I've got a session over at Warner Brothers. Maybe we can get together for breakfast the day after. Anyhow, are you okay? Everything work out?"

"Yeah. A few bumps and bruises but I'll tell you the whole story when I get back. See you soon."

"Sure, buddy. Stay cool."

I hauled myself out of the chair, picked up the flask and walked unsteadily through to reception. Tom was waiting by Linda's desk.

"Are you sure you're all right, Johnny? You really look like you need to get some sleep. Listen, eat, rest up and then give me a call. Let's have dinner tonight here at the hotel. Maybe your friend Justine could force herself to talk to me."

It all sounded good to me. I mumbled a farewell and headed out the door. I was feeling lousy. Once outside the Hawaiian Eye office I had to hold onto the wall. The hotel security guy escorting me to the chalet asked if I needed help. Somehow I pulled myself together, told the guard I was okay and we set off. The scent of the plumeria in the gardens made me feel slightly better but it still took everything I had to reach the cottage in a vertical position. The two hotel security men Tom had placed on guard duty gave me a nod as I lurched past them. I swung the door open and stepped into the room. A room I'd left a lifetime ago.

The first thing I noticed was the bamboo tray of food sitting on the coffee table. I was half-hoping that Justine would be in the lounge, eagerly awaiting my arrival. She wasn't there though so I went on through to the bedroom. She was sprawled out on the bed, face down and fast asleep. The crisp, white bed linen was only half-covering her naked body. The contrast between her honey-colored skin and the snow-white sheets was one of the most perfect things I'd seen. I had an urge to kiss her bare back, but there was too much else on my mind.

Back in the lounge, I placed the flask out of harm's way in the room's credenza and then downed the club sandwich, fries, fruit salad and the Mai Tai in five minutes flat. It took another fifteen minutes after that for my stomach to finally stop rumbling. I sat back on the sofa, closed my eyes, and tried to relax, but my mind kept wandering into the bedroom. Even thoughts of Justine couldn't keep me awake, though, and I was soon in that strange limbo between nodding off and suddenly being awake. For a moment I was back at Don the Beachcomber's and thought I was talking to Justine while grotesque alien shapes writhed and twisted on the bandstand. I tried to listen to what she was saying to me but I could only concentrate on those shapes. They become more solid. A wave of fear swept over me. I opened my eyes and I was back in the lounge. The dipping sun had slanted its way into the room and the horizontal shadows of the blinds were advancing imperceptibly towards me. The floor was divided into bands of light and dark. And someone else was in the room.

It was Justine. She stood in front of me wrapped in an overlarge white bathrobe. She yawned. I yawned. She stepped around the coffee table and sat down next to me. Tucking her legs under her, she made herself comfortable.

"Well, stranger. What happened to you? When they sent my brunch over I thought you'd be here any minute. That was over three hours ago."

"We got the flask back. It was a rush job. I didn't have time to come tell you. I actually got back a while ago but you looked so peaceful I didn't have the heart to wake you."

She stared at me with suddenly alert eyes.

"Johnny, what did you just say? You've got the flask? Oh my God. That's perfect. If we get that back to Star Crest that would help, wouldn't it?"

I wanted to say "Yeah, it's all going to work out." I wanted to tell her whatever she wanted to hear. I wanted to promise her that the future was going to be snow at Christmas, fireworks on the 4th of July, and a ranch-style home in Bel Air. I couldn't lie to her, though. I also didn't have the heart to tell the truth, so, I kept quiet and put an arm around her. She snuggled nearer to me. God, her face was so beautiful. I knew what came next wasn't going to be easy. She kept looking up at me, waiting for the words that didn't come. When I didn't speak, she did.

"Well, what is it? Having the flask makes things better, doesn't it? You've got all Eddie's latest research papers, the lab results and now you've got the flask. I know I'm still in trouble, but surely that helps my position—doesn't it?"

"Justine. It's not that simple. Eddie spoke to the FBI. He's admitted smuggling his research papers out of the laboratory to give to you but he's saying it was all your idea. He says you seduced him and then blackmailed him into giving you all that classified information."

She pushed back from me, her body suddenly taut.

"What does he mean? How did I blackmail him?"

"He claims you knew his family would have been embarrassed to find out that their sweet little son was having an affair with a Star Crest secretary. A secretary who was the daughter of a blacklisted screenwriter."

"My God. I can't believe he's doing this to me."

"Well, what did you expect? He thinks you've left him holding the baby. He's scared and he's telling them what they want to hear."

She suddenly looked tired.

"Wow, thanks. It's nice to hear those words of support."

"Look, I'm sorry to sound harsh but you have to face the truth. Eddie might have told you he loved you, but right now, he's just interested in saving his own skin."

She shook her head.

"Don't apologize. Part of me knew what he was capable of. I really think that the drug changed him. He'd told me he'd experimented with it before he met me but while I was with him it got worse."

"What do you mean, worse?"

"He started off sweet but he got stranger and stranger. He'd take a small dose of his formula and he'd sit in his apartment for hours, just listening to all those weird albums he'd started collecting. All those records that he took to Palm Springs. He'd play them over and over again until I was sick of them. He said the only way we could regain our original innocence was by letting the drugs wash away our conditioning. He wanted me to try it, but I was too nervous. It was listening to one of the albums that gave him the idea for getting the documents safely smuggled out of the States."

"What do you mean it gave him the idea? I thought all that was Fitch's handiwork?"

"No, it was Eddie. Once I'd spoken to him about the possibility of giving his formula to Fitch, Eddie wanted to meet him. Eddie thought he was doing it all for world peace. *He* came up with the idea for using those Hawaiian idols. He said that just as the wooden masks on the cover of that *Ritual* album were used to hide human emotions, so the statues could be used to hide ideas and formulae. Until then, Fitch was relying on couriers taking them back to China via Hong Kong. He told Eddie it was dangerous that way. The couriers always risked being stopped by Customs officials. No one would ever stop wooden idols. Eddie met him at a restaurant called the Royal Hawaiian down in Laguna Beach. They had statues in there that were carved by Eddie's friend, Rudy."

"How the hell did Rudy end up being Eddie's friend?"

"Believe it or not they went to Stanford together. They both belonged to the jazz society. Anyway, they stayed in touch after Rudy dropped out

191

of the university. Eddie said Rudy spent more than he earned on booze and drugs so he'd welcome the extra income Fitch would give him."

Well, well, so Eddie wasn't just some naive intellectual whose only part in this caper was to pass documents on to Justine. I'd gotten the impression he'd suffered an attack of conscience over the use his new wonder drug was being put to. But no, it went deeper than that. His ego had led him to actually planning a safer conduit out of the country for items the Reds had stolen. But how much of Justine's version of the story could I trust?

"If everything you've just told me is true, why didn't Eddie just give Fitch the flask himself? Why risk giving it to Joe Safarini?"

Justine snorted.

"That's easy. Eddie was terrified of being found out. He only met Fitch twice. After that, he let me deal with it because he was so concerned with not getting caught. That's why, when he thought Star Crest was tailing him, he began to go to pieces. If a car backfired on the street—he thought it was an assassination attempt. He was completely paranoid those last few days. That's why Joseph and I decided to get out when we did."

'Why didn't you tell me any of this before?"

"Because I didn't want Eddie to get into more trouble than he already was, and I didn't know that we'd end up together like this. When I first met you I didn't think you would uncover so much of this awful mess."

I put on a big fake smile.

"In other words you didn't think I was a real private investigator? Is that it?"

She placed a warm hand on my knee and squeezed.

"Johnny, please don't be offended by this, but Eddie told me a few times during our relationship that he thought you were a joke as a private eye. He said you chased women too much to be good at anything. I guess he underestimated you in more ways than one."

Strike three, Eddie. I'd misjudged Vicki's kid brother all the way down the line. And it was starting to look like I'd misjudged Justine as well.

"Okay, Justine, let's forget about Eddie. We have to worry about you. I'd like to tell you that my evidence and the return of the flask are going to make a difference but I just don't know. Star Crest and the Feds might want to make an example of you."

She sat for a moment in the gloom before she answered me.

"If I don't go back, it means I might not see mother for a long time. But, if I do go back and they send me to prison, I still wouldn't get to see her. Some choice, huh?"

The girl was trapped. And I felt kind of responsible. If I hadn't butted in on everything, Fitch and his buddies would have gotten Eddie's formula, but Justine and Joseph might have made enough money to get clear. I knew I'd probably regret it later but I decided what I was going to do with the money I'd taken from Ku. I pulled the envelope from my waistband.

"Take this and lay low in Hawaii until I can find out what the Feds have planned for you. If things don't work out then get to Brazil or Mexico. You should be safe there."

I kept one bundle of notes and gave her the other four. Twenty thousand bucks was maybe a lot less than Sinatra would have gotten for a couple of weeks at the Copa, but it wasn't chicken feed. Justine stared at me in amazement. I knew she wanted to ask where the money had come from, but she stayed silent. After a brief pause she flicked through the money. Halfway through she stopped and just sat there, her head bowed. A tear, then two, then three dropped from her eyes onto her lap. She stuffed the money in the side pocket of the bathrobe and flung her arms around my shoulders. I could feel her tears warm against my neck. I gently patted her on the back.

"Hey, come on. Money isn't supposed to make you cry."

She didn't reply but just held onto me even tighter. We sat there on the sofa like that for a few moments—a messed-up couple in the cool of a Hawaiian twilight. At some point, the phone rang. I unhooked Justine's hold on my shoulders and picked up the receiver. It was Tom.

"Hey, buddy. The hotel's weekly Luau starts in a couple of hours. We're all booked on the best table, so why don't you two meet us there in an hour or so. I think you guys deserve a taste of real island hospitality. If you don't like it, you're just a five minute walk from the cottage. Like the brochure says 'leave your troubles behind and prepare for a night in paradise'. And besides that, I've got some good news for you. You have to be there."

He hung up before I could say a word. What the hell, nothing we did that night was going to change anything anyway, so I convinced Justine to get ready for a luau. She took some persuading, but two hours later we were sitting with Tom and Linda at a table under the night sky. A dozen or so larger tables were laid out next to ours, all crammed with baskets of fruit, drinks and amazing bouquets of exotic flowers. There must have been a hundred or so guests from the hotel there, and every one of them was garlanded with several huge leis. Flaming torches lit up the trunks of the surrounding palm trees and, on a small stage, a Hawaiian band played while hula dancers undulated around the tables. The night air was warm and soothing. So soothing I even forgot about the half-healed cuts on my face and the bruises on every limb. We drank Mai Tai's, ate fish, pork and poi and acted like there was no tomorrow. After a couple of hours of over-indulgence, Tom leaned conspiratorially over to me and told me his good news.

"I waited until your third Mai Tai to tell you this because I knew it would sound even better that way. I had a call from the Honolulu Police Department late this afternoon. It turns out that the Polynesian Pearl Restaurant was raided today by four car-loads of the city's finest."

I had to laugh, "Let me guess, they were acting on a tip off from a concerned citizen?"

"You've got it. They found two bags of heroin hidden in a newly imported wooden Tiki, four unlicensed firearms in a storeroom, and a couple of hundred marijuana cigarettes in a laundry basket. It seems the raid caught the staff on the hop. One of them was so flustered he started blabbing about shootings up at the Wai Hale flower farm. Well, a dozen cops headed over there, were met with gunfire at the gates and ended up storming the place. Two gunmen were killed and one was wounded before they surrendered. The cops found two bodies in a freshly dug shallow grave, more narcotics and a bunch of false passports. The Police Chief seems to think they've smashed a major drug ring."

He paused as a grass-skirt clad waitress brought us a round of fresh Mai Tai's. Once she left, he leaned closer and lowered his voice to a whisper.

"My contact at Police Headquarters also told me that a couple of the suspects they picked up at the flower farm had a bizarre story for them. They claimed a crazy American burst into the main greenhouse two days ago, shot dead two employees and stole a car out of the garage. You'll be pleased to know that the police dismissed the story out of hand. They think the killings were part of an inter-gang feud over profits."

After that information, my next Mai Tai tasted even better. Despite my concerns about Justine's future, I felt Ku and the other Tiki Gods were finally on my side. Hey, it was almost like old times. I had a beautiful girl by my side, a drink in my hand and all my troubles were out of sight and out of mind. By midnight, when the party started winding down, I was pretty hammered. We no longer had to worry about a security detail so Justine and I weaved our way down to the beach to watch the ocean. The moon hung in the big, black sky like a Japanese lantern, its reflection shining across the surf to where we stood. We held on to each other and took in the view. It was a moment made for saying something deeply poetic about nature's beauty, but the soft, warm fullness of Justine's body pressing against me stirred a baser urge. I whispered in her ear and, guided by the burning torches, we returned through the dark foliage of the gardens to the cottage. The sex was drunken and intense. Rum and moonlight are a dangerous combination and I think we both knew that it could be one of the last times we would be together. When Justine finally drifted off into a deep sleep, I just lay next to her, staring at her perfect, flawless face. In the soft moon glow of light that filtered through the bedroom windows, she looked the picture of innocence. I couldn't take my eyes off her. I guess I figured that if I stared at her long enough, the image of her face would be locked in my mind forever. I wanted the present to last. The future could wait.

Aloha Hawaii

I woke to hear a gentle tapping on the cottage door. Justine was still slumbering so I slipped out of bed and, pausing only to pull on a pair of slacks, I floated like a hung-over ghost to the door. I peered through the slats of the blinds. Tom Lopaka, immaculate as usual in a black sharkskin suit, stood in the grey dawn light. A uniformed hotel guard stood yawning a few yards off. I quietly opened the door. I could hear the surf washing up on the beach. The morning air was fresh and moist.

"Hey, what's up? I don't remember booking a personal alarm call."

Tom gave a forced smile.

"You didn't, but I thought it'd be good for you to be awake right now. Grab a shirt and come with me to the office. There's something I want you to see. Oh, and if Justine's not awake already don't disturb her."

Something in the tone of his voice had me preparing for the worst. I pulled on the aloha shirt I'd worn the night before, gently shut the door behind me and followed Tom to the hotel's main building. It was so early the tourist bustle hadn't started yet. The hotel's Hawaiian gardeners were diligently sweeping up fallen plumeria blossoms from the empty pathways. The air was so fresh I shivered. Once in his lanai office, Tom handed me a cup of freshly brewed coffee. I sat down, took a mouthful of the java and waited. Tom picked up a photo from his desk and dropped it on the table in front of me. It was a black and white shot of Justine. She was wearing spectacles but there was no mistaking that face. I picked the picture up and flipped it over. Written on the back was *Justine Fiona Moore. Employee Star Crest Chemical Corporation. Wanted for questioning by Palm Springs Police Department and Federal Bureau of Investigation*. I put the photo down and looked up at Tom.

"Where did you get this?"

"The FBI wired it over to the Honolulu Police Department first thing this morning. The duty sergeant there just sent me one. They routinely send photos of people on the run over to us in case we can help them.

I'm the only person in the hotel who's seen this. This is serious, Johnny. She hasn't got much time."

"Well, what do you suggest? Could we get her to one of the other islands?"

"We could, but it wouldn't do her much good. We need to get her out of Hawaii as soon as possible. I'm saying this for two reasons. One, you two seem to be involved and I want to help her. Two, I can't drag Hawaiian Eye into sheltering a fugitive from the FBI and if anyone else at the hotel sees this photo we're in trouble. There's a chance that one or two police patrols might have picked up copies of this before they started their shifts this morning but I'm guessing that the airport hasn't been alerted yet. If we can get her there by ten-thirty there's a flight to Tahiti that we could get her on."

"In other words if we can get her past any bright-eyed cops there's a good chance she could be heading south this morning."

"You got it. The only problem is that this photo is pretty good. She's an attractive girl and most cops wouldn't need to look twice to match Justine to this picture."

I took another hit off the coffee. I was thinking that the caffeine had better work fast when I noticed a couple of magazines lying at the end of the table. On the cover of one of them was a head and shoulders color shot of a pouting Kim Novak. The photo gave me an idea.

"Tom, do you have a beauty salon here in the hotel?"

"Yeah sure, but why?"

"Justine needs a drastic change in appearance and this particular disguise comes out of a bottle."

Tom glanced down at the picture of Miss Novak and smiled. Five minutes and three phone calls later he'd convinced the beauty salon's manageress to open an hour early.

"Okay, Johnny, she's going to be there in fifteen minutes. You better rouse Justine and get her over there. Meantime I'm going to try and arrange a ticket for her on that flight to Tahiti."

I ran back to the bungalow. Justine was just as I'd left her. Lost to the world, safely wrapped up in her own little dreamland. I hated to wake her but I gently shook her shoulder until she stirred. Her eyelids fluttered open and she smiled up at me. Her arms went around my neck. I knew time was short but I couldn't resist kissing her. She tried to pull me down but I held back.

"We can't do this, there isn't time. Listen, the Feds have sent your photo over to the Honolulu cops. We've got to get you out of Hawaii. Before we get you on a plane, though, there's something we have to do. So come on. You've got time for a quick shower."

Still blurry with sleep, she slowly got up and tottered by the side of the bed, yawning and stretching her arms above her head. Then she moved towards the bathroom. She looked awkward on her long legs, like a newly born foal. Watching her naked body bending over the taps to turn the water on, I was swept by a wave of lust. I distracted myself by emptying my suitcase onto the bed and folding the bathrobe into it. I didn't want customs in Honolulu or Tahiti to become suspicious over any lack of luggage on Justine's part. I reckoned one medium sized suitcase should cover it. She was out of the shower in five minutes. She walked slowly into the bedroom, a towel wrapped around her body and a quizzical look on her face. She sat on the bed and grabbed my hand.

"Why don't you come with me? Leave the flask here for Tom to take care of. We've got the money. We could start new lives. In a couple of days we could be in Rio, or Sydney or Buenos Aires. This doesn't have to be the end for us."

She was right. It wouldn't be too hard to get to South America or Australia. With over twenty thousand bucks between us, we could live like movie stars for a few months or even a year or two, but then what? To her, truth seemed to be something that could be changed to suit her mood. Could I ever really trust her or believe her? It was kind of ironic but my life had somehow developed a laughable symmetry. I was torn between Justine, whom I wasn't sure I could trust and Vicki, who wasn't sure if she could trust me. But it was Justine sitting there in front of me, water droplets still glistening on her bare shoulders. I bent down and kissed her. Leaving with her would be so easy. And maybe, sooner or later, I would learn to trust her. I could show her that not all men were users, or were there to be used. It was hard to concentrate though with that damp, naked body pressing against me. But, I had responsibilities. I

198

had Eddie's formula and the flask to return. I had Vicki waiting for me. I had automobile payments, bar tabs and rent to clear. I had too many bridges I couldn't burn.

"I can't do it, Justine. I've got to go back to the mainland. There's a chance I can still put the Feds straight about you. It's the only way."

She stood up clutching the towel to her chest.

"Are you going back for me or is because you want to be with Vicki?"

It was the first time either of us had mentioned Vicki's name. It threw me slightly.

"It's got nothing to do with Vicki. I just want to get home to sort this thing out for everyone's sake. We have to get you out of here. You need a disguise to get you past the cops and that's what you're going to get right now. Here, put on your dress."

One hour and a half later, I met Justine outside the beauty salon. Her auburn hair was now peroxide blonde and styled much shorter. It was strange to see her like that. She was still beautiful but somehow the bleach job made her seem less unique, not cheap though, like all those Mansfield and Monroe lookalikes who frequent the Strip, but not the Justine I'd fallen for. She bought a couple of new outfits in one of the hotel tourist shops, packed them into my suitcase and then I took her to the airport. As the cab sped through Honolulu, she held my hand, smoked and stared out the window. I assumed she was resigned to her fate but who knew what was really going through her mind? We reached the terminal building with an hour or so to spare before the flight to Tahiti. As we made our way to the check-in desk I was worried the beauty salon had done too good a job. Her blonde hair made her look more like some Hollywood starlet than a company secretary, it meant every guy in the place seemed to be eyeballing her, including a couple of cops by the Pan Am desk. But they were just rubbernecking. Giving the once over to a gorgeous, classy blonde.

As we sat in the lounge bar waiting for her flight to be called, we sipped our drinks and looked at each other like strangers who had only just met. With her departure so near, it felt like the bond we'd had was already dissolving, melting away like the ice in a cocktail glass. It was ending the way most holiday romances ended, with a last drink at the hotel bar or the ship's lounge and the realization that those magical vacation days were over and that the mundane reality of everyday life was just a journey away. But the feeling I had meant more than that. I was never good at farewells so I usually took the coward's way out and avoided them. But this was a farewell I couldn't avoid, and I was lost for words. The new blonde Justine sat across from me and played with the ends of her bleached hair. She looked at it as though it wasn't her own. Finally she cupped her hands under her chin and spoke to me.

"What is it, Johnny? Are you embarrassed at being seen with a fugitive? You know, you don't have to wait with me."

There was no hint of reproach in her voice, just the slightest tinge of hurt. I shook my head.

"No, it isn't that. I want to be with you. But I hate this. I'm just getting to know you and now you have to go. I hate it when life gives you no damned choice."

I took her hands in mine and held them tight, and tried to ignore the squawking of the tourists around us. There was just Justine's face. I leaned forward and softly kissed her pale pink lips. We sat like that for a moment, oblivious to our surroundings and lost in each other's eyes. And then, over the public address system came the call for the Tahiti flight. She sighed and put her sunglasses back on, opened up the new handbag she'd bought an hour earlier at the Hawaiian Village, and gave me a sealed envelope.

"Johnny, you have to promise me one thing. Please go and visit my mother up in Santa Barbara. There's enough money here for the nursing home's bills for at least two more years. I've written the address on the back on the envelope. And when you go, try and say hello to her. She's not too aware of what's happening any more. Last time I visited her she thought I was her sister, Dolores. But she does like visitors. It might not make any difference, but tell her I love her and I'll come back and see her as soon as I can."

Her bottom lip was trembling and I fell for her all over again. She was trying to be brave, a girl without a home, without a country, about to head into the vastness of the South Seas and who knew what final destination.

I took the envelope.

"I promise I'll go see her as soon as I get back to the States. But baby, don't give up. I'm going to sort this out with the Feds. You have to stay in contact with me. You've got my home telephone number and my address?"

She nodded yes. Then she stood up, handed me her suitcase and took a deep breath.

"Okay, I've got a plane to catch."

We walked arm-in-arm across the terminal to her gate. Past the sunburnt businessmen and their clucking wives dressed in the brightest Hawaiian prints imaginable. Past the lei stands smelling of plumeria and ginger. Past the surfer kids waiting for their flights back to California, past the postcard and souvenir shops. Up to the line at the gate outside the terminal building and then it was her turn to board. We hugged one last time and then, without looking back, she took the case, turned, and went through to the line waiting to board the plane. I watched as the line moved slowly forward and she climbed the steps, and, without once looking back, disappeared inside the aircraft. For a moment, as she paused just outside the fuselage door, she looked like Vicki. The cut and color of her new hairstyle created the illusion while my crazed mind was the conjurer. And, just like magic, they were both gone. Justine. Vicki. I stood bemused, leaning on the wire fence while the door was secured, the steps were wheeled away and the engines growled into life. Ten minutes later the white and silver beast slowly taxied down the runway, picked up speed and rose into the sky. The sun, finally breaking through the morning cloud, glinted on its wings. It climbed steeply, banked to the left and headed south out across the ocean.

I walked slowly back to the taxi stand. On the way, an over enthusiastic Chinese lei-seller mistook me for a freshly arrived tourist and draped a huge yellow and white flowered lei over my head. Smiling through gapped teeth she wished me "Aloha" and kissed me on both cheeks. I couldn't raise a smile back but fished in my pockets and gave her a five-dollar bill.

I told her to keep the change and that earned me another kiss and the distinction of being the owner of the most expensive lei in Honolulu.

When I finally got into a cab, I just slumped in the back and stared blankly out at the world, a world I no longer felt part of. The driver made a couple of attempts at conversation but quickly gave up. To cover the silence he switched on his radio. I was so lost in my own thoughts that it took me a few seconds to recognize the song that was playing. And then it hit me. It was Nat King Cole singing his first Number One recording, the one and only "Nature Boy". The words, the chords, the orchestration all rubbed salt into my raw emotions. I rubbed my fist into my eyes to stop them watering. What in God's name was happening to me?

Memories

Los Angeles looked cold, grey, and uninviting as my overnight flight from Hawaii started its descent. It was one of those Los Angeles summer mornings when the cloud wasn't going to burn off until after noon and, as we circled the airport, it was hard to tell where the sea ended and the sky began. At times, it felt we were in a ghost dimension of unending, suffocating grey. Maybe that was what Hell was like. No Technicolor in the halls of Hades, just grey: shapeless, formless and forever. For minutes on end, we flew through the fog. The white-out was so total that at times there was no sensation of movement. Only the occasional shudder of the plane and the drone of the engines let us know we weren't just floating in space. I thanked God for radar and felt a huge surge of relief when the airliner finally bumped down onto solid ground.

With Justine gone, my last few hours in Hawaii felt empty. The day drifted by without me really feeling that I was in it. Linda, from the Hawaiian Eye office, helped book me a seat on the eight o' clock flight back to the mainland. Then I met up with Tom and had a long lunch. Back in the Eye office I finally got to speak to Scott Lopaka via the phone line to Kauai. We shot the breeze for ten minutes or so before his Hollywood clients demanded his attention. After that, I spent the rest of the day on the beach in front of the hotel. I was hoping the sun and salt water would help the cuts and bruises I'd picked up on my brief trip to paradise. But the whole time I was there, I kept looking at my watch. I couldn't wait to get that return flight to LA. I needed to be doing something, going somewhere. Finally, around seven in the evening Tom took me to the airport. We shook hands and said our farewells. And then I was back on a Stratocruiser, winging my way home to the States.

As I left the airport parking lot in the Chevy, I switched the radio on out of habit. After five minutes of listening to news of tantrums at the UN, riots in Venezuela and gangland slayings in Culver City I turned it off again. I preferred the silence. I hadn't felt much like eating on the plane, so I ate breakfast at one of the diners out by the airport. The food wasn't good but it was fast and it was filling. The Chevy needed refueling too so I got a full tank of gas and headed for Hollywood and home. The flight back from Hawaii should have given me more than enough time to work out a plan of action. Nine hours wasn't long enough though, because I'd come up empty. I was running on instinct.

That instinct told me to get to North Formosa so I could pick up my artillery. Whatever happened in the next twenty-four hours, it wouldn't hurt to have my .45 with me. Going back to the apartment was a calculated risk. I knew Fitch's goons had probably hi-tailed it out of Dodge days ago, but I wasn't sure about the Feds. I thought I'd let fate decide. In a lot of ways Lady Luck had come through for me lately, so I thought I'd stick with her. If they were waiting for me, so be it. If they weren't, then I was still in the game and playing on my terms.

I was on a winning streak. There were no cops, Feds or CIA spooks that I could see anywhere in the vicinity of the apartment. Maybe I was under surveillance but I didn't care. They could watch me all they wanted, so long as I could do what I'd set out to do. Karl, my landlord, had replaced my broken front door and had reused my old locks so I had no trouble in getting in. The place was pretty much as I'd left it. Karl had re-hung some of my wall decorations but the hi-fi system was still sitting in pieces on my sofa. I tried to remember if I'd kept up my insurance payments. I didn't have time for a shower so I just took a strip wash at the sink. I kept my eyes away from the mirror. I wasn't ready to face myself yet.

It was still grey and bleak outside as I prepared to leave the apartment, so I threw on my navy blue gabardine zipper jacket for warmth. Before I left, I also carefully removed the flask from the old suitcase Tom Lopaka had loaned me. I'd wrapped the thing in my Hawaiian outfits for the flight back, but now I rolled it in a couple of towels and put the whole lot in my old Marine kit bag. I draped that over my shoulder, squeezed my revolver into the inside pocket of my jacket and hit the road. Once in the Chevy, I resisted the temptation to drive over to Vicki's parents' place. She and Justine had never left my mind on the plane and I had a powerful urge to see her again. I had no idea how I'd feel when I was face-to-face with her, though. She'd become a distant voice on the phone, separated from me by two and a half thousand miles and my passion for her brother's ex-girlfriend. I constantly had to remind myself that before I'd left, I'd felt closer to her than at any time since our separation. I decided that seeing her so soon after saying goodbye to Justine wasn't fair to any of us. Did that make me caring or just a coward? Maybe both but what difference did it make? Eddie's lousy formula was supposed to help people see things more clearly, but crashing through the so-called Door of Perception hadn't helped me one little bit. I'd gotten more insight from The Three Stooges than I'd gotten from the Huxley Project.

Instinct took me south and east to Gerry's pad. His Corvette was parked in the drive when I got there and I parked the Chevy bumper-to-bumper behind it. Except for the odd automobile or two wheezing to life on various drives up and down the street, not much was stirring. A couple of young Mexican women in maid's uniforms went chattering past as I stepped onto Gerry's pathway, but that was it. I checked for suspect vehicles and guys in trench coats hiding in the neighboring undergrowth as I gently knocked on the front door. I tried that three times before I carefully let myself into the house. I knew from experience that Gerry rarely rose before ten, so in case he was there, I crept quietly along the corridor to his bedroom. The door was ajar. Gerry lay snoring on his side, one arm draped over the naked shoulders of a raven-haired girl. Her stockings, hi heels, panties, and two hi-ball glasses lay haphazardly on the floor. I hated to burst in on the bastard so I did an about-turn and tiptoed into the kitchen. I found the loose tile under the kitchen table, painstakingly removed it and lifted out Gerry's ammo box-cum-safe. I pulled the *Ritual* album out of the box, stuffed it into my kit bag and replaced the ammo box and tile. I found paper and pen and wrote a thank-you note and propped it against a box of Corn Flakes that stood on the kitchen table. The faint sound of snoring told me my host was still asleep. I crept out of the house. So far, so good.

It was noon when I reached Palm Springs. It had been a hell of a drive down. The July sun had turned every chrome bumper and window of the traffic around me into dazzling mirrors. Even with my shades on, the relentless flashes of sunlight had me squinting most of the trip. Hot air rose from the tarmac, making the near horizon appear like shimmering liquid. By the time I reached North Canyon Drive, the temperature must have been nudging one hundred and fifteen degrees. Not a good day for walking, but inside the Chevy the air-conditioning made life bearable. And at least in the desert the air was clean, unlike the air in LA, which was a constant brown haze that had been in and out of a thousand pairs of lungs before it reached mine. But the desert oxygen wasn't my reason for being back in Palm Springs. I needed to take five and do some calm thinking and I couldn't do that in LA. The law of averages also said that Uncle Bradley's place was now somewhere I could spend the night without being disturbed.

Parking outside the house gave me a creepy feeling of deja vu. It may have been high noon but the area was as quiet as that first night I'd driven down, over a week before. I sat in the Chevy for a moment looking at the house while the memories of that last visit swirled like cotton candy around my mind. I wrestled with the "what ifs" for a few minutes, but it wasn't getting me anywhere except down so I grabbed my kit bag and got out into the sunlight. I still had the front door key so I let myself in. This time there wasn't a body slumped in the hallway, so I dumped the kit bag in the lounge, switched on the air-conditioning and mixed myself a screwdriver. The vodka was for my head, the vitamins in the orange juice for my body. Two iced glasses of those and I was feeling kind of relaxed. Back in the lounge, I emptied my kit bag. The flask and album I placed on one end of the coffee table, the envelope containing Fitch's list of contacts in the USA, I placed on the other, and my revolver I placed in the middle. I mixed a third drink and lay back on the sofa. I tried not to think of Justine in Tahiti or Vicki in Beverly Hills. My main concern was Eddie. Before I decided what I was going to do with the stolen items from Star Crest, I wanted to hear his side of the story. Sure, I'd fallen for Justine, but that didn't mean I was going to believe every single thing she'd told me, especially when it came to Eddie. It was hard enough to accept that he could have been so involved in the Reds' espionage racket, let alone be the brains behind the whole thing. It came down to her word against his. The only other people who could tell me the truth were either dead or, like Rudy, on the run.

The booze made sure I slept through until about six. When I woke, it was still hot and my head felt like it was filled with cotton. I needed to get the blood pumping through my battered body so I did twenty lengths of the pool and a few dozen sit-ups. That little burst of activity made me feel better. It also made me realize that I was getting out of condition. I promised myself to get in shape by Labor Day. I showered, shaved, splashed on some of Uncle Bradley's Bay Rum aftershave and headed into town. I found a good restaurant and had a steak dinner. Two hours and twenty bucks later I drove back to the house.

Returning there alone got me kind of depressed. I couldn't help thinking about Vicki. We'd had some great times in Palm Springs, including making love under the clear desert sky, romantic dinners at the Biltmore, shows and drunken nights at the Chi-Chi and "Two Sleepy People" playing on the hi-fi. All those memories started getting to me. That was the trouble with the Springs. Something in the atmosphere of the place does something weird to your emotional state, and that desert voodoo was hitting me big time. I was starting to feel edgy—like a cat before a thunderstorm.

I switched the TV set on just for company and picked up the phone. It was time for a chat with Eddie. The Hastings' butler answered. I was glad. When Vicki was at her parents' place she often grabbed the phone before anyone else and I didn't want to talk to her yet. I needed to run a few things past her brother first. Talking to him was my last step before I went to see either Star Crest or the Feds. When he finally got on the other end of the line, he sounded apprehensive.

"Hi, Johnny. How have you been? Are you okay?"

"Hey, Eddie. Good to hear you sounding your old self."

"Oh… thanks. So, where have you been?"

"Between you and me, I've been out to Hawaii." I thought that might throw him but I was wrong. He didn't miss a beat.

"Hawaii? Why did you have to go there?"

"Because that's where the flask ended up. Anyway, there's nothing to worry about now. I've got my hands on all your research papers and the flask."

"Yes, yes. I know. Vicki told me you managed to get everything back. That's really great. But hey, don't you want to talk to her?"

"Not just yet. The truth is I really want to talk to you. About the papers and everything."

"You've got them there with you now?" He sounded excited.

"They're safe. But I can't tell you too much now—I have to get going. I'll tell you what we have to do. You and I need to get together and work out how we're going to square things away with Star Crest and the Feds."

"And then I'll get my papers back?" There was the slightest hint of suspicion in his voice but he was getting more excited by the minute. I couldn't tell if it was for real or not. Maybe he *was* on the level.

"Probably, Eddie, but that's one of the things we need to talk about. We just need to make sure you're in the clear. We have to get our stories straight for the Feds don't we?"

I played it as straight as I could. I didn't want him getting suspicious. I had to sound like I was completely on his side.

"Sure, Johnny, anything you say. Why don't you come over here to the house?"

"Not a good idea, for lots of reasons. But, as I said, we shouldn't discuss this over the phone. I haven't got much time right now. I'm going to be driving down to Uncle Bradley's place in Palm Springs first thing in the morning. You should meet me down there around 9 o'clock. It's probably best you come by yourself and make sure you're not being tailed. This thing's almost over, Eddie, so let's be careful."

"I will be. I'll leave here around sun-up and be there by nine. But what…"

I cut him off before he asked any awkward questions.

"Eddie, I've gotta go. I'll see you there. Don't keep me waiting."

And then I hung up. I'm not sure why I lied about my whereabouts. Paranoia maybe. Anyway, if I read Eddie correctly, I figured he would arrive at nine on the dot. He sounded real eager to see his research papers and the flask again. Perhaps seeing them would convince him that his problems were over. Maybe then it would be easier to catch him in a lie. Of course, he might not be the one doing the lying. That was a possibility too. And not one I was looking forward to confronting. I needed to know that Justine had told me the truth and to know that my heart hadn't over-ruled my head. Whatever happened though, I figured on getting eight hours sleep before he turned up. I dimmed the lighting in the lounge, turned off the TV and switched on the hi-fi system. Money was no problem for Uncle Bradley and his stereo set-up was the best on the market. Eddie's pile of LPs was stacked against the hi-fi console just as Vicki and I had left them all those days ago. I flipped through the albums and pulled out a handful to listen to. As they played, I tried to imagine Eddie hearing the same music while under the influence of his mind-altering drugs. Ghostly female vocals singing wordless songs, the ringing of temple bells and the ever present rumble of jungle drums. These were the exotic sounds that Eddie had chosen as the soundtrack to the unimaginable visions and emotions rampaging through his mind. And I wondered what visions he had seen. How often had he floated on the drug into paradise and how many times had he stumbled into hell? I remembered the gut-wrenching fear I'd felt in Don the Beachcomber's. Had Eddie seen and felt similar terrors? The last track on the last album I'd chosen came to an end. The arm of the turntable swung back to its start position with a click. I switched the system off and moved to the panoramic window that separated me from the desert. The stars were still there. The mountain was still there. But that night they didn't look the same as before. In bed, I thought of many things, but mostly I thought of Vicki and Justine. I can't remember which one I missed most.

Desert Fire

I woke with the sun. It was going to be another beautiful, hot day. Back in the den, I checked that the flask, the *Ritual Of The Savage*, Fitch's list of contacts and my revolver were in the kit bag. Then I made a pot of coffee and sat in one of the loungers out by the pool. It was quiet. So quiet I could hear the scampering of the occasional lizard as they ran across the paving stones beneath my feet. For a while, I sat in the morning sun, its warmth relaxed the aches and pains I'd picked up in Honolulu. All I had to do was wait.

Finally, a few minutes before nine o'clock, I heard the recognizable growl of a Thunderbird's engine. I strolled around to the front of the house and stood by one of the two giant Yuccas that flanked the driveway. Moments later Eddie's fawn colored T-bird swept into sight. The top was down and I could see Eddie wasn't alone. I should have realized he'd be too nervous to come by himself but it was still a surprise to see Vicki with him. The car came to a halt next to me. I opened the passenger door and took Vicki's arm as she stepped out. She was tanned and rested and looked like an angel in her crisp white blouse and white slacks. In contrast, Eddie was wearing a crumpled suit the same color as the T-Bird. His cream shirt was crumpled, too, and dotted with little grease stains. He was kind of like a creased sepia photograph that had been bleached by overexposure. Vicki hugged me and I held her tightly. I wished I were someone else, someone she could trust. We barely had time to catch our breath before Eddie hurried over and started shaking my hand. He seemed a little over-anxious, but his aviator sunglasses hid any emotion his eyes might have betrayed. I was kind of angry with him for bringing Vicki along, but there was nothing I could do about it. So, I went inside with them and tried to be as cordial as possible.

We sat in the kitchen like civilized people, Vicki and Eddie drank coke; I had orange juice. I apologized to Vicki for not calling as soon as I'd landed back in the States. I told her it was because I wasn't completely sure if Fitch's men might still be tailing me or not. I explained it so convincingly I believed it myself. She said she understood, but I sensed she wasn't entirely happy with my explanation. Either way, she seemed genuinely happy to see me again. She must have thought the whole sordid episode of Eddie's missing formula was almost over. It wasn't going to be quite that easy, though.

While Vicki and I talked, Eddie sat staring at me. He was still wearing his shades but I could feel his eyes on me. As the minutes passed, the tension between us grew. We were both waiting for the other to make some acknowledgement of what I'd said to him the night before. Eventually, as I was telling Vicki about Tom Lopaka's involvement in my Hawaiian visit, Eddie cracked.

"Well, Johnny this is swell," he exclaimed sarcastically, "just sitting here listening to your exploits on my behalf, but I don't understand why you wanted me to come down here alone."

I was kind of surprised at his tone. There was an aggression there I hadn't expected. Before I could respond to him, Vicki repeated the question.

"Yes, J.D., if you were worried about seeing me because of Fitch's spies, why ask Eddie to drive here on his own?"

I had little choice except to reply as best I could.

"Honey, I wasn't one hundred per cent sure that Fitch's men *were* around but, while there was the slightest chance they were, I didn't want you to be near me. I didn't want you in any danger, but I needed to talk to Eddie before I handed everything over to the Feds."

"But why?" Vicki said it first but her brother echoed the question, a sneer on his face. What the hell had happened to Eddie, the happy little jazz fan? That was an academic question I didn't have time to dwell on, so I answered Vicki's query instead.

"There's a couple of details I need to get clear before I go to the Feds. Eddie is the only one who can explain those points to me. They're the kind of things I didn't want to discuss over the phone so I needed him in person. You understand don't you, Eddie?"

I tried to put enough threat in my voice for Vicki to miss but Eddie to get. He got it all right but decided to play it the hard way.

"Well, what is it, Johnny? What points don't you understand? I'm sure Vicki won't mind us talking formulae, although I'm surprised your interest in hallucinogenic drugs has developed so rapidly."

The little son-of-a-bitch was playing a game with me. Perhaps he thought that the best form of defense was attack but I hadn't accused him of anything yet. Was a guilty conscience gnawing at him? I got a chance to find out when Vicki made her excuses and headed off to the bathroom. The second she was out of the kitchen, I grabbed Eddie's arm. I was tired of his delaying tactics.

"Listen, Eddie, sooner or later I'm going to be alone with you and you're going to answer my questions. Let's keep it polite shall we?"

"Whatever you say, Johnny," he muttered but the sneer returned to his face as I carried on talking.

"I don't want Vicki to know more than she has to, so let's step outside and discuss things properly. Besides, I've got some Star Crest property that needs returning to you."

As I spoke I half-led, half-pushed him into the lounge. I picked up the kit bag and guided him out onto the patio. Most of the backyard and swimming pool was in morning shadow, but that couldn't shield us from the heat. Even so, I wanted to be as far away from the house as possible when Vicki returned to the kitchen so I moved towards the sunlight.

"Okay, Eddie, just a little farther, and then we can have a chat about what I'm supposed to tell your new buddies at the Bureau."

We walked around the pool, stepped over the knee-high boundary wire that marked the division between backyard and pristine desert and stopped about thirty yards from the house. I sat on a rounded boulder while Eddie stood about ten foot away. His back was to the mountains. He shaded his eyes with his hand as he peered at me. With the sun full in his face, he looked even younger than he was. It was hard to believe this kid was central to all that had happened to me over the last week or so.

"So, what is it, Johnny? I'm sure Vicki can't hear us now."

His tone was smug and confrontational. I reached down into the kit bag. First, I found the cool metal of the gun, then my fingers closed on the flask. I pulled the aluminum container into the sunlight.

"Do you recognize this, Eddie? It's the flask you supposedly gave to Joe Safarini for 'safe keeping'. I want you to tell me how it ended up in Hawaii."

His eyes widened when he saw it. He stepped forward as though he was going to grab it. Before he'd gone more than a couple of feet I spoke up—my voice almost a bark.

"Tell me the damned truth!"

Eddie stopped in his tracks but then, from somewhere in the shadow of the patio, Vicki's voice interrupted proceedings.

"J.D., why are you yelling? What are you two doing out there?"

"Don't worry, honey," I shouted back at her. "Eddie and I are just having a man-to-man chat about things."

As Eddie cautiously backed away from me, Vicki hurried closer. She crossed from shade to full sunlight, her clothing going from grey to snow white in a few steps. Her voice was full of concern.

"What do you need to talk about? Why don't you tell me what you're trying to do, J.D.?"

"I'm trying to get your brother to tell me the truth. There are a lot of things about this whole case that I'm confused about. One of them is whether Eddie deliberately gave the flask to the Reds."

Obviously exasperated by my stupidity, Eddie snorted out a reply.

"Of course, I did it deliberately. I gave it to Safarini knowing that the greedy fool wouldn't hold on to it. I was counting on him to give it to Fitch and he didn't let me down."

His sudden honesty threw me.

"So, you wanted Fitch to have it?"

"Naturally. The reason I helped Fitch develop the whole smuggling scheme was to facilitate the removal of my formula. I didn't care what other inconsequential trivia he was trying to export. Compared to the formula, anything else was just a waste of time and effort."

I couldn't believe he was willing to admit his involvement so willingly. I could only figure that the drug-abuse Justine had told me about had seriously affected his judgment.

"You must be very proud of yourself, Eddie. You managed to pull the wool over Joe Safarini's eyes. Damn the consequences for the rest of us if you helped the Reds get information that could harm us. So long as your little game was going well, you were happy. I'm intrigued though, how long did it take you to figure out that Justine's industrial espionage wasn't for some rival East Coast corporation? I guess a clever guy like you saw the truth right off the bat?"

Vicki stood to my left, frozen in her tracks by Eddie's testimony. I hadn't wanted her to be there when I confronted him and now it was too late to do anything about it. For his part, Eddie seemed oblivious to his sister's presence. He seemed to be enjoying his confession. He folded his arms in front of his chest and carried on, seeming to relish his moment in the sun.

"Of course it didn't take me long to realize that Justine's contact on the outside wasn't another pharmaceutical company. I realized after a few weeks that it had to be the communists."

"Eddie! What are you saying?" Vicki sounded shocked and angry and, for once, that anger wasn't directed at me. The tone of her voice didn't stop Eddie though.

"At first, I thought it was the Russians, but when I realized it was the Chinese, it made me feel better about what I was doing. Those people have an ancient wisdom and a cultural longevity we'll never have here. I wanted to share my knowledge with them and to help create a spread of consciousness across the Pacific. And then it came to me how they could get everything out of the country. Don't you see how perfect that was? Using those primitive statues to export the future."

I had to cut in. I was tired of his mumbo-jumbo bullshit and his smugness.

"Eddie. I hate to burst your bubble, but did you really think that the Red Chinese were going to use your invention to expand their minds? Their people might have centuries of ancient wisdom to draw on, but their government enjoys ripping down Tibetan monasteries and stringing up monks. Wake up to reality. There's more to life than spending all your time in a laboratory and dreaming that it could be one great big happy world out there. The truth is, kid, you were playing at being a spy and got out of your depth."

Vicki interrupted. I could tell she was growing increasingly uncomfortable—caught between loyalty to Eddie and some pretty ugly truths.

"J.D., do you have to be so harsh? Eddie's confused. I don't think he knows what he's saying." She turned to her brother. "Eddie. Do you understand what you're admitting to? You never mentioned any of this before."

He shook his head as she spoke, squinting at me against the sun's glare. His expression was that of a professor trying to teach algebra to a very dumb child. He was bugging the hell out of me. I raised my voice a couple of notches.

"So, that's the truth, huh, Eddie? You were helping the Reds and betraying your own?"

"Don't talk to me about truth," he spat the words at me, "what is truth, Johnny? Your truth isn't my truth. The truth is like a diamond. You can look into it from a hundred different perspectives. And you, for one, really need more perspective on everything. It's a big world."

"You don't say. Tell me something I don't know."

"It doesn't have to be us against them. The more I experimented with LSD and my own formula, the more I realized that I could help change all that. Do you really think I wanted the CIA and the military to have that knowledge? They just want to control people. They don't want to help anyone. But I'd come too far to destroy what I'd created, so it seemed better to spread it. To give the whole world a chance to leave this chaos behind."

"Noble words. It's a shame your actions weren't as gallant."

"Don't talk to me about gallantry," he shouted at me, "not with your record. Besides, I did realize at the last minute that it might be unwise to let the formula get into what you would call the wrong hands. When Rhodes caught up with us and presented the evidence he'd collected on me, I was willing to cooperate. I didn't like what he'd done, all that snooping behind my back, but I saw that things had gone too far. I didn't want anyone to get hurt. It all would have been okay, except for Justine. I should have known that all she was really interested in was money."

"Maybe her motives weren't as noble as yours, Eddie. But you've always had money so you couldn't understand what made her tick. For you, this whole damned thing was just an intellectual exercise. To prove you were better than all the simpletons who hadn't had the benefit of sampling your wonder drug. Justine told me that the whole smuggling idea came from you. She couldn't understand why you told your new friend Agent Rycroft that it was all her doing."

He pounced on my words.

"So, you saw Justine? Did she ask about me?" For a moment his face was all boyish concern, then his eyes narrowed and his voice grew ugly. "You were in Hawaii with her, weren't you? I bet you couldn't keep your hands off her, could you?"

He hissed the accusation at me. I hesitated for a couple of seconds and I was lost. I glanced over at Vicki. She was waiting for my answer, her eyes fixed on me. I didn't have to say anything. She *knew*. That wounded look of betrayal I'd seen before filled her face. She shook her head with an air of resignation. I knew what she was thinking: *The bastard will never change. Never!* She abruptly turned on her heel and walked resolutely back to the house. I wanted to run after her but Eddie, oblivious to his sister's hurt, stepped towards me. He pointed at me and carried on ranting.

"You can't keep your hands off any woman, can you? The big war hero. You know, I really used to like you but then I saw how you treated Vicki and I hated your guts. Do you know how unhappy you made her? She told me once you were the only man she'd ever loved, and look how you treated her!"

He paced to and fro in the sand before seeming to calm down again.

"But that's in the past, Johnny. I don't hate you anymore. The drug made me realize that you couldn't help yourself. Your mind hasn't evolved. You're still locked into an adolescent never-never-land where other people's feelings don't count as long as you're having fun. Justine was my girlfriend but you had to have her."

His words stung, but I wasn't going to allow my sense of guilt to let him get the upper hand.

"Cut the crap, Eddie. I'm not the one who sold Justine out to the FBI. I'm not the one who dragged Vicki into this whole stinking mess. You played a game, got out of your depth and everyone else suffered. You talk about this drug as though it were the cure for all man's problems. It isn't. It's just something that will make you famous in scientific journals. If you left your ego out of this for just one second, you could see that it's just another escape route from reality. Just another cocktail, only dirtier and more dangerous."

Once again, he ignored my argument. He'd made his mind up and nothing I said was going to change it.

"I know you're not a great thinker, Johnny, but try and understand. I'm talking about creating a new world. If people could really see what was going on, things would change for the better. Once you've opened up your mind to the wonders that are out there you can't be mean or petty."

"Oh, so what are you telling me, Eddie? That your little invention gives men consciences?"

"Eventually, yes. I think it would. Once the door of perception has been opened the only limits are your own imagination."

"That's swell for you but who else would it work for? I tried your little concoction and it was the most hellish experience of my life."

"That's because you obviously weren't ready for it. You need preparation to benefit from such a new experience. But you'll never be the same, Johnny. I can promise you that, you'll never be the same."

He made it sound like a threat. He started on another rant but I cut him off.

"And how many unprepared people are you going to send through that door, Eddie? How many people like Rhodes, who couldn't handle the horror your drug opened his mind to? How many more young GIs are going to die in so-called traffic accidents before your formula is perfected?"

His face flared red. Perspiration was starting to glisten on his brow.

"I didn't want those soldiers to die. It wasn't my fault. Those stupid, interfering military doctors were on duty that day. They were the ones who gave the wrong dosage. And that's precisely why I knew that no single government should have my drug. It's the property of the world. It's not a weapon, it could be salvation."

Something in the tone of his voice spurred me into action. Until that moment, I hadn't been sure exactly what I was going to do. Now I knew. Keeping my eyes on him, I pulled the flask from the kit bag and carefully unscrewed the lid. When I'd done that, I extended the flask towards him. He looked confused.

"What are you doing? Be careful with that. That liquid took months to prepare, you don't know what you're doing!"

"Yeah, I do. I'm giving your formula to the world, Eddie. I'm giving it back to the earth. Ashes to ashes. Dust to dust."

And with that, I tilted the flask so its contents began to spill out, the amber liquid pouring onto the desert sand. Keeping the flask at arm's length, I held my breath while the drug was soaked up by the dry, thirsty dust. Eddie stood, stupefied. He watched in horror as his precious liquid formed a dark stain on the desert floor. Within seconds, the sunlight reduced the stain to nothing. The sand had acted like blotting paper. The liquid and all its potential nightmares soaked away into oblivion.

Then I turned towards the boulder where I'd left the *Ritual Of The Savage*. Eddie must have read my mind because he dove at me. He grabbed at the album and I pulled it out of his reach. As we grappled together the rest of the kit bag emptied on to the sand. I left the other stuff there and managed to push him off fairly easily. Physical activity had never been Eddie's strong point. Once I had him off- balance I punched him in the solar plexus. He doubled over and clutched his stomach. As he gasped for air, I shook out the brown envelope from the album cover. Then I removed the sheaf of papers inside that and let the envelope and album drop to the ground. Eddie was still having trouble catching his breath. I wanted to teach him a lesson. I fished my service Zippo from my pocket. He managed to look up at me, his face creased with pain. When he saw the Zippo he tried to straighten up.

"No, Johnny. Please don't do that. Look, I'm sorry. Sorry for all the trouble I've caused. You don't have to burn those papers."

I ignored him and slowly raised the lighter to the document. Suddenly he dropped to all fours. For a second I thought he'd collapsed, instead he scrambled in the sand and I realized what he was reaching for the second before he found it. With both hands, he raised my .45 and pointed it at me. I'd been so intent on making him suffer that I'd forgotten about the gun.

"Don't do it! I swear to God that I *will* pull this trigger."

By the glint in his eye I knew he probably meant what he said. I flicked the Zippo anyway. A steady yellow flame sparked into life. I held the flame close to the bottom edge of the papers.

"Johnny! I mean it! Don't do it." His voice was almost a scream. "Those papers took me years to research. You don't know what you're doing!"

I was amazed at the turnaround in Eddie's feelings about his formula. A week ago, with a dose of the drug pumping through his mind, he'd wanted the damned thing destroyed. Well, it was too late for any change of heart he might have. The fate of the formula was in *my* hands. I held the flame two inches from the paper. I could feel the sweat beginning to ooze under my arms.

"The trouble is, Eddie, is that I *do* know what I'm doing. I know that the odds are that you, or one of your buddies at Star Crest, will come up with something similar to this but at least I won't know a damned thing about it. But you see, I do know about this. If I give it back to you now, part of me will always feel responsible for whatever you, Star Crest, the CIA, or the Commies end up doing with it."

As I spoke, I had an image of a godforsaken future world where all those beatnik bums down at the Jive Hive were gobbling Eddie's little capsules. I saw them spending their lives slipping in and out of reality, drifting slowly backwards and forwards from nirvana to nightmare. A generation unhooked from the rest of society by a witch's brew of man-made chemicals. Crazy, spoiled children who'd breed even more crazy, more amoral kids. And maybe some egotistical jerk like Eddie, with the zeal of Billy Graham and the arrogance of a liberal intellectual, would convince them that they were the chosen ones. Super-enlightened beings who'd figure they could trample on laws and traditions because they'd passed the drug initiation. What was it Eddie had said, a thousand years ago, on that night in Palm Springs? "All those Indians taking peyote, going into trances." This was it. This was Eddie's very own *Ritual Of The Savage*. The same old mumbo-jumbo bullshit, but crafted for the Atomic Age. Everything changes, but it stays the same. And the new witch doctors would wear lab coats, listen to jazz, and read Kerouac. My mind was made up.

I moved the Zippo's flame closer to the paper. The edge started to blacken and char. Eddie was shaking. He knew he wasn't physically strong enough to stop me but he had my .45. He stepped closer. His arms were fully extended towards me, the gun still clutched in both hands. Its barrel pointed straight at my chest. Only six feet of space lay between us now. The perspiration on his brow had turned to sweat. It ran in trickles down his cheeks. His voice crackled between anger and pleading.

"For the last time! Give me those papers. I can't let you do this. You don't know what you're doing. You're going to destroy something just because you can't understand it!"

"Damned right I don't understand it. But just because I don't understand something doesn't mean I don't know when it's wrong."

The charred border of the paper grew a glowing red edge that ate into the typed notes. The red edge suddenly flowered into a flame. The flame licked its way onto the other sheets. The cleansing fire burnt away the laboratory notes, the chemical compounds, the performance charts, the dosage tables, the reaction reports, the whole rotten lot. Eddie screamed.

"No! No!"

His eyes closed tight and then he pulled the trigger.

Sophisticated Savage

For a split-second I imagined the impact of the bullet as it ripped through my chest. My flesh torn, my arteries severed, my blood splattering in rich crimson drops onto the desert. Several heartbeats passed and then my ears told me that the hammer had clicked uselessly onto an empty chamber and then another and another...

The gun had been empty when I'd put it in my kit bag. I'd never had any intention of shooting Eddie. I'd thought that if he got out of control he'd assume it was loaded and give it the respect it deserved. When he retrieved it from the sand he didn't know enough about guns to know by feel whether it was empty or not. Even so, I was relieved to still be alive. Eddie wasn't so relieved. Hearing the dull clicks of the hammer, he opened his eyes and stared in disbelief at the gun. As he realized what had happened, he slumped to his knees in the hot sand. Tears joined the sweat running down his face.

By now, the papers were burning brightly. Little pieces of charcoaled paper floated all around me. I felt the heat from the flames on my hand so I dropped the burning sheaf to the ground. When there was only the top quarter of the papers still left intact I stomped the fire out. I wanted to prove to the Feds that I had Eddie's formula even if they couldn't use it. I picked the charred papers up and shoved them into the *Ritual Of The Savage'* record sleeve. A souvenir of a job completed.

I walked over to Eddie. He knelt weeping. I pried the .45 from his stiff fingers and tucked it into my waistband. I patted him on the head. I should have pistol- whipped him for trying to kill me but, short of giving me some satisfaction, it wouldn't have done any good. Only time could sort out his problems.

I started back towards the house. A flash of sun on metal showed me where I'd dropped the flask. I scooped it up as more evidence for the Feds, brushed off the sand and continued on my way. I didn't go more than a few steps before Vicki was running towards me from the house. As she reached me, I could see the tears in her eyes. I wanted to hold her, hug her and explain to her that I wasn't the heel she thought I was. But she was looking past me to the forlorn figure of Eddie, still crying in the sand. She rounded on me, her blurry eyes filled with anger and hate.

"Why was Eddie screaming? What did you do to him?"

"I didn't do anything to him. He did it all to himself. But he's not hurt; he's just very upset. Vicki, listen, about Hawaii…"

She didn't give me time to finish. Her voice was cold, firm and final.

"Just forget it. I don't want to hear it. I can't be near you right now. I've got to look after my brother and I'd appreciate if you weren't at the house when we get back to it."

She strode past me to Eddie. She knelt down and put a consoling arm around his bowed shoulders. I watched for a few seconds before I turned away and headed back towards the house. When I reached the pool, I stopped. I gazed down into the sparkling blue water. The broken refractions of my reflection looked blankly up at me. He didn't look too happy. He didn't even look like me. I sighed, swung my kit bag over my shoulder, and went along the side of the house to the street. The door handle of the Chevy was hot to my touch as I opened it. I threw the kit bag onto the passenger seat, got in and started the engine.

If you act like there's no tomorrow, one day soon there will be no tomorrow. Probably the only smart thing Doc Svenson had said to me while I was recovering in military hospital. It was advice I'd never heeded though. Since the war ended I'd been unable to concentrate on the future. The distractions of the present were always enough for me. Except for those first couple of years with Vicki, planning rarely entered my daily existence. And right there in Palm Springs on a scorching July day, it all caught up with me. I'd tracked down the flask. I'd done what Vicki had wanted me to do. I'd even surprised myself by uncovering the whole sorry caper. I should have returned to the mainland a conquering hero, but I'd blown it. I blew it the second I laid eyes on Justine. I'd wanted her so much I'd kissed goodbye to what could have been a new beginning with Vicki. That new beginning had been close, but, like Eddie's formula, it had evaporated with the desert heat. It was kind of ironic. In trying to prove my worth to Vicki, I'd met Justine. Justine was the key to solving the case but also the reason I'd lost Vicki.

Well, that seemed typical of my life. The only thing that had existed for me while I was with Justine was the present. The future hadn't mattered. But the future had become the present and I was stuck with it. And unlike Eddie, I didn't have the best lawyers in the State to argue I was blameless when the past caught up with me.

Yes, in an age of savings and loans, of Mutual of New York life insurance and United of Omaha pensions and a golden American future, I was an anachronism. The only place I felt secure was the past. You knew where you were with the past. It all made sense somehow. La Canada, Mom and Dad, Labor Day picnics, playing Cowboys and Indians, track events at John Muir High School, Marine Boot Camp, meeting Vicki, the dead-end jobs, the endless cocktail parties, the barely-remembered affairs, even the pain of Iwo Jima. It was all part of me. I could deal with that. I could even deal with the fact that life could be so arbitrary. Why my legacy from the Imperial Japanese Army was a seven- inch scar, while for tens of thousands of others it was a grave somewhere far from home. Why Joe Safarini died, yet I'd driven out of an Inglewood coffee shop parking lot alive. Yes, I could just about deal with that.

But tomorrow, tomorrow was different. The future was a gaping void that would only end on Judgment Day. Maybe that end would come under a crop of radioactive mushroom clouds or maybe under the rays of little green men from Mars. Who knew? And that was the point, wasn't it? No one knew. The future didn't make sense because it hadn't happened yet. So, if Eddie was a 20th Century witch doctor, I was its sophisticated savage living day-to-day, always wanting the short-term fix of pleasure over long-term commitment. Accepting life as it came at me, never thinking beyond the next winter, spring, summer or fall. As a modern savage, I probably wasn't that different from the ancient Polynesians who had worshipped Ku and the other Tiki gods: people who could only plan for the next feast, the next hunting trip, the next sacrifice. I was just another primitive, but dressed up real nice in a gabardine suit.

Was I being too hard on myself? Perhaps, but suppose Eddie was right and that one solitary experience with his formula had changed me forever? I guess I'd never really know for sure, but, because of my involvement with his damned drug, I knew the circumstances of my life *would* be different. So, I was heading west, driving towards the distant vastness of the hulking Pacific Ocean. First to Santa Barbara to see a sad, deranged widow who wouldn't even know who the hell I was, and whose daughter was on the run somewhere beyond the pale horizon. Then I'd return to Los Angeles to face the CIA and the Feds. To try and explain that I'd stopped the Commies getting their formula but that the good guys wouldn't be seeing it either. Perhaps the list I'd found of Fitch's stateside contacts would ease their anger. Then I had to try and make my peace with Vicki. I'd failed her twice. That was twice more than she ever deserved. And once I'd done all that, then maybe, just maybe, things would get back to something approaching normal. Perhaps I could take a trip out to Tahiti to try and find Justine again.

There and then, with the wind rocking the Chevy as I drove towards Banning on Highway 99, that's what I planned to do. No more drunken bar-hopping, no more making meaningless conquests and no more frivolously performing the only ritual this modern savage knew. I hoped the spoiled kid in me had finally grown up and had learned his lesson. In the end though, I guess it all depended on how much I'd changed, if I'd changed at all. There was only one way to find out. With the sun directly overhead and the Coachella Valley behind me, I pushed the pedal to the floor and sped towards the rest of my life.

THE END

If you enjoyed *Ritual of the Savage*,

you'll love the next Johnny Davis adventure

To Kill a Cure

Sign up here for pre-launch specials and

notification about the book.

jaystrongman.wordpress.com

CPSIA information can be obtained at www.ICGtesting.com
Printed in the USA
BVOW02s1117030216

435319BV00002B/24/P